1ˢᵗ Ed

C000259119

The Hottentot Room

ALSO BY CHRISTOPHER HOPE

Fiction
A Separate Development
Private Parts and Other Tales
Kruger's Alp

Poetry
Cape Drives
In the Country of the Black Pig
Englishmen

For children
The King, the Cat and the Fiddle
The Dragon Wore Pink

THE
HOTTENTOT
ROOM

Christopher Hope

HEINEMANN : LONDON

William Heinemann Ltd
10 Upper Grosvenor Street, London W1X 9PA

LONDON MELBOURNE
JOHANNESBURG AUCKLAND

First published 1986
Copyright © Christopher Hope 1986

ISBN 0 434 34663 2

Printed and bound in Great Britain by
Mackays of Chatham Ltd,
Chatham, Kent

. . . now one would think that this wretch might have conceived his present, compared with his former condition, as Heaven upon Earth; but did not do so . . . for when he had learned a little of our language he would daily lie upon the ground and cry very often this in his broken English, 'Coree home go . . .'

(Edward Terry describing the ingratitude of a certain Hottentot named Coree, kidnapped in the Cape of Good Hope and brought to London to be put on display.

A Voyage to East India, 1665)

For Marlene Maertens

CHAPTER 1

So Biddy Hogan did, after all, wear vests. An old, unlikely report was unexpectedly confirmed. A juvenile witticism turned out to be true. Or, if you prefer, life proved to be a lot funnier than the old crack about Biddy Hogan's vests. Pure cotton, with a border of daisies around the neck.

Thus we are continually surprised by tales out of Africa which start off as incredible, even ridiculous, myths – and then one fine day prove true. It is disconcerting, it is unfair, it is seldom convenient. But there it is. Caleb Looper went to bed with Biddy Hogan and found the old joke about the vests was not a joke at all. At the same time the phone rang. This was another joke that amused only to deceive. For whenever the phone rang in the Hottentot Room, it was never for Looper. No member of the tribe could ever remember a phone call for Looper, and it had become a source of amusement. 'It must be for you,' the regulars around the bar chorused when the phone rang, which was never for Looper. Sometimes, frustrated by the absence of calls for the square-jawed gingery reporter, they would shove the receiver into his hand and he would stand there holding it to ironic cheers and laughter, while the caller squawked furiously in Looper's powerful grip.

It was the second momentous call of the day. To have been in bed with none other than Biddy Hogan was an achievement upon which lesser men might have rested with pride. It had taken him many weeks of unremitting persuasion to advance to this point with the slender Sidney scholar. But there was no rest for Looper. Having just become Biddy Hogan's lover, he was summoned by a call from his fiancée, Rose.

'Come quickly,' she ordered calmly, 'I think Mummy's finally going. She's asking for you.'

Her deliberately unemotional tone did not surprise him, nor did it deceive him. Finally going. Relief vibrated through the overstatement. As if she were seeing off some tedious guest who had overstayed. Rose had long prepared for this moment.

The first call that morning had invited Looper to view the head

1

of the Emperor Trajan in the British Museum. He found the head in room 15, standing on a plinth in the corner. Trajan wore his hair combed forward over a narrow brow and his face was sharp and tough. The head was carved from marble and the nose had been broken and glued back. The commanding, thin-lipped face shouted with power and yet there was also a delicate, almost fastidious air about him. He might have been, Looper decided, a dress designer who had turned to thuggery. Here Looper had been handed a first-class air ticket to Johannesburg by a young woman who seemed very nervous and would not meet his eye. Looper was stunned but before he could question her or react in any way she turned and hurried off. Just a messenger, he thought. Raw. Straight from the Office. Trajan turned on Looper a look of frowning scepticism. Over to his right was the figure of a crouching Aphrodite, quite naked and dreamily beautiful in her plump milky perfection. It was then that the reason for the little messenger's nervousness became clear for there stepped from the gloom of the Assyrian Gallery next door a huge black man in a beautiful dove-grey suit. This was Looper's first glimpse of the Zulu. The Zulu examined the head of Trajan with a contented smile. He examined Looper with slightly less attention than he gave the other exhibits. Then he circled the crouching Aphrodite and, when he was quite sure that Looper was watching, he patted her naked shoulder. For some reason he could not fathom, Looper found the gesture deeply provoking. Shortly thereafter Looper and the Zulu left the museum together. Later that evening, though he was by then relieved of the responsibility of doing anything more, Looper was back in the Hottentot Room where he met Biddy Hogan and they had slipped away before ten and gone home to his place, to the accompaniment of winks and nods from the assembled company around the horseshoe bar.

All this might suggest that Looper was in demand with women. After all he was in the arms of one, summoned by another to the sick-bed of a third. This, however, would be a false impression. His relations with all three women arose from duty. If he felt true affection, it was for the old lady to whose side Rose now called him. Looper's attachments to these women were hard to fathom. Why, or indeed whether, women were attracted to him was just as obscure. A body 'tending to bone', was how Rose put it in her cool, clinical way the first time she saw him without clothes. His eyes were a light green, his hands neat, his hair close-cropped, crisp, with a prickly, gingery gleam. He displayed no prominent features except for a feline agility. He was quite remarkably quick on his feet, but that was something few noticed. His face was pale and unremarkable: 'open' was the only compliment anyone had paid to it. Upon that word rode the suggestion of trustworthiness, a somewhat stolid dependability. Few had seen him angry. The rare occasion might be observed when they pushed the phone into his fist and he stood there holding it stiffly, like a club. On such crucial misconceptions a career may be built. On such misreadings of character and temperament a clever, modest man can go far by encouraging these all too easy opinions to seem to those who hold them kindly, but dismissive, analyses of a not very powerful nature. By allowing what pass for accurate depictions, abbreviated by charitable impulses, to seem fair if perfunctory generalisations (while in fact they are patronising slurs) – much can be achieved.

Whether Looper had always possessed a talent of dissimulation or whether it had developed since his deportation from South Africa in the mid-seventies, was not clear. His history was well known. He had been a journalist who overstepped the mark. His radical sympathies had led him to take action. He had hidden people; he had distributed leaflets; he had carried messages, money, equipment. He had been jailed and deported.

In jail he was held in solitary confinement. In those days, the granite seventies, there were many white people in detention and their plight attracted wide interest. There were many more non-white prisoners, of course, but they tended to attract attention only if they died in very exceptional circumstances. A black prisoner would have to slip on a cake of soap in the shower or fall from a high window, still fully clothed, before eyebrows were raised. And even then he would have to arrange for the police doctor to enter 'influenza' on his death certificate before serious questions began to be asked. Even so, the coroner would probably declare these perfectly common symptoms of influenza in Africans. White radicals, by contrast, had only to be arrested to attract considerable attention. It was this fact that probably saved Looper when he was picked up. And the fact that they began with the man in the cell next door. Something had gone wrong. Looper knew this from the face of his jailer. Since prisoners were allowed nothing to read, Looper took as his daily newspaper the broad spade-shaped face of his jailer. Usually the morning edition was cheerful – something

3

along the lines of 'Springboks Wallop Ozzies!'. But the news grew grimmer. 'Rain Stops Play!' gave way to 'Follow-on Inevitable!' and, on the third day, black borders appeared around the jailer's face 'Boks Collapse!'. And Looper knew the man next door was dead. They released Looper in case he had heard something. Then they deported him.

In London he contributed stories and articles to a variety of papers and journals which took a sympathetic line on the struggle for freedom in Southern Africa. In short, he was a hack of sorts. He was the first to say so. But only just. It was a fact that Looper positively inspired underestimates of his achievements. Yet he had taken Biddy Hogan to bed. The 'unbeddable' Biddy Hogan, as she was known in her student days, had succumbed to his patient attentions.

He had also become engaged to the daughter of Frau Katie. Blonde, blue-eyed Rose, 'English Rose' as they called her, though never to her face, down at the Hottentot Room. Rose had taken the lead in their engagement. She had worked him over in her rough, amorous way. Looper had not only withstood the trial (and this spoke for his calibre), but no one noticed. How could they? He had also persuaded Rose that their engagement must remain a secret.

'No secret, no engagement,' was the way he put it.

'But Caleb, I want to marry you,' said Rose.

He was appalled by her train of thought. Fortunately desire did not make a contract. He had wanted to marry Marilyn Monroe when he had been a boy. And where had it got him? No. Rose might claim she was engaged to him – but it was an engagement of the sort he had contracted with Monroe. And what Rose wanted was not marriage. She used the term loosely. A form of convenient shorthand. What she really wanted from Looper was not yet clear.

'I'm afraid your mother would misunderstand,' he said.

Rose laughed. 'Dear Caleb, let's get this straight. My mother loves to pretend that you and she will elope one day. You will arrive at her window with your ladder. She will run away with her beautiful gallant. I don't want to be cruel, but it's an old joke. And, really, it's wearing just a little thin. I'm serious about how I feel. This is *real*.'

If Looper had a weakness, it was for bestowing affection where it was unlikely to be reciprocated. He had done so in the case of his

4

dead mother around whom, though she had died when he was still too young to have any but the vaguest memories of her, he had built a cult of remembrance founded on a solitary photograph which showed a dark-haired girl in a picture hat, slender, shapely hands in her lap, smiling brilliantly. But she had died and left him alone with his father, the Inspector of Mines. So, too, he had fixed his affections on Frau Katie. The reasons were far from clear: she was old enough to be his mother, she was distinctly perverse, she was ill and yet she remained a vivacious, commanding presence combining a natural hauteur with the talents of a flirt and a laugh as deep as a drumroll.

'She likes men. She's always liked men,' warned English Rose, in the quasi-objective tone of voice she used when preparing to condemn someone, the way she said that the trouble with Wyngate Hossein was that 'he's too fond of the bottle . . .' or criticised Looper's flat.

Looper's flat in Sea Lion Mews, off the Marylebone Road, had been designed for a very neat dwarf. His bed occupied much of the single bedroom which, with a tiny kitchen-cum-shower cubicle, made up his home. Indeed it was the crowded nature of his flat which had eventually deterred Rose from coming home with him to his 'horrid little cupboard'. It would be one of the first things to go, she told him, when they married. 'I'm sorry, Caleb, but I simply cannot stand to see you like this.' The brisk dismissive way this was said suggested the unsightly symptom of some sad, embarrassing affliction, a pox, stain or hole, or flap, the cure of which would be a relief to patient and onlookers alike.

'We've managed to contact everyone except Biddy,' Rose said. 'Do hurry.'

Looper put down the phone and began to search for his socks.

Biddy Hogan watched him. One hand was under her head and the sheet was pulled up to her chin. It took a conscious effort to remind himself that beneath the sheet she was naked. The nature of her nakedness was no surprise. She was thin, bony, lengthy. If there was anything surprising it was that his expectations had been so exactly confirmed, even down to the vest. How odd that a girl who prized the life of the mind should leave so little to the imagination.

His pursuit of Biddy Hogan had been one of the most difficult in his career. He had first set eyes on her in Buffy Lestrade's seminar on Nietzsche. Lestrade came later to claim that she had fallen in love with him, then turned against him – 'When I refused to play Sartre to her de Beauvoir.' A tall, nervy, formidably intelligent girl with close-cropped brown hair on a small round head, green eyes, very thin white hands with fingers that waved and tasted the air like the fronds of some delicate plant, or the whiskers of some curious fish. At the same time, there was in her rather hoarse voice and her emphatic expression something disconcertingly masculine. This, together with her whole manner and appearance, the beautifully shaped, rather small head, prominent cheek-bones, the hands that tasted the air, had all marked her in her university days as a dominant force. In her English tutorials she had been an unflinching and unforgiving follower of the critic Leavis, forever on the lookout for those who shirked the high moral seriousness of true literature. For advertising men she felt the deep loathing of the devout vegetarian for the proselytising, bloody-aproned butcher. Journalism was for her solely a term of abuse. She hated implacably the remaking of great novels into movies which she described as the rendering down of the diamond-light of culture into the cheap paste of Hollywood. At the time television was forbidden in South Africa and she declared that she found this reason enough to support the government. Aggressive in debate but curiously shy, people called her Biddyhogan, the two names being run together for no discernible reason other than perhaps that they emphasised her substantial presence in the way a mere nickname, Christian name or a diminutive such as Kit or Bobs or Binkie, which undergraduates use between themselves, would never have done. It was known that Biddyhogan was not a person but a brilliant phenomenon. Biddyhogan would take a first-class honours. Biddyhogan was good academic material. It was also said, however, by some of those not well-disposed towards the star student, and perhaps taken aback by her contradictory qualities of mannish debater and shrinking violet and repelled by her disdainful air and the thin, tense, round-shouldered body, that Biddyhogan was also the sort of girl who wore vests . . . the vestal virgin.

It was meant as a joke, of course. A wicked jibe. Whoever had dreamt it up was undoubtedly male. One knew that because it was the kind of remark which could be understood properly only by those who knew her and were fascinated yet irritated by her glowing passion for poetry, drama, books – which contrasted so strongly with her fastidious, cool, virginal manner. Then there was the pugnacious thrust to her chin and the almost unnoticeable breasts. So the word went round – Biddy Hogan wore vests. Betcha! With her, all the heat was in the head.

However, the compilers of the secret report on the stern Leavisite did not understand the joke. They had recorded this item, along with other relevant facts, gathered by their campus spy, usually an overworked informer who paid his or her way through university on the pittance offered by the security police, or the Special Branch, or the Secret Service or one of the many clandestine agencies that seeded university campuses with student spies in an effort to identify the subversives and political trouble-makers of the future. It was widely known that informers operated in the universities, but then in a country where the security police could be turned on a persistent questioner at a political rally who pressed a minister for answers to an awkward question, and when members of parliament had their telephones bugged by listeners who thought nothing of interrupting a conversation that took a dangerous turn with an obscene remark, or a maniacal laugh, this sort of thing was regarded as a fact of life. What was strange was that Biddy, whose hatred of politics as a vulgar side-show was widely known, should have been selected for surveillance.

Odder still was the fact that the spy who had taken so literally the remark about the vests proved to be eerily perceptive about her later development. Biddy gave absolutely no indication during her brilliant undergraduate years that she was ever going to be anything other than a student of literature. She took no political line. Indeed she despised politics for the dangerous lure it held for writers and readers, tempting them to engage themselves in committed action and the expression of personal conviction led them into the trap of polemic and debate, a road at the end of which lay rhetoric, the ruination of literature by the clever sloganising of the ad-man and the commercial vulgarisation of Hollywood. She would no more have gone in for politics than she would have gone into a cinema showing some expensive castration of a much-loved classic novel. So it was that when after her South African degree she went on to Cambridge to write a thesis on the sonnets of Sir Philip Sidney, nothing was more natural and her path through life seemed assured.

Looper sat naked on the bed pulling on his socks. 'That was Rose. Her mother's dying. She's asking for me.'

7

His watch showed it to be just before midnight. It was still snowing. It had begun to snow when they left the Hottentot. If he hurried he might still get a tube. He and Biddy had slipped away from the Hottentot Room shortly before ten, while Rose was upstairs with her mother. The others had grinned amongst themselves when they left together. The *habitués* of the Hottentot Room regarded Rose as having a hopeless, unrequited passion for Looper. They knew nothing of his 'engagement'. It amused them to imagine that Biddy was giving Rose some competition. They teased him about Rose's feelings for him, but they also liked to cover up for him, saw him as the targeted male running before the hunting female. Rose was the sort of person who made covering up not merely a duty but a positive pleasure. And why not? Looper was a free agent. In an odd sort of way, they were half correct.

Maybe that was why he was here in his flat with Biddy Hogan while everyone, every single person who knew Looper, imagined he was somewhere else. Even expected him to be somewhere else.

'Don't you think Rose rather enjoys giving orders?'

Biddy shifted in the bed and allowed her shoulder to emerge from beneath the sheet. Behind her on the wall hung a signed photograph of a black woman with a sweet, faintly troubled smile. Biddy blinked her green eyes, scrutinising his body rather as she might have regarded a particularly knotty poem, as a suitable case for practical criticism.

'I imagine Rose is not above using Frau Katie's illness to get at you.'

Looper pulled on the rest of his clothes quickly, feeling uncomfortable beneath her cool, intense scrutiny. He could sense her resentment, and it surprised and somewhat chilled him. Resentment was not what he had expected under the circumstances. Of course Rose enjoyed giving orders. But it wasn't Rose who was commanding him to return to the Club tonight. Death was giving the order tonight. And yes of course Rose wasn't above using her mother's illness to make him do things but she was not doing so tonight. He thought of the old lady in the big bed. The disease had finally found her out. The 'old story' was coming to an end.

What Biddy would never know was that this interruption was extremely inconvenient to him as well. It had taken the most careful planning to bring Biddy to this position. He had patiently applied

8

himself to winning her trust, approaching her when she was most vulnerable and by careful attention to detail he had made himself a great comfort to her, applying the mild, good-natured charm which had proved so effective. Painstakingly, he had brought her to the point where she had begun to discuss her political connections with various groups in general and with Via Afrika in particular. She had a lot to say about its General Secretary, Wyngate Hossein, with whom she had carried on an affair for eighteen months.

What no one suspected was that this affair had been closely observed, recorded and even photographed – until detailed, colourful proofs of the liaison were one day unexpectedly brought to the attention of Mrs Hossein. It was Biddy's reappearance in the Hottentot Room, even paler than usual, shock and grief clearly visible in her eyes, that signalled to Looper that it was time to make an approach. He had known she would come back to the Hottentot Room once she was alone again. When she and Hossein had taken up they had not been seen in the Room because it was an unwritten rule of the place that no one with attachments was allowed. Some clubs accepted no cheques. Frau Katie allowed no couples – not at least in her tribe. The Hottentots, Frau Katie maintained, were a libidinous folk ... they did not practise monogamy. Hottentot women were carefree in their favours. The men visited ships calling at the Cape and for the payment of a few beads or some tobacco would perform suggestive dances and display their private parts in order to confirm or confound the widespread belief that Hottentots possessed only one testicle. And, just as true Hottentots were a wandering people loyal only to chiefs and clan, so the Hottentot Room accepted only those without homes and attachments into its inner circle – Frau Katie's selected 'little tribe'.

What would they have made, the admirers and mockers, teachers and spies of her university days, of the extraordinary transformation of Biddy Hogan? Those old colleagues of hers would have gaped to have seen the metamorphosis of the slender inquisitor, the shrinking violet with the bullying brain settling down in a Cambridge library to write her thesis on 'The Notion of Love in the Sonnets of Sidney', changed in an instant into the passionate apostle of African liberation. This alteration was of the order of some profound religious vision, so Biddy described it with no loss of her unyielding sense of conviction. One fine day she had suddenly

9

left her desk, left her university, left Cambridge altogether and gone down to London to work in the offices of Via Afrika as a poorly paid researcher. Her dramatic conversion took place, so the legend said, when she attended a political meeting out of boredom and a certain vague homesickness. There she heard Hossein speak and the scales had dropped from her eyes.

Of course Biddy Hogan remained outwardly unchanged. She brought to radical politics the same pale face, the thin stubborn shoulders, the short, straight, cropped hair, the same cold, intellectual intensity. It was about this time that she first began coming to the Hottentot Room. Wyngate introduced her. 'My young comrade-in-arms,' he had called her.

Wyngate Hossein had lived in London for almost two decades. He had left South Africa when upon his release from a ten-year gaol sentence for treason he had found himself confined under indefinite house arrest. Far away the most impressive of the exiled leaders, Hossein's name itself demonstrated how broad was his appeal to all parties and persuasions at home. There was that European, vaguely American, first-name – Wyngate; there was the surname with its Asian or Muslim echo; and there was the man himself who turned out in fact to be a Black African of Zulu stock. His universal appeal had been recognised early, and with some chagrin, by the white government he had sworn to overthrow. 'He sounds like an Indian, speaks like a white man and looks like a black,' cried the perplexed Minister of Native Affairs, back in the old days when such departments were named for their function and not to disguise their real purpose. 'Who is this Wyngate Hossein?' sneered the incomprehending minister, thereby compounding his folly and living to regret it, for in time everyone knew who Wyngate Hossein was. He was even then a benign yet commanding figure, barely thirty, with short very curly hair, prominent cheek-bones and a generous, gleaming forehead. Hossein had come up through a hard school: in the fifties he became leader of the first Union of Dustmen when that group lacked for allies even among the lowest-paid workers; reviled and arrested many times; organiser of the Walk-To-Work campaign against bus-fare increases; arrested, beaten and imprisoned. Arrested again in the great round-up which preceded the tragi-comic Treason Trial in which the accused were all found not guilty only to be re-arrested and tried again, he had

10

been sentenced to ten years for conspiring to overthrow the state. During his years inside there had circulated copies of his speech from the dock, with its theme: 'This long night is passing', and its ringing, repeated declaration: 'I see the dawn!' He emerged from jail grey, grizzled and defiant.

Once in London Hossein took over Home Front Affairs within Via Afrika and became the organisation's chief spokesman and doyen of exiles and expatriates who plotted and prayed for the long-deferred collapse of the Boer regime. It was said of Hossein that his first experience of London was the Hottentot Room. These were the sixties and the Room enjoyed tremendous popularity. He had been taken straight from the plane to Frau Katie's establishment in Antaeus Street, Earls Court, before he'd even seen his wife, Gladys, who'd been living in London for much of the time he was in prison.

Years later, when Biddy Hogan began her secret affair with Wyngate Hossein, now in his sixties, Looper happened to become acquainted with Wyngate's wife, Gladys. He interviewed her for an American magazine interested in African affairs. It was a warmly human story of the wife of a prominent exile. They talked of the house, her children, her hopes for the future. There were a number of photographs.

The interview was a considerable success. Gladys was a kindly woman who missed her African home quite dreadfully and spoke of her children with pride mixed with certain reservations at their increasingly marked European traits and habits. It was sad but inevitable that they should be westernised in this way, she confided in Looper. Africa, for her children, was a distant memory, a fading picture. She had been a nurse when Wyngate married her. She had waited patiently throughout his years in gaol. They lived now in north London, in a pleasant house on the slopes of Hampstead Hill with a fine view across to the City. Gladys told Looper that Wyngate was consumed by his work, that he burnt with the fire of freedom. Such phrases came naturally to her and she uttered them proudly. The pride with which she spoke did not entirely conceal a faint note of regret. Looper took her photograph and she glowed with pleasure. Round, kind, desperately sincere, in the light of Looper's interest, Gladys gleamed like a rich, polished plum. He had kept a copy of the picture which she had inscribed:

For Caleb – a friend of our struggle.

11

She added her large, childlike signature with a great fat *a* and looping *y* and *s* – *Gladys Hossein* . . . He hung it on the wall of his bedroom. Was that a hint of reproach in those dark eyes? Of course not. At that time she knew nothing of Biddy Hogan. Even now it seemed Gladys was unknown to Biddy who lay naked beneath her picture, pointing her sharp little breasts accusingly at Looper. Biddy had paid absolutely no attention to the photograph of Hossein's wife, who gazed down on the other woman with an expression of gently troubled sweetness.

Looper's successful interview and photography session led to a deepening acquaintance and further visits for tea. One afternoon Gladys confessed to having trouble organising the family album. Pictures not only of the children but also of Wyngate on his many foreign trips. Some of these pictures needed reprinting. Some she would love to see enlarged. There were shots of Wyngate in East Germany and pictures of their first visit to Moscow. They were not very good, perhaps owing to the poor quality of the film bought in those countries. The photographs showed them posed in a snowy Red Square. He wore a uniform, Gladys recalled, peering short-sightedly at the blurred print. Khaki, she seemed to remember. Brass buttons and green epaulets. But then everyone wore uniform in those days and she remembered thinking how very handsome he looked.

'The Russian people crowded all around us. They wanted to see who we were. In those days there weren't many Africans in Moscow, so people stopped and stared at these black people in the snow. I was wearing a big fur coat and a tall fur hat. See, you can just make me out. I look like a fat stove wearing a fur hat.'

Looper said it was a pity she did not still possess the negatives. There were modern methods of enhancing the image and perhaps obtaining a clearer picture of that snowy day in Red Square.

Gladys beamed. 'But I have all the negatives, every one!' Her eyes were moist with pleasure and gratitude. 'For me, they're a priceless record. If they could be restored I would be very happy. How do you know all these new techniques? How wonderful!'

Looper shrugged. 'It's my line of country,' he said.

He took away the album and did as she asked. He reproduced

all her family photographs in clean, clear prints, including as well many other interesting and unique pictures: Wyngate arriving in Cuba; addressing the Liberation Committee of the Organisation of African Unity; meeting Via Afrika guerrillas secretly somewhere in the Namibian bush; relaying comradely greetings in Budapest to a group of trades unionists, accompanied by other high-ranking members of Via Afrika; a rare shot of the inner council of the Movement, chaired by Wyngate, preparing for a strategy session, showing logistical maps; an uncharacteristic and rather charming shot of Hossein enjoying himself at a party to celebrate the opening of the new Via Afrika offices in Albert Luthuli Crescent, Hackney, with a particularly clear view of the new office safe in the back-ground. Altogether these pictures constituted a rich, irreplaceable dossier of the major figures in the liberation movements. Where names or dates were unclear, Gladys Hossein's excellent memory supplied the missing information and Looper's achievements in clarifying this unique photographic record was widely regarded as a considerable feat.

Gladys Hossein was delighted, too.

Lying in Looper's bed, Biddy Hogan looked disconcertingly boyish with her cropped hair and assertive jaw. 'You're not slightly attached to English Rose?' Her green eyes glinted.

He almost smiled. The idea of anyone attaching himself to Rose was ridiculous. One fell into Rose's orbit, or beneath her influence, but the notion of 'attachment' was far too slight to describe rela-tions with English Rose. He looked out of the window. The snow was very heavy. 'Cheer up,' he told himself, 'this is spring.'

'Down at the Club,' Biddy persisted, 'they say she's pretty taken with you. Which means, in Rose's terms, that she views you as the glutton does the last chocolate in the box, or the piranha some pass-ing flesh.'

'Don't be silly.'

'Or the rough philanderer the foolish virgin.'

'You shouldn't believe what you hear in the Room. They're inter-ested in talk, not truth.'

'Surely it's not as absolute as that? There must be some truth beneath all the talk. I bet you've teased out a story or two from the loose talk that goes on late at night around the bar of the Hottentot Room.'

13

'It takes time to extricate the few nuggets of fact that float around all that liquid blather. The Room's a place for people who've nowhere else to go. They sit at the bar and talk about what might have been, or could still be. Never about what is. What might be true in the Room is not true anywhere else.' He buttoned up his coat.

She leaned forward. He saw her breastbone ridged and prominent, her tiny, apple-hard breasts pointed. She eyed him quizzically, 'But you take a semi-professional interest in the talk that goes on down there?'

'I'm a journalist. Of course I listen. I can't help it. I'm a professional listener. But I don't make the mistake of believing what I hear down there. The Room's a place for relaxing, it provides a rest from the world.'

She nodded. 'I used to be a scholar. I was trained to look beneath the words on the page for what was really being said. You see, I can't help it either. We have something in common.'

He did not find this suggestion particularly agreeable. He did not like her questing tone. He found something almost, not quite, but yes, almost *investigatory* about it. He decidedly disliked this quizzical mode, the clever metaphorical associations which linked English Rose with the glutton, the carnivore and the rapist and pictured him as the victim. He felt uneasy at the sceptical air with which Biddy Hogan delivered these insults in her curiously husky, almost hoarse voice. How odd that one so thin, flat, slight and bony should possess such a growl! He did not like the way she sat up in bed to make her points, not caring now that so much of her body was exposed, she who had been so determined to hide herself when she came to bed.

Biddy Hogan had come to bed quickly, edgily and only once under the covers did she remove her vest. The vest was unexceptional; white cotton with a sprinkling of daisies around the neck. There had been something in her grasp that left him dismayed and dissatisfied. Her approach could be described as vigorously experimental. That she was clumsy and inexpert was hardly surprising; he could not believe that she did this often. But it was her grasp of him that so perturbed. She was clearly unaware when a bite became painful, she had a tendency to grip and squeeze, her fingers became the talons of an impatient crone, mother of the tribe, prodding and pinching some nubile maiden for proofs of virginity. It occurred to

14

him that perhaps, in the guise of love-play, these sharp researches of his person were actually designed to keep him at arms' length. But he revised this opinion while he was undergoing her severe parsing of his parts, when the notion occurred to him it was more likely that she went through these beaky motions of love in order to pry from him the answers to questions that were troubling her. She picked him over like some augurer reviewing the warm entrails of the sacrificial dove for signs of the best way to proceed. What she transmitted through her fingers was not love but tension and trouble. He began dimly to perceive what had changed Biddy Hogan from the dutiful student of old into the radical mistress of Wyngate Hossein. What Biddy wished for, and deeply desired to defend and honour, was a cause which the world despised. In the old days, the love of her life had been Sidney, and life at its truest, was to be found in certain approved texts which excited her, but earned her the scorn and contempt of the world which preferred instead Hollywood, journalism, Hampstead novels, television. That had been enough. However, once out of Africa, out in the world and on her own, it must have come to her when she heard Hossein speak with a sudden clarity, in a flash Damascus-brilliant, that Sir Philip Sidney and the great tradition of the common pursuit and Shakespeare as a dramatic poem simply would not do any longer. She wanted action! As happens often to South Africans abroad, what began as love ended in politics.

He learnt this from her grasp of him. Yes, her hands were a hard school and in them he was given a sharp lesson. As she rode above him he saw that what drove Biddy Hogan was not, and had never been, solely intellectual, literary or even sensual, passion. The mistake had been to see her as one thing. In fact she was neither all head nor all heart. The inner storms that left her tense and white-faced were not tempests of passion nor ecstasies of art, what convulsed her was ideology! What had once seemed, in the university student, to be an incurable need to defend the text, and the literary theory which she brandished like a weapon with its belief in good writing, was in itself a misreading of the nature of Biddy Hogan. When she maintained that great art was a criticism of life and a severe scrutiny of human existence in which moral values would shine like jewels in the mire and everything else was entertainment, advertising or journalism, that was only part of her story.

15

For Biddy had come to see that it was by no means enough. The thing about life was not to criticise it but to change it, to take it in hand and alter it utterly. Naturally she herself had not recognised this to begin with and certainly nobody else had done so. Her natural element was her suspicion which she sent before her like a secret police force. Those who did not survive her investigation were branded. In another life, a former time, she would have made a great inquisitor, or a sniffer-out of witches. That was why she so disliked Frau Katie, for there was certainly a whiff of sulphur about the elderly, wild-eyed, domineering Berliner.

There was so much that was deliberately obtuse and mystifying about Frau Katie. Biddy had come only recently to the Hottentot Room and, despite her acceptance into 'the tribe' by the old lady, she had never really taken to it. Then just as she began to understand at least that nothing was what it seemed in the Hottentot Room, and that it was the magnetic will of the old lady that held all in place, she had been obliged to withdraw because of her relationship with Wyngate Hossein. She wanted everyone to know that he was in love with her. Frau Katie objected. That was something else she held against Frau Katie. Why should couples be barred from the Hottentot Room? Why should Frau Katie be against the convention of coupledom while seemingly tolerating any sort of promiscuity? Why, look at the affair between Mr Govender and his so-called daughter. Calling her his daughter only made matters worse, said Biddy, and, if true, quite horrible. If she wasn't his daughter, then they were having it off like any other couple and Mr Govender was a dirty old man because Anagupta was certainly young enough to be his daughter. And if she really *was* his daughter, then it was incest. And what exactly was the mystery about Frau Katie's illness? And why did the others call it Debussy's complaint? And what on earth was 'the old story' and why was Frau Katie so obsessed with it? And why did she go on about eloping with Looper?

These were some of the questions Biddy had plied Wyngate Hossein with during their time together. He, on the whole, had preferred not to waste time talking. Now, hurt, angry and bewildered after Hossein's rejection of her and abrupt return to his wife, Biddy directed her questions to Looper. He suspected she had allowed him to seduce her, partly at least, so as to detain him in a secure place and ask him certain questions. Yes, that was what he was doing – he was helping Biddy with her enquiries.

'What does an old German lady know about Africa? That's what I can't work out. I don't see the connection. When you think about it, Caleb, she doesn't relate. She doesn't relate to anything. Not to old Berlin, because that was destroyed long ago. It doesn't exist. And she's never been to Africa. And yet she talks as if she owned the place. Like she was a queen of both places. If you look at it carefully, at its very best, it's misdirected, this attachment. And very sad. At worst, it's grotesque, when you consider what she really is. It's Rose I'm really sorry for. What with her mother's dreams of German greatness. When you consider the sort of people who use the Club, and the sort of persecution they've suffered back home – it's odd that they should be so attached to Frau Katie who is an out-and-out Zionist. You might even say it was morally offensive.'

Looper pulled on scarf and gloves and took from the top of the cupboard an old green Tyrolean hat with a prominent feather, somewhat frayed at the edges, but still showing a broad sheen that hinted at more confident, assertive times. There was no immediate need to put on the hat indoors, after all the snow was falling outside, but when Biddy Hogan talked of morals it was better to be well covered. Looper began to understand why she detested Frau Katie. It was not because of his friendship with her. That wasn't what Biddy meant when she questioned the basis of the connection. What Biddy objected to was not Frau Katie's Club, or her age, or her witchery, or even her nationality. When Biddy said 'German' she meant something bad. When she said 'Zionist' she meant something worse. Looper was in a rush now. He checked his pockets as he always did before going out. He even remembered to pick up the letter from his father that had arrived that morning and stuff it unopened into his pocket. Time for that later. Besides, he could guess what it said. But he was in a rush and, as things turned out, haste made him careless. 'She is not a Zionist. She wouldn't know what the term meant.' It was meant to be his final word. It was meant to be goodbye.

Biddy persisted. Sitting up, quite naked now. 'She's a Zionist. Zionists persecute Palestinians with Hitlerian vigour,' Biddy added. 'Africans from white Africa are the last people to have dealings with Zionists.'

Looper stopped and turned. The overhead light danced blackly

17

on the green feather. 'The words you use are all just ways of not saying what you mean. You'll find it easier to call her a Hottentot.'

'You know what I mean.'

Naturally he knew what she meant and so he turned and left the flat, hurrying away from her meaning.

Earls Court station after midnight was an eerily empty, echoing cavern, still breathing the sweat and impatience of the fretting thousands who jostled through it every day. Outside the snow was falling heavily, giving the liquor shops, the grimy pubs and unlovely restaurants a soft shapely outline. Tonight all was dark, cold and clean. Usually he would have to pick his way among the drunks who crowded the entrance begging for cash. They thronged the area, bumping up against the windows of the liquor shops in their old, filthy coats, like elderly bumble-bees. This part of Earls Court was the domain of tourists, hikers, transients, bums, brightly dyed youth and a sprinkling of the dismayed elderly who shied away from the buckled and studded local punks and glanced in bewilderment at the foreign hikers with their maps, bulging backpacks, fresh faces and out of season suntans. The travel agency on the corner advertised the rates for air-freight to Johannesburg and Melbourne: £23 per carton, £26 per tea-chest. It was cheaper to Melbourne, he noticed. One pound less for cartons but the same price for tea-chests. Melbourne was much further than Johannesburg but then of course there were *more* Australians in Earls Court. Doubtless this brought the price down. Australians, New Zealanders, Arabs, Lebanese, South Africans and West Indians favoured an area of cheap hotels and rooming houses. Fading ads for Foster's lager wished passers-by a cheery 'G'day!'. Small red neon signs winked in the doorways: 'Vacancies'. Here were abortionists, bookies, many late-night grocers. The hotels had names like the Airport, the Student, Down Under. They had once been houses and the houses had once had pretensions: Hotel Weimar, Brinkley Court. But now even the late-night grocers were shut and the shop windows were reduced to a dull, neon hum. Only the clubs were still awake: La vie en Rose, the Black Cat. He could feel the muffled thunder of cellar rock beneath his feet. The traffic continued along Earls Court Road, it never stopped though hushed now by the snow it passed like a silent movie. The snow fell on all

18

conferring a momentary shocking purity. In winter the place was cold, wet, disconsolate. In summer it was hot and sticky. But now, in the snow, it looked almost well-kept. It was, thought Looper, a most unlikely London.

The snow peppered the air about his face until he could almost believe he saw the teeming molecules of which the atmosphere is said to be comprised, if only we had the eyes to see them. Then again, the snow did not so much fall, it poured from the sky. It raced, it fell, it needed to blot out everything as quickly as possible, it collapsed in an overwhelming need to be down and done, it ran, raged, smoked, it tore the air out of its way. It was as if on high a cloud had burst. No, not burst – exploded. Fragments rained. Had the Israelites wandering in the desert seen the manna falling from heaven like this? Had the story that we know perhaps been based on a misreading, a mis-memory? Perhaps it had not really been manna they saw, but snow falling, flakes of heavenly bread sailing into their parched mouths. Perhaps that had been the real miracle of the manna, a desert snow storm and the wandering Jews had lived on the miracle, a fabulous diet of snow and astonishment. The London snow grew gentler, now flocked and flew about his eyes and ears as the breeze sent the flakes this way and that. He was glad of his hat. In the upstairs room of one of the houses, someone was playing the violin. He recognised the Franck sonata. Moments of dreamy longing interrupted by storms of passion and sudden menacing intrusions by the piano. The snowfall thickened the sound, drew the long sobbing notes out into the night air, where it stifled them quickly.

Until he came to England, Looper had never seen snow. The small Transvaal town in which he had grown up offered no such exotic phenomena. The seasons were divided in two. In winter you wore a jersey and the grass of the front lawn burnt to a fine ash. In summer you wore shorts and the heat melted the tar on the road past the house. Snow fell only in books. Such was its rarity that the few boys at school who had seen and touched it were looked upon with awe. Yannovitch claimed to have seen it when he travelled to his sister's wedding in the Northern Cape. It had fallen beside the national road. It had been thick, white and woolly, according to Yannovitch, soft and not at all like ice. It felt soft and crumbly and he compared it with frozen sugar. He said he had tasted some and it had tasted like salted milk. There had been a great deal of it,

19

enough for a snowball fight and a snowman. Yannovitch said they would even have gone sledding, had there been time but they had to get on to the wedding. Now of course it was known that Yannovitch was a tremendous liar. But the others who heard him were not prepared to quibble about this. They looked on Yannovitch with enormously enhanced respect and felt tremendously grateful to him for the quality of his description. In their town there had once been a most ferocious hailstorm, some two or three hours of smashing stones. Hailstones clogged the drains and filled the gutters, banked up against walls and fences in white, frozen masses and if you looked quickly you could almost persuade yourself that it had been snowing, if your ears weren't still ringing from the cacophony of the huge ice stones bouncing on the corrugated iron roof. Then, within a couple of hours, the blazing African sun was out, the ice turned grey and ran away down the gutters. He had preferred Yannovitch's stories to this near glimpse of the almost real thing.

The traffic continued in Earls Court Road, but sedately and noiselessly.

Looper wondered if he was being followed. The snow made it very difficult to tell, closing down everything beyond eight or nine feet away. He could see very little. He shrugged. If he was under observation then the snow provided him with the equivalent protection. A snow storm had some use then. You could get lost in it quite easily.

Back at the flat Biddy Hogan was going through Looper's cupboard. In the pocket of one of his jackets she found an air ticket. She studied it incredulously. It was a first-class air ticket made out for that very night, in the name Caleb Looper. She walked over to a chest of drawers and leaned against it, still shaking her head. Then she looked to left and right as though wanting to ask someone, anyone, if what she saw on the ticket was true. London to Johannesburg! It was impossible. The ticket said Caleb was going home. He should have been on the plane that night. Yet Looper was prohibited from returning home. It was then that she took notice of the framed photograph above the bed. Possibly she was drawn to this woman with the sweet, sympathetic face. She had not recognised that face. She had not known the amiable countenance

20

was that of her former lover's wife, Gladys Hossein, until she peered at the round script.

> For Caleb – a friend of our struggle.

Biddy deciphered the signature. Then she looked again at the ticket. Then she sat on the bed and began to tremble.

CHAPTER 2

Looper had not intended to come to London. And when he had been obliged to come he detested it. Going to London had seemed the final insult to his father, the former Inspector of Mines, who had become convinced that his son's departure had something to do with the perfidious British, or more particularly, with one Briton whom Looper senior regarded as summing up in his person all the perfidy, arrogance, hypocrisy and humbug of which that nation was capable. That person was Dr David Owen, former Foreign Secretary in the Labour Government, and, more recently, leader of the Social Democratic Party. But recent developments did not interest Looper senior. For him Dr Owen was still British Foreign Secretary, the man who had set out to betray the white settlers of Rhodesia. In the sixties Looper senior drove petrol trucks to break the oil blockade against Rhodesia. When the white regime of Ian Smith finally capitulated and Rhodesia yielded to Zimbabwe, Looper senior began planning the defence of South Africa.

In the seventies in his very unsuccessful dealings with the rebels, Dr Owen had sometimes been accompanied in his attempt to solve the Rhodesian crisis by an American official, Andrew Young. This fact, however, failed to interest Looper's father. Indeed, Andrew Young did not even catch his eye. The reason for this, Looper suspected, was because Andrew Young was black and so once he arrived in Africa he simply faded into the background. Looper senior did not see black people in Africa. They became invisible. Once in Africa, the American official became just another African. So it was only Dr Owen Looper senior had eyes for. Or, as he put it, the Doctor loomed large in his sights. The approach of Dr Owen loomed so large that Looper senior began to feel about him as a Roman citizen might have done when Hannibal cleared the Alps and began rolling into Italy. Looper senior wrote frequently to his son in London. A long letter had been received only a few days before. The latest lay unopened in his pocket. In phrases choleric and declamatory, perhaps once a month, the former Inspector of Mines wrote in characteristic style:

I must warn you that any attempt by Dr Owen to take advantage of the country's present troubles, most of them caused by Britain and its international gang, will be stoutly resisted. I am now a man of advanced years, as you may or may not remember, but I shall be among the first to take up arms if Owen shows his face in this part of the world. Old man that I am, I will take my gun and I will use it. I am prepared to die for my beliefs. You may tell that to 'Doctor' Owen when next you see him. Our currency may be depressed. Black agitators may stalk our townships inciting peaceful people to riot and revolution as no doubt the good doctor chuckles to read in his morning paper. But we are not finished yet. We are not Rhodesia. We intend to fight. You can tell him that from me . . .

Clearly Looper's father imagined that his son saw Dr Owen every day and discussed steps in their subversion campaign. Indeed it was probable that Looper's senior's sole use for his son since he had been deported to London was as a useful conduit through whom he could communicate with 'that smarmy lounge lizard and greasy con-man whose first step upon our soil will be met with lead . . .' In Looper's experience, people who proclaimed their willingness to die for their beliefs usually meant that they were prepared to kill for them. Looper also knew that threats of violence against Dr David Owen were intended also to apply to him. That did not surprise him in the least. How could it have done? He and his father had already attempted to kill one another once before. That they had not succeeded still rankled with them both.

Looper generally located the origins of his murderous feelings towards his father in the Affair of the Bridge which had taken place when he was six or seven. One afternoon he had ridden his bicycle down to the railway line which ran near his house. There was a bridge across the line which it was forbidden to cross on a cycle. Caleb had dismounted and pushed his bike across. On the other side of the bridge the station master sat in a concrete box with a glass window. The station master came out of his box and settled his cap on his head. His hands were hairy and freckled. The way he put on his cap alerted young Caleb. Something bad was about to happen.

23

'What colour are you?' the station master demanded.

Caleb was astonished by the question and rather frightened. He repeated to himself the same question quietly and carefully before answering – to make sure he had heard right. 'White, sir.'

The peaked cap shook violently. 'No you're not. I can see you are a non-white little boy.'

'No, sir.' He was now seriously worried. Maybe this man knew something he didn't. He was an official, wasn't he? Like a policeman?

'Do you know why I can see you're a black boy?'

This question was too terrifying even to answer. Caleb felt nauseous. He felt as if he were falling into a deep pit. His stomach churned. The station master had a brown, creased face and he smelt of tobacco and hair oil.

'I can see that you're a black boy because you've come across the bridge which is only for non-white peoples. It says so on the noticeboard. Therefore you must be a native. Now if you want to change from being a native, you are going to have to go back across the bridge again and cross by that other bridge over there which is the bridge reserved for the use of white people only.'

But Caleb hadn't time for that. Perhaps if he had not felt so ill, if he had not been on the point of vomiting on the black polished toecaps of the big station master, he might have done as he was told and pushed his bike across the black bridge and made himself white again. Instead he pushed forward past the station master, flung a leg over his saddle and pedalled like a madman until the man's angry shouts faded behind him.

Later, of course, he had to cross the tracks again to get home and dared not go anywhere near the bridge, so he crossed the railway line at a point some miles away from the station though he knew this was dangerous because they had been warned never to cross the tracks except at a bridge or level-crossing. From that day on he was to avoid the bridge and the suburbs which lay beyond and this custom continued for many years.

When he got home that day his mother noticed immediately that something had disturbed him and soon had the story out of him. It was the first time she ever showed herself angry. And the last.

'I would like to go to the man's superiors and complain. He has no right to talk to you like that! What does he mean by frightening a child by calling him non-white?'

But his father had taken another view. 'Serves him bloody right. Teach him to use his eyes. We have a law in this country, Kitty –' this said in his 'you must be a visitor from Mars' voice '– a law which says one bridge for whites and one bridge for non-whites. Separate development. Separate facilities. If he doesn't learn that soon he's going to be in a lot of trouble one day. That station master did him a favour.'

'Shame on you! Caleb's a little boy. He doesn't understand.'

'Then he better start learning – chop, chop.'

At this time, Looper senior was just learning to scuba dive. The house was full of rubbery clothes, oxygen cylinders, snorkels and goggles. Mr Looper trained with a group of enthusiasts in the municipal pool. Plump men with hairy, freckled backs, wallowing in the water. Soon after this altercation, Looper's mother died. He still did not know why. He never asked and his father had never said. After Mr Looper lost his wife the underwater diving became an obsession. He spent his days down a mine, his spare time underwater. He took to stressing his military usefulness as a trained diver in time of conflict, pledging himself to serve his country should an underwater war erupt. The Transvaal town where they lived was many miles from the sea but that did not deter him. He had grown up by the sea, the Loopers were an old Cape family, 'Old and Pure', he liked to declare. 'Make no bloody mistake. Or if you do, in the part of the country where I come from, where the colours, so to speak, shade one into another, and if you can't tell the true stuff from a trier-on, even on a dark night with a lot of cloud, you could find yourself in the magistrate's court, bloody chop chop, I can tell you.'

Mr Looper did not seem grieved by the loss of his wife, in fact he seemed to feel himself rather usefully placed to get down to important matters. He took to wearing his diving gear around the house. He banged a large blue flipper on the table to emphasise a point and his temper, never good, grew ungovernable. He kept harking back to the incident on the railway bridge. He threatened to go and thank the station master, or buy him a drink. He spent most of his free time away on diving business, humping clanking equipment into a red Buick packed with his sunburnt, freckled friends. 'Now we're alone, Caleb,' he told his son, 'we better get ourselves sorted out. Know what I mean?' Caleb began to realise what he meant. Soon father and son began circling each other like

25

wrestlers, or knife fighters, looking for an opening, looking for the kill.

Looper brushed snow from his eyes and ears, hurrying down Antaeus Street. Halfway down Antaeus Street stood No. 31, the mock-Georgian house where a black sign swung rustily outside the front door. About eighteen inches tall, it depicted a woman with a grotesque protruding half-watermelon rump, the fabled steatopygous buttocks of the Hottentot. Looper paused in the driving snow and looked up at Frau Katie's bedroom window on the third floor. No light showed.

At the end of Antaeus Street, where it met the Old Brompton Road, stood a pub called the Joustings owned by jovial Siamese who would supply hot food to the Hottentot Room upon request. The Joustings was a favourite with two groups of expatriates, Australians and Sumatrans, between whom, for obscure reasons, bitter enmity existed. Battles sometimes erupted on Friday and Saturday nights when the two nations clashed bloodily on the pavements and full-breasted Australian girls screamed, 'Hurt him, Lance!' at huge, violent men who flung themselves fist and boot against small, dusky adversaries whose side-on stance and flashing blade-like hands suggested some deadly Sumatran martial art. The cries of the wounded sometimes floated through the windows of the Hottentot Room mingling with the hysterical wail of police sirens. The speciality of the Joustings was its traditional cooking: oxtail and bubble and squeak were among the specialities offered and this made it acceptable to Frau Katie's daughter, Rose, who objected deeply to the increasing numbers of foreigners thronging the cheap hotels of Antaeus Street. Across the road from the Joustings lay a cemetery protected by tall, black railings. The gravestones were mossy stumps, crooked and overgrown. In spring, when the rampaging grass threatened to choke them completely, Rose could be seen behind the railings, with other members of the Cemetery Preservation Society to which she belonged, hacking resolutely at the foaming greenery with a large scythe.

No. 31 Antaeus Street was flanked by two hotels, The Bella Vista and the Highland Glen. Across the road was the Melbourne. Frau Katie had bought the house on her arrival in England during the war and the Hottentot Room had opened its doors soon afterwards. The Club occupied the ground floor. In the cellar beneath, the

26

liquor was stored. On the two floors above Frau Katie and her daughter Rose lived in separate suites of rooms, the décor and colours of each reflecting the widely different tastes of mother and daughter. Light colours for Rose, Swedish furniture, chrome and glass. For her mother, heavy maroon velvet curtains drawn tight against light and air. Too much fresh air, said Frau Katie, was 'over healthy'. Heavy wooden cupboards, big brass bed, all the furnishing solid, heavy and rather ugly, gave her apartment a look of impressive permanence.

'Combed from the junk shops when she first came to London in the forties, looking for German furniture,' Rose said. 'She told me she had no choice because she was poor.' Rose shook her blonde head firmly. 'I believe you always have a choice. This is hers. And besides, she wasn't exactly poor. She had her pension and I believe she brought something with her when she came.'

When Morris, who knew about such things, pointed out that Frau Katie's furniture was English, Rose was not deterred.

'Yes, but it looks German.'

Looper stood in the porch at No. 31 stamping snow from his shoes. He removed his Tyrolean hat and banged it on the railings, taking care to avoid damaging the feather. The hat was a present from Frau Katie. Parked at the kerb was Frau Katie's car, an enormous black Mercedes from the 1950s with monstrous head-lamps covered in wire mesh and rust eating into the doors. In this vehicle she went shopping at Harrods and Liberty's, piloted by Gerrie the barman. He drove at a solid, stately pace which befitted the appearance of his ample passenger, who sat in the back with her pale powdered skin and her red hair, glancing neither left nor right, unperturbed by the stares of passers-by.

Once inside the hall that smelt of rubber boots, he hung his coat, hat, gloves and scarf in the cupboard that smelt of wet afternoons and mud and blew several times on his cold hands. His shoes were wet through. He cursed himself for a fool; ten years on a damp island and still he did not understand how to dress to keep warm and dry. More than once over the years, when Wyngate Hossein had reminded him of 'our friends on the Island', meaning that distant prison on Robben Island off Cape Town, Looper had reminded him there were other island prisons in which to be in-carcerated.

'God, don't let me become old and cold in England,' had been

27

his prayer, as the years abroad lengthened. He foresaw the day when, weakened by successive misreadings of the treacherous seasons, he would step briskly, one layer too few, into a falsely beckoning spring morning which deceived with its glittering sun in a clear blue sky, only to switch in a trice into the rawest winter day, and would be sent coughing and wheezing to his grave. Well, in the past few days God, it seemed, had answered his prayers in His own curious fashion. Looper had been called back home to the warmth. But it was a call he did not wish to hear; a call that he found himself unable to accept.

CHAPTER 3

The Room was quiet and dim, lit only by the curious lamps on the horseshoe bar. On some, Cossack horsemen in red and black, brilliantly glazed, carried where their saddle-bags should have been, fat yellow bulbs. On the veined parchment shades of others, soldiers in blue tunics and brass helmets goosestepped briskly. The lamps threw an uncertain light on the circular tables and narrow benches, covered in elderly red plush, that filled the room. At one end of the horseshoe bar sat five or six drinkers crowded together, as if for warmth and comfort. Above the bar hung a fading, striped blue and white canopy which gave it the look of some forlorn Continental café. The bar was beflagged and fringed with bank-notes from African countries, many of which existed now only in the distant music of their names – dominions and dependencies of vanished powers, extinguished kingdoms, forsaken colonies – Tanganyika, Rhodesia, Biafra, Nyasaland, various Congos, the notes hung in sheaves like witchdoctors' medicine. All were dead. Some had died from inflation, or history, or army coups. Some came from countries which had renamed their currencies with each succeding coup, so that no one knew any longer which treasuries of which brief presidential reign these gaudy paper tokens represented. Gifts of members of the Hottentot Room long gone. Often these donors had been swept aside in the revolutions they had gone home to serve – shredded, consigned to flames like these same banknotes, with their heads of national redeemers, sacred elephants, *kabakas*, tanks, gods, queens or flywhisks. In one dark corner stood a grand-father clock with the face of a spiky-haired peasant, wearing a lunar grin. More banknotes were pinned to the awning like the pelts of small animals.

Behind the bar, where old Gerrie the barman resided, were displayed among the bottles wooden carvings of little men with enor-mous erections, scowling masks with sack hair, geometrical facial incisions and sad slit eyes; there were drums of various sizes made from cow-hide stretched over beer cans or paraffin tins; pale and roundly gleaming calabashes strung in bunches; ostrich eggs illus-

29

trated with scenes of Bushmen hunting buck; there was any amount of garish copper ware, flamingos feeding, presentation dishes bearing the arms of the City of Bloemfontein and the military memorials of Salisbury. Gerrie polished the copper daily. The copper had a deep orange colour, darkening in certain lights to red, giving it the look of some kind of artificial, almost metal meat. In fact it looked rather like some of the artificial foodstuffs with which the former philosopher Buffy Lestrade liked to terrorise the other members; protein made from seaweed, or, for the incorrigible flesh eaters, a look-alike meat manufactured from mushrooms (or a look-somewhat-alike, as Gerrie sourly observed). It would have looked rather sad and tawdry in the daylight, but the daylight never penetrated the Hottentot Room. The curtains were always drawn.

Pride of place behind the bar was given to a short piece of cane, about two feet long and not unlike the sort of thing once used by teachers. On one end of the cane was a copper grip. Below the cane was a brass plaque which read: *Coree's Cane*. Coree's name was also inscribed on the copper grip. It was said by Frau Katie that this was the original Hottentot cane given by the Dutch to the Hottentot Captain, Coree, in the seventeenth century. Hottentot canes had been presented to various leaders of the Hottentots whom the Colonial Governors in the Cape of Good Hope, both Dutch and British, had regarded as helpful and loyal. Coree had been a noted Hottentot captain under the brutal regime of the Dutch governor, Simon van der Stel. Such canes were rare. The chiefs who had carried them were assured of good relations with the white authorities in the Castle in Cape Town. At the same time those who carried the cane were widely despised among their own people for having collaborated with the detested Dutch invaders.

The Hottentot cane was a symbol of the relations between the people who had once lived in Southern Africa and the white Dutch who took it over. The indigenous Coloured people of Southern Africa had felt from the very start, as the earliest records show, the feeling of unremitting hatred for the white invader. And the Dutch, in their turn, viewed the Hottentots with immovable contempt. So it had been and so it continued to be. The British also continued the custom of the Hottentot canes when they occupied the Cape of Good Hope.

'I possess,' said Frau Katie proudly, 'perhaps the only example of a Hottentot cane. The only thing more rare than a Hottentot cane is a Hottentot!'

A British expedition had kidnapped Coree and brought him, together with his cane it was presumed, to London.

'He took one look at the place and refused to be kind,' was the way Frau Katie put it. 'He told them they could keep it. It was dirty, damp and so dreary! Thanks, but no thanks! said Coree. So they took him all the way back to Africa and dumped him back on the beach from where they kidnapped him, thinking they were doing him such a big favour!'

Frau Katie had found the cane years before on the Bermondsey market. 'Maybe they took it away from Coree for being such an ungrateful visitor,' Frau Katie suggested. She often toasted his memory. Coree was the patron saint of the Hottentot Room.

Now into this wanton display of Africana, Frau Katie had introduced memories of her home town, Berlin, as it had been during its heyday in the early decades of the century. Behind Gerrie the barman was the head of an old lion with soft, glazed brown eyes which gave him a kind, faintly pleading doggy look which contrasted greatly with the strong yellow teeth bared in a frozen roar. From one strong molar there hung a collection box exhorting the charitable to *Save the White Rhino!* Beside it a brightly coloured poster behind glass depicted the Potsdamer Platz in Berlin in 1915. A newspaper-seller in a blue coat and cap lounged by a lamp-post. Behind him was his stall showing an extraordinarily colourful range of illustrated papers. A flower-seller, clearly posed, with a great wide basket of blooms proffered a bunch of red carnations to the viewer of the poster while behind her little boys in straw boaters, men in bowlers, drivers of carts and passengers in yellow trams gazed with round-eyed astonishment at the invisible photographer. Various other views of the old city were offered, ranging from the Luther Memorial to the arrival of the Kaiser in the Pariser-Platz, driving in an open carriage to an enthusiastic welcome of his loyal subjects, who cheered and waved their handkerchiefs.

The Hottentot Room, founded in 1950, had been one of the very first clubs for expatriate Africans. Their best days were long passed. In the fifties and sixties there had been a number of such establishments scattered across London: The Zanzibar in Baron's Court, The Safari in Chelsea, the Laager a few blocks away on Earls Court Square, the Calabash in Knightsbridge (though that was really a

31

nightclub and strip joint). First to open, last to close, that was the boast of the Hottentot Room. Most of the clubs had been formed in the days when entry to Britain for exiles and tourists alike had been easier, when universities opened their doors to African students, and the newly independent states sent their young men and women for a glimpse of what was still regarded by black and white Africans as the mother country. Such establishments comforted Africans newly ventured abroad who suffered quite terribly from the homesickness which the Continent inflicts on those who think they can escape her. These clubs eased the shock which accompanied the discovery that although English might have been the home language of these visitors, England was not the home country. Despite the books one had read, the films, the illusions of the shared culture, England was a foreign place. The clubs provided delicacies sorely missed, local beer and cigarettes, as well as political gossip, offers of accommodation, job contracts, rivalry, love and camaraderie among whites, blacks, Coloureds, Asians, men and women, Muslims, Christians and Jews. A form of mixing which was very often unthinkable in the countries from which these young visitors originated.

Not even the racial intolerance of the native English, then in its sullen, muttering *sotto voce* infancy, could dilute the pleasure of being abroad in the great capital. The sixties were the high years of these convivial, boozy organisations. The seventies saw them dwindle. The Africans who came to Europe in the seventies were not as clubbable, perhaps because they were not as vulnerable. The independent countries from which they now came were older and wiser and the mother country was, in any event, not quite so maternal. The immigration barriers had been rising steadily, racial hatred was an everyday reality. Then, too, there were far fewer of the true exiles, expatriates, refugees and drifters who had once constituted the solid core of the clubs, those desperate, unhappy, uncertain souls who were not sure if they would ever return home, or even if there would be a country to which they would be allowed to return. As the tide of independence moving down from the north reached even some white states in the south of Africa in the seventies, as worries about drought, exports and genocide overtook the potent rhetoric of the freedom struggle, the Africans who travelled abroad were, increasingly, professionals: aid officials, medical students, trainee fighter pilots, agriculturists. This new breed did not go into the clubs. They did not need to remind themselves of their African image and when they did they visited the Africa Centre, or the Commonwealth Institute, or the ethnic restaurant of their choice. Increasingly, many of them preferred not to be reminded of home at all and lived in Chelsea or Buckinghamshire and went wind-surfing at the weekends.

One by one the clubs dissolved. Only Frau Katie's establishment remained and prospered. It was helped, no doubt, by the fact that it represented members from white-ruled Southern Africa where political development remained at a stage which most other African states had experienced some twenty-five years earlier. Then again, unlike many of the clubs which were run by committees of like-minded individuals, the Hottentot Room, by contrast, was founded and owned by Frau Katie who did things in her own way, oper-ating, as her daughter Rose said, 'upon private capital for obscure motives . . .'

Frau Katie with her pale skin, her green eyes, and her dyed red hair, was a friend, a confidante, an institution. Her whimsical rules for entry to the Club were accepted without question. Indeed, while not quite understanding them, members approved the methods by which she selected those admitted to the inner circle, to the little tribe of which she unashamedly professed to be queen. She alone selected new members. There was no method of applying. You were chosen.

By and large, those who sat around the bar in the Hottentot Room on most nights were a collection of refugees and escapees from Southern Africa, exiles, expatriates who had been washed up on this small northern island. A keen observer might notice how they would sometimes pause in mid-conversation, glasses frozen between bar counter and lips, and cock an ear as if they heard the distant thunder of surf upon another sunnier, southern shore. Or they would mop their brows in an involuntary habit, though there was no sweat to wipe. Or bat imaginary mosquitoes. There came, too, wild-eyed young radicals in the flight from a township mass-acre, or a political raid or a house arrest or a banning order. These were orphans of the frequent storms which broke in the black townships when stone throwers took on armed police and were cut down. And then there were the plain tourists, the curious, the hangers-on who had heard of the Hottentot Room and who paid their pound for one night's membership and came to gape at such

33

legendary figures as Buffy Lestrade, or Wyngate Hossein, or perhaps just for the South African beer served in the Hottentot, or perhaps simply because they were homesick and hated Europe for its crowds, its endlessly complicated, tedious politics and its cool indifference to the very heart of the world which they knew Africa to be.

However, there was a most crucial difference between those who attended an evening in the Room, and those people who were selected to become members of Frau Katie's little tribe, her band of Hottentots. To become a member of the tribe presided over by Frau Katie in the Hottentot Room was a complex business and a privilege extended to very few. The induction of Wyngate Hossein was perhaps the most famous example of her method of extending an invitation. Hossein had only recently been released from prison and fled from house arrest in South Africa, arriving one evening in London, tired, disorientated and confused. A friend had taken him to the Hottentot Room on the way home to his wife, who had been patiently waiting for many years for the release of her husband. Hossein had become very drunk very quickly, not surprisingly, after his years of prison abstinence. Frau Katie had mothered him, fed him and then settled him down on one of the red plush benches, as she had done with many another member when he or she was too drunk or too sad to go home.

'Your wife waited and waited all those years when you were in prison. Don't you think she can wait one more night? One night will not harm her. Believe me, darling, I know how you feel when you flee the disease. I, too, did it. Apart from your grief at leaving your home, you are also confused. Tell me nothing! I know, certainly. You feel like a country pumpkin when you come from here to there.' Frau Katie's throaty Berlin accent deepened in sympathy. Taking a tartan travelling rug from behind the bar and throwing it on the bench, she ordered: 'Snuggle up for some shut-eye, sweetie-pie. Relax! Frau Katie welcomes you to the Hottentot Room.'

Invitation was by photograph or by postcard. The prologue was a tale of childhood.

'We lived in Dahlem, which is a suburb of Berlin. What you would call a good area.' Frau Katie pronounced this 'aria'. At this point in the selection process the unwitting candidate might be shown the photograph. Yellow with age it pictured an elderly man, bald, pleasant and smiling, sitting beside his wife, who was round and dark and wore a calm, gracious smile. They sat on chairs on a lawn. Behind them stood a young boy and a girl in their late teens. The boy was wearing uniform. 'That is me and beside me my brother, Max. Behind him, in the left-hand corner, sweeping the drive, is Dieter the gardener. We had three gardeners. You are looking at the family Brahm as they were years ago when we were at home. And happy. And no one had heard of the old story.' She sipped a glass of champagne and eyed the prospective recruit, watching him or her closely, for this was the test and the reaction to it, which only she could read, was crucial. No concession was made to the fact that the person addressed had probably lately come from Soweto, or Germiston, or Luderitz or some South African desert town and could hardly be expected to have any acquaintance with the suburbs of Berlin some fifty years before. None the less she would watch closely as if she was searching for some sympathetic gleam, some imaginative attempt to comprehend the great changes, the long journey between the girl in the white dress on the lawn and the old foreign lady with her champagne, her brilliant eyes, her vivid green or blue silk dress and her red hair. Gerrie the huge barman, once a boxer, would watch her closely when she was at the bar and fill her glass the moment the level dropped. Gerrie himself drank heavily, which was something Frau Katie approved of, saying she could never have trusted a barman who didn't hit the bottle. Her other opening gambit, when assessing a possible member, was to mention some of her former friends . . .

'Believe it or not, I was a friend of Von Ribbentrop, once. In his better years. My husband, the General, played bridge with him. But of course I also knew Pastor Niemöller. We mixed with all sorts. And until the end, I corresponded with Dönitz.'

Out came the postcards from the Admiral, written in green ink. To be shown the Dahlem photograph or a Dönitz card was the secret sign admittance to the tribe was being favourably considered, and membership would sometimes follow. However these symbols did not always evoke the response she was looking for. And then the unsuccessful visitor, unaware often that he or she had even been an applicant, was returned to the outer circle of the Hottentot Room, to the crowd of gawpers, bruisers and casual visitors who crowded the bar most evenings, swapped gossip from the distant townships, regaled each other with instances of the bitterly amusing idiocies of apartheid, swapped van der Merwe jokes, cricket scores,

35

sang old rugby songs, cursed the white nationalist government or defended it as the only hope for the future, pointed out to each other well-known exiles, many of them banned by the South African government and therefore never mentioned or quoted at home – figures such as Wyngate Hossein and the deported journalist, Caleb Looper, and Mr Govender, president of the Congress of Allied Democrats, who had had that affair with the white gynaecologist in Durban so many years ago. Her name they could never remember but they recalled she had killed herself before the case came to trial under the Immorality Act. Among those who paid their pound for a night's admittance were increasing numbers of young people whose wild angry looks proclaimed them to be students who had fled the killings in the black townships and now fumed in Clapham bedsits waiting for the revolution, or gave wild drumming displays in the Commonwealth Institute before enthusiastic but incomprehending audiences of local well-wishers who tried not to tap their feet for fear of giving the impression that they were moved by the drummers' sense of rhythm. If these crowds of casual members became too excited, or attempted to overstay their allotted time, then old Gerrie Germishuis moved in. The visitors pointed incredulously, for this was the boxer with the steel plate in his head who had killed several white opponents and a number of black burglars back in his South African heyday, and had been widely admired on both counts. At the time punch drunk and slipping badly in the ratings, Gerrie had travelled to Brighton for a fight with a young southpaw – his first ever visit abroad – and was dropped in the fourth with a looping right that put him in hospital for a month and left him with a steel plate in his forehead and a tendency to mumble or twitch whenever the booze he swallowed began to wear off. Ruined, twitching and ashamed to go home, Gerrie had found his way to the Hottentot Room and Frau Katie had taken him on as barman, chauffeur, bodyguard – this last function was necessary, she told him, because the Gestapo were still after her.

Although the Hottentot Room being a private club possessed a late-night licence, pub hours for the visitors were strictly observed and Gerrie called 'time' each night around about ten-thirty. The Room was clear by eleven and returned to the possession of the tribe, who in fact were rarely to be found there in any numbers before the crowds had left. Thereafter they drifted into the room in

36

ones and twos and might spend an hour, or the night, at the bar. The red plush bench seats and the tartan rugs, kept beneath the bar had bedded down the various members on many occasions when they were too tired, or drunk or bored, to return to their legitimate couches.

Looper looked at the human beings with which Frau Katie had bedecked the bar, the odds and ends held on to against good advice and common sense, even the ridicule of Frau Katie's daughter, English Rose, who declared them to be worthless, quite possibly dangerous. Certainly ineffectual. But Frau Katie treasured them because they represented a stubborn faith in the capacity of the tribe to survive. Those who saw them as she did would know them for what they were – her strength and support. And they were more important than good advice and common sense which was in huge supply in England. Everyone had more of that than they needed. Or perhaps wanted. The Hottentots then, saw themselves as having fetched up, by great misfortune upon a miserable island. They had fallen among the master race. They wished to register their objections. They had, it was true, learned too many of the master's ways. They drank his liquor, caught his diseases, traded with him and accommodated him. All right, they'd compromised. But they would not give in. They would not go under. They would never go over to the enemy. And if some of the Hottentots did not believe this with all their hearts – then Frau Katie believed it for them. Her faith and their gratitude made the bond between the queen and her Hottentots.

CHAPTER 4

Sitting around the horseshoe bar Looper found most of the tribe. Buffy Lestrade in a pale cream suit was there. Mr Govender of the Congress of Allied Democrats, for once without his beautiful daughter, Anagupta. Morris Morrison, the copywriter, in dark blue suit, red rose in his buttonhole, with his look of slightly furtive respectability. Elize from Zimbabwe puffed a small black cheroot and wiped her eyes on the back of her sleeve. Her tweed jacket was too tight across her powerful shoulders.

'Looks like the end of the road,' said Gerrie. His eyes were red and moist. He poured Looper a whisky.

Spare and elegant, with the head of a bird of prey but with that curious brown, bruised look about the eyes, Mr Govender said: 'We've all been in to see her. It's difficult to say whether she recognised me, but I hope she felt my presence.'

'My visit was too short,' Morrison said with a wan smile. 'I'd like to see her again.'

'The doctor's been and given her a shot, pain control. That's all they have to offer, at the end, these allopathic chaps,' said Lestrade, rubbing his massive forehead.

'Rose is with her,' said Elize. 'Wyngate dropped in. He'll be back later. The boys from Soweto haven't been. Wyngate's trying to reach them. Mona came for a while, but she was too upset to go and see Katie so she went off on a long run. Biddy Hogan hasn't come. We don't know how to contact her. Frau Katie told Wyngate that he looked overworked. She said his revolution wouldn't be won from a desk. She told him the master race would be very pleased if he died from paperwork.' Elize grinned through her tears. 'She asked after you. She said she wasn't going anywhere without you. Her old joke.' At the thought of this old whimsical joke of Frau Katie's Elize began sobbing again.

Looking embarrassed, Gerrie the barman gave her his tea towel. Lestrade clicked his tongue and took his silk handkerchief from his breast pocket. 'Cretin!' he said to Gerrie. *'Jaap!'*

'Don't call me a *jaap*,' said Gerrie. 'You fat freak.'

'Shut up, both of you,' said Mr Govender. 'Do you want Rose

38

to find us squabbling when her mother is dying?'

'What does it matter?' Lestrade asked. 'We can't sink much lower in her esteem.'

'Does she want me to go up?' Looper asked.

'She'll come down for you,' said Elize.

'We thought you might know of a way of getting a message to Biddy Hogan,' said Mr Govender with feigned innocence.

'Me? Why should I know?' Looper enquired with matching lack of guile.

The phone on the bar rang abruptly. They all looked at it. No one spoke. No one suggested it might be for Looper. Gerrie picked up the receiver. It was Wyngate Hossein. They could hear his booming voice. He had been to the house in Balham where the Knights lived and there was no sign of them. He asked if Biddy had arrived. Gerrie said no one knew where she was. Hossein said he was on his way back. Too bad about Biddy. Gerrie agreed.

'Why can't I go up?' Looper demanded.

'Rose insists we only go up with her,' said Lestrade. 'She's very much in charge tonight. Ordering everyone about. It's awful, but there you are. Frau Katie *is* her mother, after all. Hard though it is to believe. If this is how she is now – can you imagine what she'll be like when Frau Katie's gone? Our days are numbered. I can tell you that.'

Looming particularly large that night, as if drawing sustenance from the time of crisis, Lestrade was very much on form. Byron Francis Elisha Lestrade had been named for a poet, a saint and a prophet. Reduced, when such associations embarrassed him, to B. F. E. Lestrade. Afterwards, and always, he was 'Buffy' Lestrade. Well, almost always. In later years there were very few who ever knew that Lestrade's name derived from his initials and even fewer still knew what those initials stood for. Indeed it could be said that one of the greatest achievements of Buffy's life was to put so much distance between those early given names and the extraordinary person he later became. This disconnection had to do with his father. It had, after all, been his father who named him and thereby had shown the extent of his ambition for his son. It had even more to do with the fact that Buffy's father had, once upon a time, reputedly played right wing for a semi-professional football club in Pretoria called the Comets. There was even the story that Lestrade *père* had been a traffic policeman. The young and very incredulous among Lestrade's students heard these rumours with utter disbelief;

the more envious learnt and repeated them with feelings of delicious relief, because the point about Buffy was that he did nothing to scotch the rumour that he was the illegitimate son of an eminent mathematician from Cologne. To the intellectual faithful, however, the distant rumour that he was in fact the progeny of a traffic cop from Pretoria seemed like sacrilegious mischief; while even to those who disliked him it seemed unlikely.

Lestrade had been, in the days when he worked in the university, quite simply the most famous Marxist in the Southern Hemisphere. Impressive to behold, he was a large, solid man with the head of a massive river boulder, a smooth and gleaming ovoid, sleekly ornamented with a few fine hairs. He had begun his intellectual career as a Heideggerian specialist. No one else had ever heard of Heidegger and so Lestrade's knowledge was rare and powerful. He would alternatively terrify and delight his students by confronting them in German, enunciated in great round syllables, with the formidable question: *'Was ist das Sinn von Sein?'* What is the meaning of being? This would be snapped out with unexpected force. Though they seldom knew what he meant, so impressed were they by the foreign brilliance of it that the younger, newest students, frequently broke into applause and then threw their hands to their mouths and sat red-faced, eyes popping with embarrassment at their own reactions. Lestrade read aloud in German. He thought nothing of thinking aloud in Spanish. He decorated his lectures with French phrases. He had a particular affection for the phrase: 'le néant', which he expressed with a sudden extension of the fingers of his right hand and a loud braying sound as he fell on the final vowel and swallowed it. He *wrote* in his books. He bent their covers back until they cracked. He swore in Italian. He thrilled his students with invitations to his 'book cave' where all was solid with foreign titles and Wagner played very loudly on the hi-fi and delicate oriental teas were offered. As a student of Lestrade's, taking a course in German philosophy – 'From Hegel to Nietzsche and Beyond', Looper had never been invited to the book cave and feelings of intellectual inadequacy soon drove him from the course. Biddy Hogan had been a regular visitor.

The size of Lestrade's head, the fluency of his foreign tongues, his rough way with books, scratching underneath the phrases with a blunt pencil, the volume and violence of his cerebral processes, the stabbing forefinger, the way he had of raising his pudgy fist and smashing it down upon the text under examination to emphasise a

point with the sort of force one associated with men at fairgrounds
swinging a hammer to ring a bell – all tested his students severely.
He discoursed loudly and with a somewhat disdainful air on the
concepts of Heidegger's thought – on *'Sorge'* or care, on 'being-in-
the-world', on the 'fall into everydayness'. He managed to give the
impression that these pearls were quite wasted on the bone-headed
mono-lingual provincials he had the misfortune of instructing. He
sang snatches of favourite *Lieder*. When he retired to his book cave
he sometimes donned an Arab jellaba which flapped about his
portly frame and made him look rather like Mr Toad after his
escape from jail disguised as a washer-woman. He would sing:

> *'Dunkel, wie dunkel in Wald und in Feld!*
> *Abend schon ist es, nun schweiget die Welt.'*

Buffy Lestrade openly declared his profound respect for Mao
Tse-Tung and considered Russian communism dull and vulgar. He
was described by his senior students as being 'left of Moscow' and
the thrill this gave to those who heard it was still recalled with
excitement years after Lestrade had left the university. It must be
remembered that very few students on the campus had met anyone
of the left in those days, none of them had ever been to Moscow
and the designation as being to the left of Moscow suggested a
political position so extreme that it disappeared off the radar
screens of their minds. Lestrade was in every sense deliberately outrageous, at times he invited ridicule yet no one laughed at his tall,
portly figure in the flowing, floating, white cotton jellaba or refused
his offers of Darjeeling tea, or dreamt of attempting to answer his
questions about the meaning of being.

Lestrade taught Heidegger's concept of the 'dwelling-in-the-
world' of the *Dasein*, the there-being of existence, which he always
pronounced buzzingly – *Existenz*, using English and German terms
interchangeably thus hopelessly compromising the spelling ability
of his students which had never been good, as well as giving them
a taste for German compounds, a love of hyphens which pock-
marked the prose of a generation of political radicals who learned
their Hegel, Heidegger and Marx at the knee of Buffy Lestrade.
Looper remembered Lestrade on the campus when he was at the
very height of his fame, when he blew, as the student newspaper
said, 'like a fresh wind across the stale acres of the campus'. Stale
acres they may have been but Looper had never been able to think

of Lestrade as anything so ethereal as a wind. He was too corporeal, too solid for that.

His departure from the university had been as sensational as his politics and his exotic tea ceremonies. This was provoked by the affair of the Registrar's nephew. Lestrade, it was said, had seduced the boy, a very beautiful young physicist named Justin to whom he had been giving special classes on the philosophy of science with special reference to Heisenberg's uncertainty principle. This principle held that it was possible to plot the position of sub-atomic particles but then you couldn't tell their speed. On the other hand, if you could tell their speed you couldn't work out their position. The uncertainty principle delighted Lestrade and frightened many of those to whom he expounded it. Its effect upon the Registrar's nephew was never clear.

Lestrade resigned in a blaze of publicity, pinning his letter of resignation to the Principal's door. People were reminded of Luther. He gave away his selection of exotic teas. He sold his books. The sale took days and students could be seen streaming from his rooms carrying thick expensive texts in foreign languages. People were reminded of Faust. Then Lestrade announced he was leaving the country, but not for any academic post abroad. He forswore philosophy, he abjured politics, he announced that he intended settling in Cologne where he would open a male brothel, or perhaps begin an opera troupe dedicated to bringing opera to the people by giving performances of *Aida* and *Carmen* in football stadia. Whether one or other of these projects had failed, or never got off the ground, did not much matter. All the appeal of Lestrade's plans lay in their enunciation. Expression, intention, articulation, style – these were more compelling and exciting than the boring matter of seeing them into being. These plans, like his philosophy, his politics, were a matter of oratory, a form of private music which he sang in his booming organ tones and which, while the music lasted, his listeners found utterly beguiling and convincing. But their belief too was not important to Buffy. He made this music for himself. If others enjoyed it, well and good. But he was himself the audience which he most wished to please.

'Cologne,' said Buffy, when asked about it later, 'fell through.' And what a fall was there! Cologne had been tested and found wanting. Cologne would grieve, Buffy's tone suggested, when it discovered its loss. But it would be too late. Buffy came to London where he fell among faddists.

For those who remembered, as Looper did, the booming savant of the early days, London represented the beginning of the falling off. Buffy Lestrade, philosopher of authenticity and *Existenz* and the meaning of being, the Maoist to the left of Moscow, Germanist, Sartrean existentialist, tea drinker extraordinaire became a food freak, with a brief spell on the way down as an animal liberationist when he had joined the military raids on an Essex mink farm, released animals from various laboratories and tormented fox hunters. But as Lestrade now freely confessed, this hadn't been his line. He had always intensely disliked animals and as a result he soon moved into the field of militant nutrition.

'Enough of theory, time to act,' was the way he put it. Action included exposure of the hidden substances which contaminated our diet; sugar, salt, fat, preservatives. Lestrade's group raided supermarkets, slapping labels on suspect foods, identifying their poisons. They especially hated all dairy products, mixed gravel in pots of cream, put sugar into butter, punctured milk caps. The more radical among them attacked restaurants which used butter in their sauces and served cream with their sweets; a few hotheads attacked and beat up fat men in the streets for flaunting their capitulation to the food merchants. It was said, too, that Lestrade had once belonged to a group of militant joggers who ran along pavements early in the morning and late in the evening deliberately jostling slower pedestrians in their path, choosing those they regarded as being slow, or plump, or out of condition. Whether they did this to cause injury to the pedestrians or to attract notice to themselves was never certain. In any event, there was wide disagreement as to whether Lestrade had ever belonged to this band. It wasn't that people couldn't imagine him doing it, in principle, but he was such a square, solid fellow, that one could not imagine him jogging at all.

Frau Katie's analysis of Lestrade's condition was merciless. 'Once he was a philosopher. He taught about the big moment when someone chooses to be true. When you take your freedom. When you live – whatever the consequences! Once he believed in the thinking hero. He took a proper interest in death. Now all he believes in is living to be a hundred! Ah ja . . . Pity he never read his Nietzsche since he came to London.'

Lestrade grew very irritated under these attacks. 'That was all talk. This is action.'

'Oh yes, oh yes. Frightening people about what they eat, that's

43

some action. Spoiling meat, that's action. Smashing eggs. And when people won't listen, smashing heads! That's action.'

'We try to persuade. People should learn that these food merchants package the poison that gives them cancers, allergies, heart failure.'

'And those that won't be persuaded, you liquidate. Ja? But I don't blame you, my poor friend. It's coming here that has done it. Once you were a big atheist. Fearing nothing. You threw out God and heaven and fire and devils. And now you go around frightening people with stories about salt.'

'I really can't argue with you if you're going to simplify everything.'

'Who's simple? Listen who's talking! No, Herr Professor. The fault is not your own. You have fallen among the English and in England they free themselves from God only to terrify everyone with their moral fanaticism . . .'

'Very clever,' said Buffy.

'Not me,' Frau Katie replied sweetly. 'Nietzsche. Remember him?'

The grandfather clock with the peasant's face struck one. Elize from Zimbabwe was drinking steadily. Short, square, powerful with smooth, handsome looks and darkly curled hair, Elize should have been the calmest of them all. She had been a nursing sister for many years and had seen death often. Her name was something of a misnomer. She actually came from the Cape Province and was a Coloured. She had been closely involved in the violent clashes between Coloureds and police that had scarred the Province. At first she had coped with the stream of wounded carried into her hospital in the way to which she was best suited: she nursed them. The violence grew worse. She herself had been teargassed, whipped and imprisoned for going to the aid of demonstrators shot by the police. Then, one night, when she was on duty a number of young men in her ward who had been admitted to hospital earlier in the day suffering from buckshot wounds jumped up and, still in their dressings, demanded to be allowed to rejoin the battle raging in the Coloured townships. Elize, thinking she was doing her duty, tried to prevent them leaving. The young men were angry, Elize was firm, fighting broke out and she was punched and knocked to the ground while horrified patients looked on. The young men accused her of being a government stooge and a traitor to her people. Then they ran off to rejoin the battles in the streets.

44

The attack shattered Elize. As she put it: 'When the wounded leave their beds to rejoin the war, then I feel my work is useless.' The wild charges of treachery also grieved her terribly.

She moved to Bulawayo, in Zimbabwe, believing she could place her nursing skills at the service of 'a post-liberation' government. But after working for a time in a mission hospital Elize found herself treating men and women who had been beaten and tortured. Before long she discovered that those abused tended to be opponents of the government and the methods used against them were those of the previous, despised white regime. 'I felt as if I were travelling back in time,' she said. She made her complaints known to the authorities and was promptly deported. Since it was impossible for her to return to South Africa, sympathetic organisations to which she had sent details of the torture and mistreatment of prisoners, arranged for her to be granted political asylum in Britain.

In London she devoted herself to Frau Katie, on the one hand, and to Mona May on the other, both needs being supplied by attendance at the Hottentot Room.

Mona May was the brilliant young high-jumper from the Bushveld, who at sixteen had already cleared just under two metres and trained, it was said, back home by competing against a tame springbok named Hendrik, which she had rescued after poachers had made off with its mother. As a South African, Mona May was unable to compete in international meetings and so, following the example of other sportsmen, she had taken British citizenship on the basis that her great-grandfather, who had absconded from London with a large sum of money in the late nineteenth century had been proud to be British and his descendants had always renewed their claim.

Mona came to London and hated it. When interviewed by the press and asked what she wanted, she invariably said she wanted to go home. She missed her farm, she missed Hendrik the springbok. Demonstrators attended her sports meetings and barracked her. Sections of the press suggested she had taken citizenship for reasons of expediency. Mona could not answer these accusations herself as her English was inadequate. In this miserable state she was grateful for the Hottentot Room and the warm friendship offered to her by Elize from Zimbabwe.

Elize now went to the window and drew back the curtain. 'I do wish Mona wouldn't run after dark. It's past one. And snowing hard.'

At this news Buffy Lestrade lifted his massive head. 'The trouble, I always think, is that Mona does these things for the wrong reasons. I think it most commendable that she is in such physical trim. A perfect specimen. But she runs, not for health, but in order to win. She eats properly, but for the same reason. It is a contamination of motive. Frankly, it is more honest to be fat.'

'You have your honesty then,' said Elize.

'To exist only to jump – that is an odd way for a woman, surely. Or even a girl,' suggested Mr Govender.

'We know how you prefer your women, or girls,' Elize rejoined 'Where is your little Anagupta tonight, Mr Govender?'

Mr Govender was president of the Congress of Allied Democrats, an organisation smaller than Hossein's Via Afrika to which it was fiercely opposed. Only in the Hottentot Room could the two top men of these rival liberation movements meet peacefully because the Club represented neutral ground where the most radically opposed people could and did come together.

The division between the organisations went back to the old simple days when their political colour could be described in terms of 'alignment'. Thus Via Afrika was said to be aligned to Moscow and the Congress of Allied Democrats to Maoist China. Since then much had changed. Mao was no more and the Chinese appeared to be embarked upon a programme of unabashed pragmatism. The Congress of Allied Democrats had flirted briefly with Albania but the relationship had not matured. Increasingly, as if to compensate for the disappointment, Mr Govender took more and more interest in his family, most particularly his daughters, a succession of whom accompanied him to the Hottentot Room over the years. All his daughters worked for Unesco in Paris, said Mr Govender. Against vicious jibes about the nature of his feeling for his daughter, Mr Govender merely replied that he was to his very toes a family man and the family was at the very heart of African politics – even if some people appeared to have forgotten it.

'Tonight my little Anagupta took the last plane from Paris and went to an important meeting. I expect her shortly. She will wish to pay her respects to our queen. The poor girl has been working so hard lately. As you probably know, Unesco is in crisis. The capitalist governments are threatening to leave. The socialist governments are trying to persuade them to stay and my little Anagupta finds herself caught in the middle.' Mr Govender screwed up his face, as if he suffered with her. Hawkish elegance, a great beaked nose and

46

an air of confidence which disappeared when you grew aware of the hurt, frightened look about his eyes.

These quarrels between members were growing more frequent. This was something unheard of during the years of Frau Katie's prime. No one would have dared to give way to bitterness and recrimination in the Hottentot Room, it was against the rules, unwritten and unspoken. All the rules of the Club went without saying – though, of course, Frau Katie reserved the right to say them as loudly and as often as she liked, if anyone broke them. What they were experiencing, and they all knew it, was the disintegration of the cordial bond that had for so many years held so many unlikely people together. Without the dying lady upstairs they had nothing left but each other, and they did not much like each other.

The other silent member at the bar was Morris Morrison, the advertising man. Formerly a priest in a rural mission, Morrison had left the ministry and fled abroad. Now, in his dark blue suit and flame pink tie he looked the very picture of an ad man. The reason why he was silent was because he was praying. The old religious urges had been returning frequently of late and Morris found he could no longer resist them.

Looper felt sorry for Morrison. He was the victim of urges he could not control. Looper knew how he felt. Morrison felt himself to have fallen – from service of God to selling soapflakes. Leaving the priesthood had been intended, in the liberated seventies, to be a blow for freedom and independence – not a *coup* for Unilever ... What Morrison was suffering from was conscience. As Heidegger said (or rather as Frau Katie liked to remind Lestrade, Heidegger said), Morrison had heard the call from afar to afar. So, for that matter, had Looper. Hence this urge to heed the call. The symptoms were the tendency towards emotion, the urge to weep in public, to confess on street corners, to preach at the horseshoe bar. Morrison wished to save her soul. And Frau Katie deserved saving – if not from divine judgment which would in any event surely deal kindly with her – then at least from her daughter, English Rose. Looper knew that dying would not be enough to save her from English Rose. Death was only the beginning of Rose's plans. Something more radical would have to be done. The difference between Looper and Morrison was that the copywriter believed he knew what the call meant. Looper was still waiting to find out.

47

CHAPTER 5

How the others shied when Rose came into the Room! They threw agitated glances at each other and nervously chipped away at the brass foot-rail around the bar. Rose was calm and full of sympathy. 'Poor Caleb. Come, she's waiting for you.' Without a glance at the others she led the way upstairs.

She was wearing a chequered black and white blouse and white skirt. Her blonde hair was in place, her blue eyes bright. Rose, who had been utterly exhausted by the past weeks of nursing, now looked quite remarkably relaxed, free from strain and fatigue. In charge. He detected in her a mood of watchful expectancy. He could not help but feel that Rose sensed, finally, that things were proceeding, if not happily, then at least inevitably. There would be no further delays. 'The doctor was here a short while ago. He's given her a shot for the pain, which was bad. She may not know you but she keeps calling your name.'

Long acquaintance with Rose had shown her to be tough and paradoxical. Her sentimental attachment to a bucolic England of the sentimental past, of daisies and thatch, witnessed by her choice of Laura Ashley dresses, her fondness for fringes and fronds, herbal soaps, lavender, old lace and cameo brooches on which anaemic girls turned their thin-lipped profiles on the world, all this contrasted significantly with her murderous instinct for dealing with the present. Looper remembered the time when a single look from Rose destroyed his erection as surely as anything she might have said. Her look was truly withering.

Rose despaired of her mother's refusal to let go of her German characteristics (what Rose always referred to as her 'Germanity') and become properly English.

Frau Katie would say simply: 'I was not different to begin with. My difference came about because others said it was so.'

'I would have thought after what you'd been through, Mother, you would have given up those Teutonic attachments. I don't

48

know how you could remain so Teutonic and yet deny you're German. Frankly, I think you are more German than you are Jewish.'

'We, my darling, say *we*.'

'It's not we, Mummy – it's *you*.'

'Jewishness, I happen to know, is passed through the mother, so you must please say *we*.'

'I will not say we. I will not put up with this guilt by association. I reject it.'

'So did I,' her mother retorted sharply. 'What made me Jewish was the discovery of others. What keeps me Jewish are my memories and my bad dreams.'

'Well, it's about time you put them behind you. Give up those memories.'

'If I gave those up, my past would vanish and with it, my future.'

'What future can you expect to have if you don't give them up?' Rose demanded. 'You can't have any further effect on that old world. It's behind you. Dead and gone. It won't come back. And you can't go back.'

Nor would she. Rose liked to remind her of this odd refusal to return to the motherland. After all, why not? If she loved it so and hated Britain – why not go back – to the new Germany?

'Not Britain. England,' Frau Katie would counter with expert provocation.

Britain, Rose would insist and then return to her original question: why not go back?

Frau Katie had her reasons. 'People are just waiting for me to do that. The disease is ready and waiting to catch this lady which it failed to catch so many times. But so close! So close it was!'

'I think you're scared.'

'Sure I'm scared. Wouldn't you be? With the old story just waiting to take up where it left off. Katie's back in Berlin, they would say, now's our chance.'

'I mean you're scared because you can't stand to face the truth. The old Germany only exists in your head. Good and bad – it's gone, Mummy.'

'I will go back, one day. In my own time. Caleb and I. Like young lovers. We shall go to Berlin. No – we will escape to Berlin! One day I intend to make my presence felt,' Frau Katie promised. She turned upon her daughter a look of regal disdain. Her tone

49

was full of calculated pity. 'You should go to South Africa. There you will find what it means to be declared a dangerous species by government investigation. You do not know what you are until they tell you. They are crazy Aristotelians. They are mad about classification. Nowadays they say – Look! We are changed. Forget the past. We have put it behind us! Like you say I must do. What? Put it behind? No! These people have done things to us. They have made us what we are. Jews or Coloureds or corpses. What they have made us. That is all we have – and you tell us to put it behind us!'

'I wonder why you've never thought of going to South Africa?' Rose asked coolly. 'I get the impression that it would suit you rather better than me. It would lend weight to your comments. People might listen if you'd actually visited the place you speak about with so much authority.'

'But *you* are the one they need, my darling. You are the one who supports the government there. Tell me this – *who* was glad when we stopped showing pictures of their riots?'

'The South Africans stopped the pictures.'

'Yes. And weren't we relieved!'

Rose welcomed the chance to repeat her feelings on 'appetite', and on what she called the 'Berta' government. 'I've made my feelings clear.' Rose's feelings reflected perfectly the thinly disguised racialism of the right-wing British press and its almost erectile sympathy for the wielders of the truncheon and whip. Rose always began the expressions of her feelings on South Africa with the traditional disclaimer: 'I find racialism wicked. Abhorrent. But –'

'Ah – the *but*. Now we come to the *but* . . . Behold the *but*!'

'I don't believe in shutting them off.'

'You support them.'

'I do not. And you know it. I abhore "appetite".'

'That's an expensive word. Can you use something cheaper? I don't know what it means.'

'You know very well what it means.'

'You don't want us to see pictures of their riots. You want to censor news from South Africa.'

'At least I look at the place as it is now. I don't have some romantic dream about it.'

According to Rose it was her mother's association with African exiles that led to this romantic linking of her trials under Hitler

50

with the sufferings of 'the Coloureds under Berta'. 'I'm all for free speech. But, yes, I *object* to the continuous stream of television pictures we get from South Africa. I'm afraid it's very possible that pictures of the riots there encourage people here to do the same.'

Not unnaturally this view caused some amusement amongst the Hottentots who in depressed moments cheered themselves by planning a version of the Nuremberg trials for the Berta regime, one fine day.

'It's a-part-heid, not "appetite"' – Morris would correct her.

'The next thing we know, the "Berta" government will be claiming that it's pictures of your race riots in England which are inspiring our people to go on the rampage,' Hossein had suggested amid general laughter.

'That's right. Mock my accent. I simply cannot get my tongue around those Dutch words,' said English Rose. 'And don't be ridiculous.' Even she laughed.

Perhaps they should not have laughed. A week later Looper received a letter from his father:

. . . and I must tell you that we now have unassailable proof in this country that it is by watching pictures of your riots in Britain that our normally placid and easy-going township dwellers have been inflamed. We never used to have petrol bombs. Petrol bombs are unknown in this country. But what has happened? For weeks we have watched them exploding on the streets of London and Birmingham. Now we are suffering a positive rash of them over here. Doubtless the good Doctor is ready to fly in to sort out our troubles. I hope you're satisfied . . . However, we will not take it lying down. You may tell the Doctor that from me. We support the police who we know have been made to look like maniacs on your TV screens. When the time comes we will show our appreciation to the forces of law and order and civilisation in appropriate fashion . . .

The difference between mother and daughter could not have been more marked. Even now, in her seventies, mortally ill, Frau Katie remained a gracious and imposing foreign lady. The great gifts of her youth, the expectations of comfort and ease and privilege, though they had been strategically overlaid by her careful upbringing, were still discernible rather as an old painting will be covered

51

with successive layers of varnish which although it darkens and deepens the picture over many years never obscures that elusive, gleaming quality of the masterpiece.

Rose, by contrast, was what she seemed. A pretty woman in her early forties, blonde, quick-witted and thoroughly English. Hard-headed, practical, intelligent, she worked as a buyer for a big department store and dressed in flowery, flouncy prints of some imaginary Albion. She regarded her mother as a quixotic, eccentric and imperious woman, whom she called La Tyranta, a name which did not stick. Frau Katie, on the other hand, long ago called her daughter 'English' Rose, a nickname which stuck very fast indeed. Rose found very trying her mother's continual insistence that she had 'lost rank' by leaving Germany. If she were only in Germany today and things had been different, Frau Katie tirelessly repeated, 'I would be treated with the respect according to a general's widow and my pension would be paid promptly.' To which Rose would retort that had she been foolish enough to stay in Germany she would have been dead.

Frau Katie would sigh and shake her head at this, calling it pure anti-German prejudice and cited it as an instance of the lamentable lack of a European sense among the English in general. If Frau Katie responded to the question as to why she'd stayed in England and not returned to Germany after the war by saying that she 'got stuck', her daughter put it another way. 'Mummy cannot be said ever to have lived in England. I think she spent the years since the war in Africa.'

They also differed in their surnames. Frau Katie had retained her husband's surname: von Sturz. Her German passport, stamped with a large J, gave her name as Katerina Margarita Abrahamsohn. This of course being the name the Nazi investigators declared to be her real one, while Brahm was merely her alias. Rose, however, had kept the shortened surname which she pronounced with the short English 'a', as in bramble. Rose Brahm sounded acceptably English, even if to some ears it might have had a slight Chinese or Vietnamese chime. Frau Katie was scornful of this. 'My poor little English Rose, has done a Händel.' She gave the word its nasal German intonation.

'Not Händel, Mummy – Handel,' said Rose.

'Precisely,' said Frau Katie. Thus she explained the difference between their names by reference to the Englishing of his name which the composer had affected when permanently settled in England. 'It was like he did a nose job on his name.'

Rose's response was an air of calm, clear superiority.

'Doubtless, at that time, my daughter would like to believe that all the English went around in clothes like hers. Their hair was clean. Complexions good. Teeth excellent. Maybe they didn't even have the English disease.'

'And what is the English disease?'

'Rickets.'

'Oh really, Mummy! What nonsense you talk.'

'Nonsense? Let me tell you that's what all of Europe calls it. We worried our children should get it.'

Needless to say, Frau Katie disapproved of the daughter of a general becoming a 'shopkeeper' and would confess quietly to Looper, when she was sure Rose was within earshot, that she was grateful that her husband was no longer alive to see it.

As time went on she left her bed less and less. Propped up on her pillows in her bedroom above the bar she would listen for Gerrie to call 'Time', and she would hear the casual drinkers and the one-night members leaving and then would come the summons to the tribe drinking below. She began a loud insistent banging on the floor with her walking stick, a great cudgel of black oak encircled with silver bands, surmounted by the head of a troll, carved with fierce precision, and tipped with a buttery-yellow brass ferrule.

Night after night in her last weeks her Hottentots perched on a variety of chairs and the stool from the dressing table, while Gerrie would ply between bar and bedroom with a loaded tray. Frau Katie, wig carefully combed, sat up wearing a pink bedjacket and all her rings, 'As a testimony, dear friends, to the importance of your company.' A good deal of serious drinking went on into the small hours, until at last, one by one, the guests would slip away, or Frau Katie, overcome by the mixture of drugs and champagne, passed out in mid-sentence and a red-eyed Rose hurried them from the sick room.

It had been after one such late night sick-bed session that Looper had stayed on at Rose's invitation, 'for a night-cap'. He should have suspected something. Rose never offered drinks and she had no use for night-caps. Indeed the word in her mouth represented a concession to what she vaguely imagined as that quality of cordiality which stamped a friendly invitation in that social world she had only heard about. The invitation was so studied that one felt she had probably read it in a book, one of those guides which help you to find ways of making your guests feel at ease. She went further: she told him that she wanted to ask his help and advice. Now this was utterly new. Rose was not in need of advice and she looked with contempt on offers of help. What Rose principally required, as the Hottentots all knew, was obedience. What she praised was efficiency. What she desired was success. But of course there was the question of just what she planned to do with the Hottentot Room after her mother's death. All Rose had ever said on the subject was that she was full of plans. This sent a shiver through the tribe.

Thinking perhaps that he might learn something of these plans, Looper accepted her invitation. He sipped his drink and watched English Rose become very drunk. He watched her pour whisky inside her with the straightforward commitment which was her trade-mark. Rose very rarely drank but when she did so it was with the same kind of purpose that stamped all her actions. It did occur to him that she looked as if she were fuelling herself for something. She was wearing a black dress, cut low, which set off quite strikingly her blonde hair and pale skin. On a chain around her neck she wore a diamond pendant in the shape of a unicorn. Its eyes were tiny emeralds, its horn silver and sharp.

'I want to talk to you about something vital, Caleb,' said Rose and led him over to one of the red velvet settees, removed her shoes and sat down, tucking her legs beneath her and patting the place beside her. 'Here, sit. I want to talk about the future. The fact is, I need an ally, Caleb. One of these days decisions will have to be taken. You follow me? This house will be mine. Now I think it has potential. Mind you, it's a lousy area, but it's coming up. Bound to. Must do. I want to make something of this place. Do you understand?' She fixed her eyes on him, steel blue and shining. The whisky was getting through to her.

'What will happen to the tribe?' he asked. 'They think you want them out.'

'Exactly. I knew you'd understand. Please believe me – I don't want to turn them out. They're welcome here. They always will be. My place will always be open to them. Hell, I've grown up with them!'

54

'But it won't be the same.'

'Nothing stays the same. The Room remains because my mother preserves it by an act of will. It's an old-fashioned museum where she locks up her dreams. Her curious imaginings about Africa. In the Room there are only two realities: old Berlin and the new Africa. They are totally unconnected and quite false. They have no historical link. This place is built on illusions. Her memories of old Berlin are distorted by time, sentimentalised, romanticised. Even at its best it was never as good as my mother thinks it. Her visions of Africa are based on nothing more than ignorance. If she saw it she'd hate it. And not only that, most of her tribe, this collection of soaks, dreamers, failures, wouldn't know old Berlin if you showed it to them. And if you showed it to them they wouldn't like it. They wouldn't have it if you gave it to them!' Rose got up now and snatched an old map of Zanzibar from the wall and shook it in his face. *'Cloves! Copra! Sugar!'* The words shrieked at him in custard yellow capitals. Rose tore the map across, dividing the island of Zanzibar from its sister island, Pemba. Then she screwed up the fragments and threw them on the floor.

'Tell me how you'll change things when the Room is yours?' Looper plunged in blindly, dismayed and frightened by her rage.

The question calmed her. It forced her to think. She came back and sat down beside him. 'We are here, now, in a room in Earls Court in England. We settled in this house over forty years ago. That is fact. I want that fact recognised. I want to make this place what it *really* is! Nobody, repeat nobody, is going to stop me getting things straight, when my turn comes.' She took a large gulp from her glass and burst into tears.

Looper put his arm around her. It was instinctive. He had never seen Rose cry. The storm of tears astonished him. He was also faintly worried that Rose's loud sobbing would waken the sick woman in the room above their heads. There was just the slight chance that this humane consideration tipped the balance. Later he realised it had been a mistake.

'But Rose, there is a connection between the Hottentots and old Berlin. At least there is for us. It's your mother. Your mother connects us.'

This was clearly a second mistake because Rose simply sobbed more loudly and he tightened his embrace to compensate, as if increased tenderness would govern volume. She smelt of peaches

55

and whisky. He was conscious of how broad her shoulders were. He could tell from the tension of her body that she was not crying because she felt sorry for herself. These tears were not an invitation to sympathise or even to understand her frustration. The Rose who spoke in phrases like: 'I'm afraid you misunderstand my meaning' and 'I'm sorry, but I find your explanations quite unacceptable' or 'Frankly I prefer not to discuss hypothetical questions' when faced with her mother's emotional recollections of the perfect life Unter den Linden, or the obsessive political responses to the British imperial mission in Africa which so frequently dominated conversations among members of the Hottentot Room, was not crying because she wanted Looper to pity her. Rose was weeping over the obtuseness and unreliability of foreigners, their stubborn foolishness to face up to plain evidence, their inability to grasp the facts of the matter, their weakness for rhetoric, their love of large crowds and empty gestures, their want of pragmatism, their lack of common sense. Rose wept because her stubborn foolish mother was dying and her Club was a seedy hole where sentimental exiles played silly games of let's pretend.

Rose put her head on his shoulder. He stroked her hair, fair, fine hair which lifted in the static currents his fingers stirred. She gradually stopped crying and he thought she had gone to sleep. Very gently he began to release his hold. But as he attempted to draw away from her she slipped her arms inside his jacket and held him fast. Then she kissed him, a long, steady pressure of cool lips. Precise and professional. When it was over she drew back her head and smiled. But she kept her arms around him.

'When I get my turn, I am going to turn this place around. It deserves to live. It has taken every penny of my mother's pension and died on her. Speak to the others, Caleb. Make them understand that changes are inevitable. I have the financial backing. A banker friend is most eager to invest. We have been living on borrowed time – and money. I don't want to drive the others away. Some of the older members like Wyngate and old Gerrie were like uncles to me. I grew up with them around. I want them to stay on. It's their choice. I can do it with everybody's help and understanding, or I can do it without. But do it I will.'

– 'Yes, but why do you want my help?' he asked desperately, testing the strength of her embrace which held firm.

'Because you know what I'm talking about. You're not like the others, locked in the past. Journalists have to be aware. They see things. We're in the mid-eighties and moving forward towards the next century. The war is over, the colonies are free, Germany is divided, and this country is home. For you as much for me. You're never going back to South Africa any more than my mother is ever going back to Berlin.'

'Would you like another drink?' Looper was growing increasingly nervous.

She did not answer. Instead she leaned over him and very deliberately unsnapped his belt. 'Come,' she said. Then she reached a hand behind her and unzipped her dress, shrugging it off her shoulders. It fell to her waist. 'Come,' she said again and removed his jacket, ignoring his feeble protests.

They made love on the plush bench. He caught a momentary reflection of them in the mirror behind the bar which advertised Jamieson's Scotch Whisky and showed a surprisingly dusky kilted Highlander carrying a musket on the brow of Mount Majuba. In that brief glimpse he looked like a swimmer rocking on a pink lilo on some agitated sea. At her moment of climax Rose cried out one word, 'Mine!' For a heart-stopping moment he took this to indicate her possession of him, then realised it was the Room she was dreaming of in her pleasure. Immediately afterwards he felt a stinging pain in his chest. The unicorn which hung around her neck had gored him with its silver horn. A drop of dark blood rose into a little spherical hill among his chest hairs.

It was from this encounter that Rose dated their secret engagement. This, it seemed, was what she meant by calling on him to become her ally. It had been a proposal and in her book the act which followed, when Looper buried himself in Rose's broad, pale flesh, and her unicorn stabbed him, was the outward sign of that agreement.

Looper, of course, immediately objected to the so-called agreement. He also refused Rose's permission to use the term 'understanding'. There was no engagement and no understanding. None the less, the approach which English Rose took after this event always tended to show that she expected their relationship, whatever one called it, to continue. She was quite clear in her mind that they had a business arrangement on which love had set the seal. She amazed him by confessing that she had made the approach to him because her mother had told her Looper was somebody to be relied upon in a crisis. She'd also said that she felt sure Looper would be open to her proposal. Whether Frau Katie had hinted at some further romantic attachment or whether her daughter Rose had deliberately misinterpreted what her mother said, or, as was perfectly possible, was incapable of distinguishing between a business proposal and a romantic proposition, he could not say. Rose was quick to tell him that her mother was delighted to learn that she and Looper had, as she put it, 'come together to plan for the future'. It had, said Rose, made the dying woman very happy. She was sure Looper would not wish to spoil that happiness which was not likely to endure for very much longer.

'Mummy dotes on you, Caleb, It's surely not very much to ask. Just keep up the pretence. It's not going to be for long. Let her go on believing that we have an understanding. After all there is some truth in that, isn't there? We both want the best for the Hottentot Room. Give her a little happiness in the end. You're the one she really loves, remember? You're the one who she's going to elope with. You're taking her back to old Berlin and her house in Friedrichstrasse. You've never let her down. You've kept up the little joke. She's thrilled to hear we have some arrangement. She's even a little jealous. She says she can see she will have to carry you off sooner than she thought! Please, Caleb. Help me to humour her, I won't hold you to the engagement, or the other thing.'

By 'the other thing' she meant sex. Which, after their first meeting, she took to expecting regularly, usually coming to his flat late at night and practising upon him exotic and exhausting vagaries often conned from a sex manual that very day, as she told him without a trace of embarrassment while he lay panting on her breasts or her back or scissored between her thighs. She had a very direct attitude to sexual pleasure. She took sex as she took exercise, another English trait. Beneath her calm, quiet controlled manner she possessed a lusty, uninhibited appetite which he was employed to satisfy under the loose arrangement of their 'understanding', this ambiguous status satisfying that need in Rose which was almost as strong as her sexual drive, her desire for respectability.

Frau Katie grew more gravely ill. She now no longer ever left her bed and the drinking parties round the bed had ceased. Downstairs at the horseshoe bar the Hottentots sat talking in whispers, left without news of Frau Katie's condition. Only Rose and the doctor saw her and they said nothing. In the last month Rose had not come to Looper's flat at all. As it happened this was a stroke of luck since it was over this period that he had begun his careful pursuit and capture of the pale, unhappy Biddy Hogan, so deeply wounded by Wyngate Hossein's sudden and inexplicable desertion of her that she had welcomed the consolation he offered.

Looper knew that he was playing a dangerous double game. There was always the chance that Rose might discover his affair and this would complicate matters. But he counted on Frau Katie's final illness to preoccupy Rose and, not for the first time in his life, the delicately judged gamble had paid off.

Not that this relationship with Rose was one that he had wanted. It had resulted from a moment of weakness, or, if you like, kindness. What concerned Looper were the pressures on him to maintain the link, the 'engagement' to Rose. She wanted it herself – as a way through to the Hottentots, judging that with Looper's help she would make the transition to the new post-Frau Katie era in Antaeus Street more easily. The Hottentots also wanted it. They saw Looper as a kind of insurance against Rose's more radical tendencies. They knew how she regarded them. To her they were a spineless, weepy lot. They wanted stiffening up. Drying out. She disliked their sex lives, their politics and their clothes. She did not care for them. The exceptions were people like old Gerrie who had been around for so long she regarded him as a fixture. And a servant. He always chauffeured her mother and good chauffeurs were hard to find. One of the first things to go would be the elderly Mercedes. Looper knew its fate. It would simply disappear, put down like an elderly pet when its mistress had gone. There would be a new car. Something small, sensible, economical. Gerrie would drive Rose to the bank. Poor Gerrie. It would be better to be put down – like the old Merc. Of course Rose was not being cruel. She was being sensible. That somehow seemed worse. Rose took sensible things seriously. It was in this that she differed so drastically from her mother. Rose meant business.

Frau Katie took seriously her pretence at royalty. As the uncrowned queen of the Hottentots she mounted great shopping expeditions to the various curio shops of the West End to buy gifts for members of her tribe, setting out in the big black left-hand Mercedes with Gerrie at the wheel, peaked cap resting on his raw, brightly veined nose, muffled in his grey chauffeur's coat, and progress through the West End like some strange private parade. Frau

59

Katie glanced neither left nor right as they drove down Regent Street, very much the grand lady with her serene and somewhat haughty expression, her face thickly powdered and very pale, her brilliantly dyed red hair. Even after Debussy's complaint struck, these expeditions continued for a while. The only clue to her condition was that she looked a little taller, the extra height being due to her big new wig and the inflatable rubber cushion upon which she sat.

She bought assegais and fighting sticks heavy with blue and white beads worked in intricate chevrons; ostrich eggs painted with scenes from bushman life; snag-toothed bush pianos made from calabash gourds with ragged steel keys that made a distant splashing music like the sound of pebbles landing in an immensely deep well; black leather bags filled with witch-doctor's bones; yellow, animal-skin shoes for the men; pungent sausage and dry salted meat, beads for the women, copper bangles, recordings of penny whistles and jazz from the black South African townships. Of course she bought also German specialities: silver coins, sugary cakes, *Lederhosen* and Tyrolean hats, Berlin bears fashioned from nougat, medals bearing the head of the Kaiser, old prints of Bismarck. Presented to the Hottentots they were immediately re-presented to Gerrie who stuck them up around the bar. Buffy Lestrade told Frau Katie, after having seen her processing down Regent Street, that she reminded him of the aged Queen Elizabeth the First. It was a comparison which Rose found particularly painful and her mother regarded as being insultingly inaccurate. Frau Katie found associations with English royalty to be quite preposterous. It showed, she said, that Lestrade's brain had gone soft, probably because of his longstanding vegetarianism and his cranky ideas about food in general.

'You need a good steak,' she told him, 'and you should never have abandoned Martin Heidegger.'

'The philosophy of Heidegger was a stage through which I was destined to pass,' replied Lestrade, bowing from the waist and clicking his heels.

'I seem to remember that Heidegger was a Nazi,' said Rose.

Lestrade peered at her pityingly, his great domed forehead gleamed. 'That is problematical. If there was an attempt to grasp the accession of the Hitlerites and to analyse it in phenomenological terms, and to see it as a manifestation of being in time or history, that is not the same thing as being a Nazi.'

'The trouble with you is that you try and speak English as though it was German,' Rose retorted, 'and a man who made a speech welcoming Hitler sounds like a Nazi to me, to put it in plain English.'

'Many academics welcomed Adolf,' Frau Katie interjected. 'Those who didn't got kicked out. I do not think this makes Heidegger a Nazi. But he was one of the "blood and earth" men, as we called them. They looked forward to Hitler getting things done for them. They hoped a lot, I'm sure. Martin Heidegger sat in his rector's study in Freiburg and hoped as much as anyone. These people saw Hitler as a weapon. I remember the rectors of the universities put on uniforms and marched about the colleges saluting the saviour of the nation. They looked ridiculous. Everyone knows academics cannot march – and I speak as the wife of a general!'

Lestrade was another on Rose's hit list. And all the women. Such juxtapositions of English queens and German philosophers were over. Gerrie was OK. And Wyngate. And Looper. Wyngate was distinguished and Looper was useful. The other Hottentots were going to have to shape up or move out. They knew that. They were going to knuckle under – or face extinction.

More puzzling for Looper was the effect of Rose's affair with him upon his feelings for her mother. He knew he felt for Frau Katie something very like love. If not the thing itself, it came so close as to make no difference. He felt pretty sure he knew why he felt the way he did. She knew him, felt for him. Rose might talk of her mother's illusions, complain about her lack of sense or reality, imply that she was full of dreams and sentiment, unaware of the real world, and yet Looper sometimes had the feeling that it was Frau Katie alone who really understood who he was. In the very serious game which he played, with its requirements of a delicately based sense of timing and capacity to bluff, to gamble, and where necessary to act, however ruthlessly, perhaps certain characteristic features arose in skilled players recognisable to somebody who had played the same game. There were occasions when he caught in Frau Katie's glance an ironic question.

'We who come from countries which kill people for their beliefs, imprison them for their poems, train racial inspectors to sniff out the blood of sub-species, we understand that it is best to be certain

61

of nothing. We understand how people can betray their friends for bread or they can betray them for the good of their souls. I remember one night in '34 I was at the opera with a friend of mine, Maria Braun. We were sitting in the front row of the gallery when there entered this collection of brown-shirted gentry. It was the first time I saw such brown. It was a shit brown. The sort that hurts the eyes and makes you realise that you're facing problems when you see that colour. That was my very first glimpse of the brown and Maria said to me: "What are you going to do about this? Those Brownshirts are all bastards." And I asked her if she'd ever wear a uniform like that. "Are you crazy?" she said. About a year or so later I met her again and she was wearing the uniform of the Bund Deutscher Mädchen – like Hitler's Girl Guides. All brown. I asked her what happened to her vow never to wear a uniform. She shrugged her shoulders. "I joined the BDM. It's better this way," she said. I didn't blame her then, or now. Under such circumstances who knows why people do things? Isn't it so, Caleb?' And again there was that sidelong, ironical glance. Such reminiscences, so real for the old lady that she flushed and paled as she told them, were over.

Frau Katie in those last days had been guarded by her doctor and Rose. He was losing the only person he really cared for. Like Morrison, he suffered from excessive agitation of the spirit. Like Morrison he felt he was being called back to where he had once been. His love for Frau Katie called him back to being a boy who had loved and lost his mother when he was very young. He had hated his father. All he had felt for his dead mother he had given to this older woman. This was so obvious it was banal and so banal it was probably true. He had a mother fixation. Too bad. Looper knew he was a lot of things, not many of them creditable. But the important thing was not what he was, but what he was being called on to become. He had hoped Frau Katie would show him the way. Frau Katie was going. Yet she was going without him. She had always joked that they would leave together. Well that was not going to happen.

He followed Rose up the stairs. She had good legs. Wasn't it terrible that he should notice such things at a moment like this? He did not even like Rose and here he was admiring her legs. Why had the old lady encouraged this affair with Rose? Even connived at it? Possibly she felt that Looper would act as a moderating influence on her daughter when she was gone. So he was being thrown into

62

the arms of Rose, as if to slow her down. As a burglar might throw the watchdog a piece of meat to slow down the pursuit. But throwing him to Rose was not going to slow her down. She would roll straight over him. Like a tank.

CHAPTER 6

Frau Katie's room was dark, lit by a single ormolu lamp cast in the form of a cherub wrestling a dragon beneath the shade of yellow parchment on which were vividly depicted whiskered soldiers in blue tunics and glittering brass helmets changing the guard Unter den Linden. Beneath the lamp were old family photographs, including one he had not seen before, a photograph of her husband, Erich von Sturz in uniform, a large eagle on his cap. His lips were compressed giving his thin, handsome face an anxious, somewhat foxy expression. In a firm hand he had written beneath his picture in German: 'To my beloved Katerina from her Erich ... Berlin, 1933.' There were also photographs taken at her wedding, showing the bridal couple and their families. These precious images in their heavy silver frames were arranged in a semi-circle, within reach, like sacred charms to comfort and sustain.

Frau Katie lay with her eyes closed, breathing so faintly he could not hear her. The effect of her illness was most marked in the way in which it had reduced this once large, tall, ample woman to a shrunken childlike waif. It had thinned and greyed her eyebrows. Her face was chalky white, the lips dry and she licked them in her sleep. Debussy's disease had reduced her to a point where little flesh clung to her bones. Looper could have picked her up in his arms and carried her away. She lay like a child far too small for the big mahogany bed. Behind him Rose closed the door softly. At the click of the latch Frau Katie's eyes flickered and opened. The instant she saw Rose she shut them quickly, like a child pretending to be asleep. Rose settled Looper in the chair beside the bed. Then very quietly she left the room. After a moment or so Frau Katie's eyes opened slowly and a claw-like little hand ventured from beneath the blankets and found its way into Looper's palm. She closed her eyes but she did not sleep. The grip on his hand told him that.

Frau Katie, in her old age and even after illness struck her, remained a handsome, gleaming woman. She possessed tact, sensitivity and a kind of smooth, intelligent charm which was utterly

European and suggested a careful grooming and training during a childhood directed towards the expectation of a position of great importance and power. The word which suggested itself when one contemplated Frau Katie was 'breeding', were it not for the fact that it carried connotations that made it quite impossible to use. This did not stop Frau Katie who used it frequently herself, usually as a means of pointing to deficiencies in others, to the amusement of the Hottentots and to the deep embarrassment of her daughter. There was the celebrated use of the word in a famous conversation with Oscar, a member of the Soweto Knights.

Frau Katie took great interest in the story of the exiled student leader from the township slums who had escaped from custody by impersonating a police commandant. It was, said Frau Katie, a fine example of 'breeding'. But why, she asked Oscar in a somewhat puzzled fashion, had he been in police custody at all? Why had he not been in school that day? Oscar replied that at the time he had been burning down the school. Frau Katie remarked that this must have been extremely distressing to his mother. Oscar explained that his mother had abandoned him as a baby.

'Poor Oscar!' Frau Katie cried. 'That means your upbringing must have been left in the care of your father? How terrible to have been brought up by servants!'

Having been brought up to expect to inherit the world the emphasis of Frau Katie's education as a young girl had fallen on matters of tact and on the skilful exercise of wealth and power so that they did not become too apparent. She was taught the intelligent study of courtesies by which the well-bred avoided giving offence to those less well endowed and took the edge off social advantage. Katerina's father had a horror of ostentatious display and vulgar materialism. Her wealthy, happy family lived in the suburb of Dahlem. She had been christened Katerina Margarita Brahm. Her father was an industrialist who made ball bearings, her mother was a noted musician and a Schiller scholar. Her brother Max was in the army. It was through her brother that young Katerina Brahm had been introduced to the young army officer, Erich von Sturz, then working in military intelligence on the staff of General Ludendorff.

The Brahm family were very patriotic and regarded the loss of the Great War as a tragedy. They agreed with Ludendorff that Germany had been 'stabbed in the back'. They were forthrightly, if not excessively, anti-Semitic. Mr Brahm, in particular, deplored the cheap and nasty jingling show made by some Jewish merchants which, he said, strengthened the case of the communists and of those on the right, such as the new Nationalist Socialist Party, who held up these individuals as examples of grasping exploiters and profiteers who bled the German working man. Her family's solemn, serious concern with the Jewish 'problem' was something that young Katerina had been aware of since her very earliest years. And, truth be told, she found the subject of national 'hygiene' which her father talked about so often to be faintly boring. In fact she had to admit that she really could not tell the difference between Jews and other Germans. The Brahm parents drew a distinction, however, between Jews and what they called 'Germans of Jewish stock'. It was towards the florid, successful entrepreneurs and towards the groups of foreigners arriving in increasing numbers from the East, from Russia and Galicia, the vulgar ugly creatures of Grenadierstrasse, that Katerina's parents felt especially hostile. This invasion was caricatured in cartoons and journals such as *Simplicissimus* which portrayed the fat, thick-lipped men and swarthy women, whores, pedlars, noisy babies, anarchists, loungers, platoons of rabbis who made up the problem. Katerina's father even took her and showed her what he meant. Mr Brahm pointed to the stock type so tellingly portrayed by Arnold in his wickedly accurate caricatures of the mobs of speculators, who made up the free stock exchange of the streets, showed Katerina the drunks and the bumpkins who congregated around Nussbaum's restaurant on the corner of Grenadier and Hirtenstrasse. This human flotsam of pedlars, quacks, freebooters and criminals were disliked, Mr Brahm would point out, even by thinking Jews. Such people were in fact enemies of the Jews, said Katerina's mother, because they gave decent Jewish Germans a bad name. Katerina's grandmother, whom she remembered as a beautiful round lady with skin as pale and soft as milk, went further; she deplored these *Ostjuden*, Jews from the East, as a disaster for all right-thinking people. They were, she said, 'advertisements for Hitler'.

In 1930, Hitler was principally known, apart from his highly charged and eccentric notions about the Jews, as a patriot. One who was opposed to the payment of reparations to the allies, a supporter of Hindenburg and a man of sound economic views. He was the leader of a party with over one hundred seats in the

Reichstag and a man of firmness. However Hitler and his party were not the government and were never likely to become the government, Mr Brahm declared with firmness. Without question, Hitler would never be Chancellor. Hindenburg would 'see things through', Katie's father confidently announced and 'decent German nationalists' like Franz von Papen would back him up. None the less he respected Herr Hitler's 'position'. Herr Hitler's position was that he was against paying money to Germany's enemies, he was for a strong Germany and spoke with the bluntness of the soldier he had been. Katerina's father said that the only way out of the recession and the inflation that threatened them all was to wage war against the enemy within. Mr Brahm applauded action against illegal foreigners who were holed up in the tenements of Grenadierstrasse and other ghettos and he approved of their shipment to concentration camps such as Stargard and Cottbus by the government. The concentration camps were one of the few British inventions of which Mr Brahm approved. He pointed out to his daughter that the idea had been formulated during the Boer War and was a way of concentrating the enemy or hostile foreigners in a single place. It involved no cruelty, he went on, since these *Ostjuden* insisted on squirrelling themselves away in wretched tenements and forming ghettos and so it was better that they be moved to some place on the outskirts of the city where proper order and decent laws of hygiene might be applied.

Katerina Brahm married Erich von Sturz in 1933, in the Lutheran church in Dahlem. Her brother Max was best man. The photograph of the wedding party which stood by her bed had been shown to the tribe with considerable pride and affection. She kept it for practical as well as romantic reasons. It constituted visual proof of her marriage to a general-to-be. She pointed out the grandeur of the room in which the photograph had been taken, the gilded mirrors and huge chandeliers, the sideboards loaded with silver plate, much of the furniture so large it dwarfed the bridal party. This was a glimpse of the life she would have lived. She would have been very comfortably placed and, more importantly, assured of status as a general's wife had not history, the war, Hitler – all those things summed up in the term 'the old story' and sometimes as 'the disease', not cruelly intervened to cheat her of her due.

The photograph of the bridal couple was very revealing. It showed them sitting on a heavily padded sofa. Katerina, perhaps

67

slightly plumper than one might have imagined, wore a smile on her face which one could not have mistaken for anything but triumph. Her husband, Erich, sharp chin, thin nose, a coldly handsome face, was sitting to attention in the brass and tufted dress uniform of the Prussian regiment which, if one was to believe Frau Katie, his family had virtually owned. Arranged in a semicircle behind the couple stood the families of bride and groom gazing on the newlyweds. Katie's father was tall, bald and relaxed, one hand in his pocket, a firm but humorous mouth. Her mother, musician and scholar, strikingly elegant with her close-cropped hair and large dark eyes. Her grandmother, comfortably plump, gentle and gracious. Then the Prussian in-laws: the men in rich, complicated uniforms, and all casting long, suspicious gazes into the camera, as if to be kept waiting to no visible effect by this contraption and perhaps by the man who worked it, was unpleasant and rather demeaning. They clutched their swords and hugged their helmets to their chests. They were reminding themselves, Frau Katie liked to joke, of their Prussian duty – and perhaps of the bride's dowry. The Prussian women showed a similar iron composure, their huge floral hats looked as if they were cut from steel.

Another treasured photograph showed her parents sitting in the garden of their grand summer place in Baden-Baden. Again the family group was carefully posed. This time a couple of chairs, they looked like wicker chairs, had been carried out on to the gravel driveway and mother and father, both dressed in white, smiled into the camera. At their feet this time, Max and Katerina, both in tennis dress. Behind them horses, a cobbled courtyard, stables, the butler standing somewhat eerily in his winged collar in the middle of the lawn with silver salver in hand: and in the left-hand corner of the photograph, the gardeners in their green aprons raking the gravelled drive. Undoubtedly Katerina Brahm had been fully entitled to believe that the world was a kind and brilliant place and that the pulsing excitement she felt in Berlin was its very heartbeat.

'Hitler came in '33, the year of my marriage. We Berliners didn't much mind, or care. Mind you, we were Berliners. We did not share the admiration so strong in the country for the *Wunderkind* Adolf. Clearly he had certain qualities. He seemed the right man in some ways. Maybe he hadn't got all his cups in the cupboard, people said, but he had some good ideas. And if he gets funny, people said, then we know that Hindenburg will kick his backside.

68

That's what people told themselves. Hindenburg's president, isn't he? He'll keep Adolf in line.' Frau Katie threw up her hands in dismay. 'But then Hindenburg goes and dies the following year – what then? We were worried, a little, I don't deny it. We were worried. Who wouldn't be? Hindenburg was old. But to die! He should have asked first, people said. And then we would have refused permission. Now there was no one to kick Hitler's backside. I have to admit that we still found him funny, this young Adolf. Perhaps that was the trouble with us. We looked at him and all we saw was how funny he was. His lack of breeding.'

The first years of her marriage had seen her husband rapidly promoted. With Hitler's succession to the Chancellorship in the year of their marriage, 1933, her husband Erich caught the eye of Goering, now a General of Infantry and Reichsmarschall. As Goering's protégé it seemed that von Sturz was bound for the top.

Frau Katie recounted her memories of these events with great fondness. She was never in the least embarrassed by her early connections with men, names and events which later earned the revulsion and contempt of the world. It never occurred to her that there was anything for which to apologise. Her remarks on these subjects often left her listeners, newly come from Africa and quite unable to speak certain names without blushing, with the most curious sensation. They heard what she was saying but they could not entirely bring themselves to believe it. It wasn't that they denied that she had been there and knew the people she named. It was her easy familiarity, her naturalness with her past, that filled them with awe. She spoke without the faintest trace of regret of reproach and that in itself astonished them. She might have been reminiscing about any past, any old friends. 'I knew Hitler's pianist,' she told the group of musicians known as the Soweto Knights, soon after she admitted them to the Club. 'He was a pretty boy. His name was Hanfstangl, but we called him Putzi. Hitler took him everywhere.'

When English Rose pointed out that such declarations might embarrass or anger those people who didn't know her background and particularly those people fleeing from systems not very far removed from that of the Nazis, Frau Katie dismissed the objection with a gentle smile. 'Why should I not talk music with these musicians?'

When she had a mind to it, she would deliberately set out to

69

enrage her passionately Anglophile daughter. She liked to return to her father's remark about the English invention of the concentration camp. She liked particularly to appeal to the Hottentots to back her up on this, for after all hadn't it been the British in South Africa who had concentrated the Boer population, women and children, behind the barbed wire? And had they not died in their thousands of disease, cruelty and neglect?

'The English think them such big cheeses,' said Frau Katie.

If she felt that way – why had she come to England?

'By mistake,' said Frau Katie. Up went the champagne glass in ironical salute. 'Hullo darlings!'

And why then had she not returned to Germany after the war? Why had she stayed in England?

'I got stuck.' This with a flick of the eyes at her furious daughter.

She would also remember instances of the English presence in Berlin in the thirties. A particular favourite was a concert given by the London Philharmonic in 1936 in which Dr Goebbels, Hitler and 'that rather nice but stupid' Marschall von Blomberg sat together. The reference which was always certain to enrage Rose was the story of the Duke and Duchess of Windsor. The Führer had got on so well with them, Frau Katie recalled, 'why, he even went so far as to call them the real King and Queen of England . . .'

'Why must you live in the past? Why must you rake over the coals?' Rose would cry. 'The old Berlin is dead and gone. Forget it! You cannot live there ever again. It's gone and good riddance. It brought you nothing but pain and grief. Why must you keep returning to it?'

'Na,' her mother retorted. 'My daughter is allowed to live in old England but she forbids her mother her memories of home.'

Memories of home led naturally for Frau Katie to her celebrated enumeration of the Five Ambitions, familiar to every member of her tribe and a source of deep, abiding frustration to her daughter who, Looper had observed, would literally flee when Frau Katie began to recount them once again across the bar to an audience resignedly inebriated. Those who heard them for the first time grew cold as they listened.

'Ambition the First – and who can object to it in the young girl who knows nothing from Adam and has been raised to open the world's oyster? – was simply to have a good time. It was late in the

70

twenties and Berlin was so gay! We went and took coffee in the old Fishermen's Huts at Schlachtensee. Such crowds beneath the trees! I wore a special dress, I remember, and I met Erich there. It was a dress with red and white polka dots; under it I wore a white blouse with full sleeves, a large white beret and my hair, which in those days was thick and smooth, I had cut short, and I wore earrings, dropped earrings, considered very fast! Later, in the winter, we would go skating on the Neuensee in the Tiergarten; first they had the brewery horses to drag a weight to check the ice was safe. And then, in the spring, to Werder to see the sights of the may blossom, for sweet cherries and to drink red-currant wine. We sat on wooden benches, the blossoms above us were so thick and heavy they hung down and rested on the tables. Then to the opera! Naturally we went, who didn't? I remember the first time I saw President Hindenburg. He was in the honoured box, of course. He had with him the King of Egypt and all his courtiers. I remember in particular the show, Lehár, I think, called *Land des Lächelns*. And Gitta Alper singing – oh! – she was very ugly with a huge mouth out of which came the most beautiful sounds ... oh yes, and I also remember how the Egyptians wore round hats which they kept on throughout the performance. This must have been about '28 or '29. How healthy Hindenburg looked! As if he knew we were depending on him. A few years later von Papen became Chancellor, just as my father thought. He was so pleased. Papen was a fine choice, he said. Papen would hold the line.'

There followed the Second Ambition, which began in 1933, with her marriage. That had been the greatest event of 1933. The chancellorship of Adolf Hitler was coincidental.

'Papen did not hold the line. What a blow for my father! Papen went. Hitler came. It's an old story. But what did I care for politics! My Second Ambition, as a young wife, was to please my husband. Unlike my daughter – was I not modern. We moved into a little apartment – at number 55 Friedrichstrasse. Ah, my home! I can see it now!'

And she could. She could see it all. Frau Katie liked to take her listeners on a little stroll down the Friedrichstrasse of the time she referred to as her 'happy bridal days'. This was a walk of about four kilometres and tiring to those who took it for the first time and yet fascinating, even for those who had taken it many times before. There was always something new Frau Katie found to point

71

out along the way. There were no small villas or small private houses as such in Friedrichstrasse.

'It was a street for real business and the apartment houses, three to five floors high, were built of cement or grey brick, no balconies. When you walked through a ground-floor corridor of one building, you came upon a small yard which separated the house from another one, at the back of it, the so-called '*Gartenhäuser*' which had the advantage that one did not hear all the traffic noises of the main road as loudly and were, therefore, sought after. In the front building, facing the Friedrichstrasse, there were often shops of various descriptions. Ladies of easy virtue were to be found in the Friedrichstrasse. For tourists the attractions were places where girls served drinks in bathing costumes and restaurant Steinmeier was known for its '*Eintänzer*' – i.e. a solitary lady could hire a dancer. In certain parts the area was a bit like this. Only much, much more fun!' And Frau Katie would wave her hand at the world beyond the heavy curtains of the Hottentot Room where the traffic, the whores and the hikers flowed along Earls Court Road.

'We lived in the garden house at number 55, Erich and I. It was close to his office, a few blocks away. Now, look, here are the Café Kranzler and the Café Bauer, both equally famous. Now we come to the corner of Friedrichstrasse and Behrenstrasse where you see the Metropol Theatre. Pretty isn't it? Today they're staging the operetta, *The Jolly Robbers*, by Suppé. Do you know it? Here now we are passing the Bouillonkeller. But don't go in, because you get more than soup in there! It's full of criminals. The police raid daily. And now we come to the Imperator-Diele and what we call the House of a Thousand Armchairs where we can take tea. And dance. Only the House of a Thousand Armchairs is respectable. How do we know? Because this is 1933 and single ladies are not allowed. So I must have an escort. Who will dance with me today? Caleb, of course.'

Of course. He must have chaperoned Frau Katie a hundred times to the tea dances in the House of a Thousand Armchairs ... Of course they both knew that in 1933 Frau Katie was a married woman and married women did not go dancing with strangers, but they did not mention that.

It was with the recounting of the Third Ambition that new recruits to the Hottentot Room, who had not heard the story before, began suddenly to hear the note deepening and to feel the growing horror of young Katerina von Sturz's cruel and sudden change of fortune. And those who already knew what was coming never found that this helped them in the least to make the transition from the golden days of the earlier Ambitions into the gathering darkness of the Third.

'One day my husband came home for lunch and said he must take me out. There had been a catastrophe. In order that I should understand the nature of the catastrophe he wished to take me to see something. He took me to the Jewish quarter, not far from the Alexanderplatz. It was the ghetto. He took me to Hirtenstrasse and Grenadierstrasse and Dragonerstrasse. The same places my father had shown me when he wanted to explain from where the Jewish problem came and also from where came the cartoons I had laughed at in *Simplicissimus*. We went in a taxi and saw the urchins, whores, Hebrew bookshops, rabbis, money-changers all again – all the same! – and we saw then the big stars drawn on the glass shopfronts, the warnings pasted up: *Germans! Don't buy from Jews.* And then I knew it was not the same. There were police clearing the streets. They were stopping men and searching them for weapons and checking their papers. Erich asked a policeman why they were lining the roads and the policeman said it was because the SA were marching through the district. Erich said that surely the police could stop the march but the policeman said they were there to keep the peace and there had been rumours that communists and Jews would fight the marchers. The police were there to see the marchers were allowed safe passage and to keep the peace.

'Erich, I said. Why are we here? He said: "Katerina, this is 1938." I asked him, why do you tell me this? I know the date, Erich. Why have you brought me here? "Let's go home," he said. At home he told me: "Katerina, your family are Jews." Naturally I did not believe him. I laughed. My family were Lutherans, Germans, Berliners. He told me then that Berlin was full of Catholic Jews, atheist Jews, blond Jews, Lutheran Jews. It made no difference to those who were checking such things. My family thought they were Christians. It was an honest mistake. He was prepared to believe they had had no suspicions of their Hebrew antecedents. They had been lied to by their parents. On both sides of my family, my father and my mother, both families had drifted away from Judaism under Bismarck when things were easier for the Jews. Later they called themselves Lutherans. It was not true. My family name was not Brahm, even that was not true. My name was Abrahamsohn.'

73

When Frau Katie related the details of that fateful lunch she would grow still and pale, her eyes would become glazed and she was clearly back again at the table in her house at 55 Friedrichstrasse, attempting to comprehend what her husband had told her.

'For God's sake, Erich, what madness is this? Many bloods mix in a family, especially if you go back far enough. Even if this foolish story is true – why must we care? That was years ago! Erich told me: "I'm sorry. They take such things pretty seriously now. There is a department within my office devoted entirely to such things. It is their job to examine the racial content of certain families. They are particularly sensitive to the unions of non-Aryans and pure Germans, particularly Germans who may occupy sensitive posts in the government service."

'Perhaps I began to understand what he meant. He was already by then a Colonel in the Military Intelligence and he had just discovered that he was married to a Jew. Because of his job, he told me he could see the way the tide was running but still I struggled against what he had told me. I said to him that this thinking was madness. If it were applied throughout the country who would be safe? Who was to say what racial mixing had occurred in families in previous generations? Just how far back was this department prepared to investigate? His answer was terrible – "They are being really scientific. They're going back to the beginning. They're going back as far as it takes. They'll go back as far as the Old Testament if they feel the need." I think I went a little mad then. I screamed at him that I was German, just as much as he was German. No one was going to take it away from me. I attacked him. Erich was very strong. He wanted me to speak to my parents, but I refused. Why should I go near them? They must have known. They should have said. A few weeks later my brother resigned his commission in the army. Erich said he was determined to help us. He said that my family would have to think of leaving. A few weeks later there was the Kristallnacht. You know what is the Kristallnacht? It was autumn and the glass fell like leaves in the streets of Berlin. We call it Kristallnacht because of the smashed windows when the Nazis went berserk. They broke up the department stores. They said a Jew had tried to kill the German ambassador in Paris. Soon after they began assembling Jews, all Jews, for the transports. There were pictures in the papers. You saw lines of men in coats and hats carrying briefcases like they could have been going to the office

74

except they were lined three abreast and marched between SS and police guards to the assembly points. Again Erich took me. He made me go and watch. This time they were not the Jews of the ghetto. They were men in suits and hats. The crowds came to see them marching away. Mothers held up their babies for a better view. Bystanders took photographs. The men marched without looking left or right. They were so respectable! They looked just like the people who were watching them. They looked like us. They looked like my father.

'Afterwards Erich said, "Katcha, you must go." But I screamed and he said no more. However, he set about helping my father and mother. First, an acceptable buyer had to be found for the factory and a price agreed. The Party had to approve. Everything went through the Party. Erich found someone in the Party who would support the application. The price given was half its worth and then again only half of the price paid was actually given. But the business was sold. Then there was the question of permission to emigrate. My parents wished to go to Ameirca, which was then issuing visas, thousands of visas, but maybe only a tenth were being taken up. You see the government made difficulties for the people applying. Again, Erich got the visas. He booked the passage on the ship and then, to make everything look normal, he said to me: "Katcha, we must get a divorce." By this stage I said nothing. I had still not seen my parents. Also I found it impossible to talk to my husband. I remember Erich came home with our passports. I looked at the photograph of myself. I said – this is not me – then I looked at the big J they had stamped on the passport and finally I looked at the name: Katerina Abrahamsohn and I *knew* it was not me. I feared my passport. Worse was to come. A few days before the ship was supposed to sail my father went upstairs to his study. He sat down at his desk and shot himself in the head. He left no note. No message. There was no need. I understood. It was not suicide. Mr Abrahamsohn killed Mr Brahm. That's what he meant. Until that time I had refused to discuss these matters. I had not seen my family and I would not speak to my husband. When he spoke to me I screamed. I did not wish to hear his plans. I did not wish to know about the divorce. I did not want to go to America. What I wanted was to go dancing. I wanted to go to the theatre. I wanted all talk of the war to stop. I wanted to live with my husband in my home. I wanted to scream. But the time for screaming was over. The night before we were due to sail I left the house and disappeared.'

Here began the Fourth Ambition. Young Katie von Sturz on the run in Berlin in 1938. She knew she was pursued by the disease. Her ambition was now to outrun it, to remain a German in her beloved Berlin.

'I lived for a long time among a very rag-tag group of artists in Friedenau, a kind of hippy colony, you might say. Poets, anarchists, communists. There had once been a lot of them there but they had been torn apart by the raids. You see, this place had been raided from the very beginning, back in '33, when Goering was still just a captain trying to make his name. The place itself became a kind of religious symbol for the Nazis. They raided it often. Even when there were only a few people left there. Just like they kept re-membering the Munich beer hall. The police and the army could come and shoot the place up. The walls and doors were always full of bullet holes. Spent bullets dropped from the ceiling while you slept. They would find books and papers and burn them in the street. They would arrest a few people. Then they would stand around and sing the Horst Wessel song with interested members of the public. Soon of course I had to move on. In '39, when the war started, things got harder. I worked for a baker, in a bank, in a bar and then I worked as a children's maid. In this way I survived for two years, can you believe it? Mind you, in Berlin, Jews were still relatively safe, even when the war came. It was only in '41 that the first big sweeps began. It was October, I remember, when they began to get serious. I hid in the underground until spring of 1942.

'At this time Erich found me again. His police connections you see. By now he was a lieutenant general. Oh yes, at the very least! He told me I was in great danger. If the Gestapo found me they would send me directly to a concentration camp. Erich was very kind, very understanding, very tender. It was from that meeting that I date the conception of my daughter, Rose. Naturally I didn't know that then. Afterwards, Erich gave me a Mauser revolver and said I would know what to do with it, in need. He also offered whatever help he could, but I decided to move on. Jews were hiding deeply now, like moles. The police were everywhere and the Gestapo said they would make Berlin *Judenfrei*, once and for all. There were even trained Jew-catchers, usually other Jews, operating from Iranischestrasse. It was very, very dangerous. Illegals like me

76

had to keep moving or bury themselves in some dark hole. But pregnant women can't run. So it was then I knew I would have to leave Berlin. At that time I was living in a secret compartment beneath the stairs in a flat of some friends in Bleibtreustrasse. It was nothing more than a glorified cupboard. I could not bring up a baby there. These friends arranged through other friends that I should be smuggled out of the country from a German port on a freighter bound for Sweden. I wept. But what could I do? Then, one night, shortly before I was due to leave, a man stopped me in the street and asked me for my papers. I knew immediately he was Gestapo. I pretended to be terrified. I said I didn't have them with me. I said they were at home. I offered to take him back with me to my apartment. He agreed. He seemed to be enjoying himself. I led him into my flat. With my knees shaking I took him to the secret room under the stairs and then I confessed to be living there, illegally. He was very surprised and pleased. I could see him thinking that he would be commended for this discovery. He became very officious and insisted on searching the room. He walked inside. I followed him and I took the Mauser and shot him. My friends and I sealed up the room and I left Berlin that night. I think he is still there today, the dead Gestapo man in my cupboard under the stairs in Bleibtreustrasse.'

And this gruesome, astonishing escape of which she was so proud brought Frau Katie to London and to her Fifth Ambition, which was to safeguard her tribe from the onset of those hostile forces she described collectively as 'the disease'. They were the sorts of people who would understand what it was to be selected for infection by the disease. She and her Hottentots were '*Kameraden*'. Like her they were fleeing the disease and in the Hottentot Room they were offered a safe house. Evidently, when she'd come out of Germany she managed to smuggle jewels or gold because she bought property in Antaeus Street almost immediately after her arrival in London. She had kept it going since the war by using her pension and the reparation payments made by the German government. She complained bitterly, however, that she did not receive a pension due to a general's widow. The reason for this was, in the first place, that while she had been married to Erich von Sturz he had not been a general, and secondly the divorce had been perfectly legal. Frau Katie compared her case with that of Ingeborg Dönitz, the wife of the admiral who had received only a pension of a captain since, the

British argued, her husband had been promoted above this rank by Hitler. Frau Katie frequently complained about what she saw as the monstrous injustice towards the widows of gallant soldiers.

This feeling of injustice burned very deep in Frau Katie. She felt that her own dilemma had been insufficiently realised, and that the degree of her sacrifice went unappreciated, particularly in the light of the way her husband died. Erich von Sturz was one of the officers involved in the abortive coup against Hitler in July of 1944 when a bomb exploded under Hitler's map table. Von Sturz, along with other conspirators, was hanged in the dungeon of Plötzensee Prison while a cine camera recorded their agonies as they dangled from meat hooks. The manner of his death absolved her beloved Erich, in her mind at least, from any question of complicity with the Nazi regime. He had died, as he lived, a 'good' German. To Rose's question as to why he did not rebel earlier, Frau Katie rejoined haughtily that 'He was a soldier, not a traitor.'

That Frau Katie never believed that she had entirely escaped the relentless and ever-pursuing Gestapo who wished to kill her but merely evaded its attentions for a period, became clear when she was discovered to be suffering from cancer. The type of cancer she never mentioned, regarding it as demeaning, a deliberate attempt to humiliate her. In that regard as well, she clearly regarded her illness not as something distinct from her persecution in the years she had spent underground in Berlin, but as a continuation of that ordeal. Her description of her illness as Debussy's complaint confused still further those who heard her refer to the disease. But Frau Katie was not in the least confused. Debussy's complaint was simply another manifestation of the remorseless affliction which shattered her Berlin dream. The horror had several names, sometimes it was 'the disease', and sometimes 'the old story', and sometimes 'Debussy's complaint'. The proliferating rogue cells threatening her life were a lethal insurrection of the very stuff of life. Very good. She penetrated the disguise. Here were the old hunters who had stalked Katerina von Sturz through the streets of Berlin and very nearly ran her to earth in her secret cupboard under the stairs in Bleibtreustrasse. She claimed to have felt no surprise when her illness was diagnosed, maintaining that she'd always known that the enemy would strike again. It had not given up the hunt when she had fled from Germany to England in 1942, rather it had travelled with her. 'It went underground inside me,' was the way Frau Katie explained it.

' "The disease" knew it was in enemy territory when I landed in this country, so it hid itself, but it was waiting for the day when conditions would improve. And now here it is, popping up its head and saying–"Na, ja, remember me, Katerina?" And I say right back to it: of *course* I remember you! But be careful! I finished you off once before and I'll do it again.'

But most extraordinary was Frau Katie's grudging admiration for the forces ranged against her. Nothing about the old lady was more impressive or more terrible. She admired her adversary – for its tenacity, cleverness, its ruthless pursuit. It was as if she recognised, to the horror of her friends and the despair of her daughter, that her enemy was, after all, properly 'German'.

An operation was performed, which only proved that the course of her illness was such that an operation would not stop it. Treatment by powerful chemicals led to unpleasant side-effects and hair loss. Frau Katie now began wearing a red wig. It was richer, redder and darker than her own hair and contrasted startlingly with her pale face. The refusal to distinguish between her Berlin ordeal of the 1930s and her present illness was an ever sharper source of disappointment and frustration to Rose.

As her mother grew weaker and the medication required to control the pain more powerful, Rose found the strain of nursing the old lady increasingly demanding. She worried particularly about what she regarded as the morbid connections her mother made between the present and past. There was the occasion when Katie had been caught up in a political demonstration. 'I was walking in the city after a visit to the doctor. Suddenly I found myself in the middle of a mob who were out to get the Jews. "Blood," cried the mob. "Murderers!" They carried banners. "Death to Israelis!" said the banners. I got confused. I saw the police. They seemed to be there to keep the peace. For a moment I thought I was in Kaiser Wilhelmstrasse when the SA marched. And Erich was asking me if I knew the date. Sure I knew the date. "It's 1938. But what does that mean?" I wanted to ask him. Only he wasn't to be found, although I looked for him everywhere. I said to myself: how silly can you be? Erich's been dead all these years . . . But it was there all over again: "Blood!" screamed the mob. They were marching to kill the Jews and suddenly I knew what this

79

meant. It meant that the Disease had come out of hiding and was ready to attack.'

'Mother,' Rose said patiently, 'what you saw was not an anti-Jewish march. It was probably a demonstration against Israel. You're confusing it with the march you saw in Berlin. That's past. It's gone. This is London – and it's 1983, not 1938.'

Frau Katie shot her a side-long look. 'Aren't you frightened when you go to your job in the City?'

Rose became angry and embarrassed. 'Oh Mother, don't be preposterous! What you saw had nothing to do with anti-Semitism. It was against *Zionism*. You were in no danger. The police were there to see that things didn't get out of hand. The trouble with you is that you can't tell the difference between the anti-Jewish marchers of Berlin in the thirties and a peaceful demonstration in London today.'

Her mother looked disconsolate, even mortified. She hung her head. 'Of course, you're right, Rose. I am silly. I cannot tell the difference. But, you see – I am from Berlin so I know nothing.'

Frau Katie grew weaker. However, she continued to spend her evenings in the Hottentot Room where it was a rule of the house that no one ever asked her about the state of her health. She very rarely referred to her actual illness. But the steady emaciation, the deepening lines pain cut in her face, the inflatable rubber cushion without which she could not sit for more than a few minutes and which, when placed upon a bar stool, made her sway so alarmingly that Gerrie the barman had continually to steady her or she would have fallen off. All this marked the deterioration. The only concession she made to the fact that she was ill was to drink even more champagne and to talk lightly of the tiresomeness of 'Debussy's complaint'.

It was when they looked it up in the encylopaedia that the Hottentots learnt that the queen of the tribe was suffering from cancer of the rectum.

Frau Katie stirred in the huge bed, opened an eye, crooked a bony finger at Looper and with a quick, suspicious glance about the room, whispered fiercely in his ear: 'The disease thinks it's so clever. For years now it has been waiting its chance to take me. It hunted me in Berlin and I beat it. So it followed. It waited. It hated. The disease is not so stupid. It is determined. So is Frau Katie. We are not at the end of the old story yet. Only time is running out, my dear Caleb. I must take you away soon.' Here she very slowly and painfully closed one eye so that her face rose into a grotesque grimace as she tried to wink at him. 'Soon we will elope!' Then very slowly the other eye closed. The nervous licking of the lips began again and he knew that she was asleep. Her wig and her pillows were too big for her. She was out of place in this big room, dwindling away. She might have been a child dressing up in adult clothes. Very slowly he began to withdraw his hand from hers. The eyes opened: 'Well, Caleb, time to be going? Do you have the ladder ready at the window? Is our elopement running to plan? Don't be taken in by anything you see here. I'm just waiting for the call. The disease thinks it has me, but I'm lying low. I have plans for us.' The eyes closed.

'But Frau Katie, so have I. What I can't understand is why you've encouraged my relationship with Rose.' He tried to keep his tone light, faintly amused. 'After all, I can't elope with both of you.'

The eyes opened, glittering fiercely. 'That's right. Maybe I wanted to make sure that my Hottentots would be protected. Or maybe I wanted you to escape. Or maybe I wanted both. But both is impossible. Isn't it?'

Perhaps that was it. Having both, as she said, was impossible. Yes. He understood. She wanted him to choose.

'What do you do when you think there is no further to go? What must a person find, make, when the end comes? When you are against the wall? Where do you go when you can go no further?'

He said nothing. These were unanswerable questions.

'Well?' The shrivelled child in the bed demanded.

'I have the ladder ready.'

'Good. Then you have chosen. In return I shall tell you what you can do when you can do no more. Keep your eye on me! The disease was waiting and watching for me. I knew I must be prepared to move. I knew I must be ready if ever the hunters came for me again! Those who do not obey must be careful.'

With that her eyes opened very wide and began darting quickly about the room as if trying to find in its dark corners the forces she now felt were so close, so hot on her trail. It took considerable willpower for Looper to stop himself turning around to see what it was that menaced her from the shadows. He knew, he told himself, there was nothing to be seen. At last the little darting glances

81

stopped and her eyes fixed on him again, this time, astonishingly, with traces of amusement and a hint of something that with a shock he realised might have been pity. 'Dear Caleb. Your face is so white, so clean. You practise wiping your face so clean so that nothing can be seen there. Your face is as plain and as empty as the statues from Greece and Rome. Clear as water. Pale as marble. It pretends that it knows nothing. Do you know these heads, Caleb? You've seen these heads?'

'Of course I've seen them. I was at the British Museum a few days ago looking at them again.'

'But what did you see there? Which heads?'

'I saw the head of Trajan, the Emperor Trajan.'

'Ah.' The satisfaction with which this was said was almost palpable. 'Then you do understand. You know that they painted the faces! They coloured the cheeks and the lips and hair and eyes. In Berlin we have a wonderful museum which together we will visit one day. In our elopement! It is called the Pergamon. They have remarkable Roman – how do you call them? – friezes, I think. But they are in the latest style, from the time when the Empire was crumbling. So they are very agitated, a little oriental. I guess they were made at the time when just about anyone could call himself a Roman. The real Romans were down and out by then. What the hell, they said, anyone can join. The colour on these statues must have been even wilder. Perhaps the people who looked at those statues thought them all the rage. Very modern, they said. It's argued that when people are on their last legs they long for the modern, they long for new blood to save them. People thought that of Adolf. He may be funny, they said, but he wants the best for us. He wants Germany great again.' She struggled upright on an elbow. 'But you know what I mean. You've seen the heads.'

Gently he lifted her up, smoothed the pillows and laid her down. Her wig slipped to reveal the pale skull beneath. 'Enough. Too much talk, Frau Katie.'

She grew calmer. 'Then you understand that history deceives us. The faces look pure, simple, timeless. But there is nothing simple about the past. History wishes to make us think so. That is because it has so much to hide.' She lay back panting. Her wig had come off now and she looked like a wizened, bald baby. She closed her eyes and waved a feeble hand to him. 'Now you run along, darling. It's been very lovely to see you, but Frau Katie must rest. Go and have a drink with the tribe. Give them my love. Tell them the drinks are on the house. Tell them – tell them that Frau Katie is saving her strength.'

'Yes. But enough talk. Come – now you must sleep. Sleep . . .'

'Is this the way to talk to a respectable lady? Sleep?'

But like a child doing as she was told, she screwed up her eyes tightly, releasing his hand.

Behind him the door opened. Rose was back.

'Wyngate and the others have arrived,' she whispered in his ear. 'They would so like to visit briefly. Would you mind?'

That was it. Looper stood and then, stooping quickly, kissed Frau Katie. A tiny finger travelled to her lips, touched them briefly, continued upward in a gentle loop. She was blowing a kiss, though whether to the General in his silver frame by her bedside or to himself, he could not say for sure. Gently he resettled the wig on that hairless pate where the thin network of veins pulsed.

Rose busied herself at the curtains, pulling them closed, although they were tightly drawn. Then she drew the covers up to the old lady's chin and led Looper from the room, closing the door firmly behind him. This fussing over a scrap of flesh in the big bed seemed excessive and heavy-handed. Rose must have sensed something of his feelings because she made a response which surprised him. 'Mummy's terribly weak. She mustn't move about if she can possibly help it.'

The implication of the statement, seemingly so sensible and innocuous, was apparent in the way she made sure the curtains were tightly drawn and the door shut behind them. But the implication was not one that he wished to face. At that moment he felt too unhappy to think. He knew what she meant. Yet somewhere on the crude frontline of his mind he saw the ugly, primitive emotion which possessed Rose rearing up challengingly. She saw the end of her long servitude and she wished for no last-minute hitches.

CHAPTER 7

Rose led the way downstairs to the horseshoe bar where the others were waiting. Mr Govender's daughter Anagupta had arrived. So had Wyngate Hossein. Morris Morrison went immediately to Rose and pleaded his case for a second visit to Frau Katie, and was denied permission. Mona May was still out running. Nobody knew where Biddy was. In the corner the German grandfather clock with the face of a lunatic bumpkin, perhaps a caricature of some sweet-faced idiot in the clock-maker's Black Forest village long ago, beamed its fat, pink-cheeked beatific smile and its heavy black hands showed the time to be ten to two. Gerrie passed Looper a whisky and soda and then began polishing the vivid copper decorations behind the bar. Morrison and Lestrade contemplated their drinks. The little tribe was almost complete. Rose parted the curtains and stared into the darkness. When he had finished the copper, Gerrie buffed the gleaming ostrich eggs into an even deeper yellow. Upon the egg the crouching bushman loosed a tiny arrow at a distant buck. Lestrade told Gerrie to stop fidgeting. 'This is hardly the time to be playing house.'

'It keeps me busy,' said Gerrie. 'And, what's more, it stops me crying.'

Mr Govender and his daughter, Anagupta, sat whispering together in Hindi, their heads dipping and rising over their glasses of Perrier water bubbling before them. The high-jumper, Mona May, arrived in her tracksuit from her lengthy training through the dark snowy streets of Earls Court. Elize feared for her safety. Her anxious eyes scanned the athlete for signs of molestation. Buffy Lestrade, dressed in a crumpled cream linen suit more appropriate for some distant Egyptian veranda, rested his huge head in his hands. He was drinking vodka, an unusual event.

Gerrie the barman had evidently recently polished the floor for the medicinal smell of Cobra white wax was very evident. There was nothing now for them to do, Looper reflected, but to drink and wait. Rose sat by the window staring into the night. Under the street light a small white dog sniffed inquisitively. That part of

Earls Court, around Antaeus Street, was being increasingly occupied by West Indians. Rose took them for Africans, an error which amused and embarrassed the others.

'I am not racially obsessed,' Rose retorted. 'I can't tell at a glance who is what.'

The West Indians liked to gather on the pavement at the head of the street outside the all-night grocery. Rose attributed to them the rise in petty crime. She talked of burglar bars on all the windows. She was alone, late at night, she said. The Hottentots nudged each other and winked at Looper. But they knew this wasn't the time to provoke her. Her mother was ill upstairs. She had reason to feel uneasy.

'Rose reminds me of the early colonists at the Cape of Good Hope,' said Buffy Lestrade. 'They had trouble in telling the difference between Bushmen and Hottentots.'

'I have no colour sense, it's true,' Rose responded languidly without looking around. 'It's too bad, isn't it? What's more I don't have any moral feelings about it either. Can you understand that? What I find bloody tiresome about it all is that it's simply inefficient. To always have regard for purity is just stupid. It doesn't get things done. Do you see?'

'Certainly we see,' said Looper. 'Rose, you are merciless in your simplicity.'

'I'm so pleased you understand me,' said Rose.

Hossein stood behind Rose and placed his hand on her shoulder. His face puckered and his shoulders began to shake. Rose was very good with him. Still without turning around she patted his hand firmly and deliberately.

'The whites at the Cape couldn't deal with the Hottentots,' said Elize. 'The Hottentots simply refused to make good slaves. So the colonists had to import lots of slaves.'

'Hottentots didn't get things done,' said Mr Govender.

'Really? I wouldn't have thought the colonists saw much to choose between slaves and Hottentots,' replied Rose with cool provocation.

'There is everything to choose,' Buffy rose to the provocation and to demonstrate the anger he felt, he called for a double vodka. He hardly ever touched alcohol and allowed himself, on occasions of considerable stress, only ice-cold vodka providing it was certified to be the best Russian available, because medical testimony

85

declared it the very purest of spirits. Lestrade gave to medical testimony the kind of credence once reserved for the gospel and where medicine failed, as was the case at deathbeds, he fortified himself by falling back on philosophy. Frau Katie, he declared, had her very own way of dying. She bore out Heidegger's contention that the dying of others was not something we could really know and understand. All we could really do was 'to be there alongside' someone else's death – or *'dabeisein . . .'* How he relished the sheer pronounceability of those syllables.

'I resent the use of German at a time like this,' said Rose.

Hossein embraced her. He looked old, tired, frightened. Looper was struck by the way he clung to Rose. As if the loss, the bereavement were his alone and Rose was giving him strength. She led Hossein upstairs.

'How did you find Frau Katie?' Lestrade asked quietly.

'Dying,' said Looper. 'Dying but fighting. It's a very funny thing – I don't know how to say this. I don't even know what I mean by it. But you know how she always was when she got hold of some idea. She'd never let go until she had given it an explanation she was happy with.'

'Say an interpretation,' said Buffy.

'Yes. An interpretation. She made things work for her. Well, I got the impression that she's doing this now. Don't ask me how. But she's working on something. I don't understand it.'

'But she's too weak to move,' said Gerrie.

'And very confused,' said Mr Govender. 'She really didn't know who I was. Or, I suspect, who she was. She certainly didn't know where she was.'

'I know,' Looper said. 'It was just an impression. But I got the feeling, well, I felt strongly that she was up to something.'

Elize nodded. 'I know what you mean. She's defiant!'

'Yes. She is. But, you see, I don't understand the basis. She has no ground for it. Yet she is going ahead with something. And I know she expects me to do something. But I can't think what it is.'

'Perhaps not to do – but to be something,' suggested Lestrade.

For once he sounded sensible. Yes. They were of course all called on to be something. Mr Govender, for instance, was called on to be the spirit of vengeance. He spent a good deal of time planning the Nuremberg trials he wished to hold for the 'Berta Regime'. He answered charges that it was unfair by charging the others with hypocrisy. Those responsible for the racial policies of the country ought to be tried as war criminals. Just as had happened at Nuremberg. Of course it was not fair. The Nuremberg trials were unfair, too. They had been called to provide legal justification for death sentences the victors demanded. Rightly demanded. But they would have been more honest if they had put selected Nazis against a wall and shot them. Mr Govender would like to have been a political leader but his base was shrinking. He would have liked to love his daughters freely. But that was not possible. Instead he dreamed of prosecutions, scaffolds, vengeance. When he closed his eyes he saw the gallows. His dreams were full of tumbrels. Young Mona May wanted to be a farmer's daughter, increasingly she was likely to be a wife – to Elize. Elize had been a nurse with a horror of violence. Increasingly Elize felt the need to become Mona's protector, to guard her against her trainers, detractors, memories. Increasingly she felt she would willingly kill for Mona May. And Morrison? He dreamed, though he did not know it, of sacrifice. He wished to repent, to expiate his sin. He wished to wipe away the advertisements. And Looper? Why did he want to be. He had no idea. Certainly he knew that the calls for him differed from those on the others because he began from a position they knew nothing about. He was not in the same position. But Looper knew that he was soon to find out. This was the time of finding out.

'I feel as if I'm coming to.'

'Coming to what?' Gerrie asked.

'It's as if I've been in a coma for a long time. Or under an anaesthetic. Now I'm coming round. I get glimpses of things. I begin to see where I am, but my head's still too fuzzy. Frau Katie might be drugged, and old and dying – but she sees perfectly clearly.'

Gerrie shook his head. 'What a woman!'

'I feel I must try and do something,' said Morrison. 'Then I realise it's pure vanity. There is nothing I can do. I'm helpless.' What he wished to do was unclear, but Looper realised that this yearning was not simply recognition of the inevitability of Frau Katie's approaching death. The wish to do something referred also, he suspected, to Morrison's old religious inclinations. In his grief he was reverting to his original role as a priest. He didn't suppose for a moment that Morris encouraged this retrogressive compulsion. But it was that area of his character, or soul, or psyche that was now being challenged. What Morris Morrison wanted to do was to *minister*, to offer spiritual consolation to the dying woman and to her friends and especially to himself. He knew of course that it was inappropriate in Frau Katie's case and unacceptable in the case of other members, whom, even if they wished for spiritual consolation, did not expect it from Morrison. To them, and they all knew something of his religious background, his former calling was a youthful peccadillo, a failed and not very serious hobby, something like photography or water polo, which he had had a stab at long ago in a half-hearted way and, quite understandably, never kept up. What the Hottentots saw when they looked at Morris was not a sensitive, palpitating soul attempting to express the spiritual pangs he experienced as the imminent death of an old friend challenged his lost vocation. They saw instead a solid, successful businessman. Worse still, they saw an advertising man. Perhaps it says something of the world that they registered far more strongly the copywriter that he now was than the priest which they all, if somewhat vaguely, knew him once to have been. What struck them about Morris and even led to a certain, grudging admiration were his good suits, his expensive jewellery, the chunky gold watch, the onyx cuff links. However, this feeling was mixed with a kind of pity which itself verged on disdain since Morris was not even a 'proper' businessman, but an ageing copywriter. His dark blue suit and the red rose in his buttonhole suggested something more substantial, but of course they knew that his job was to make up slogans, headlines and jingles for toothpastes, gas ovens and little girls' frocks. They felt about him then, as they might have felt about an elderly poet, that his very job description, to use Buffy Lestrade's phrase, was a contradiction in terms. They could not help feeling that after a certain age men simply shouldn't do things like that, not if they wished to cut sensible, respectable figures in the world. There hung about an elderly man practising the profession of advertising copywriter a faintly shameful and comic air, there was something rather indecent about it, like an elderly bachelor's passion for little girls. When Morris said that he wished to do something, the others flinched, for what could Morris do? – besides extolling the delights of chilled vermouth, or, at his most profound, warn in public service advertisements of the dangerous relationship between cooking fat and kitchen fires. What Morris meant, of course, was that he would have liked to have heard Frau Katie's confession, to have comforted her and to have prayed for her soul, to have beaten his breast and called on God for mercy, to have knelt in silent prayer – anything but let Frau Katie fade out like a dying fire in an empty room.

Hossein arrived back in the Room. 'She didn't know me. Sleeping. What's to say? Or do? Rose says she knew who you were, Caleb.'

Looper nodded slowly. 'Yes. That's right. She knew me. She knew exactly who I was.'

'Well, I don't know,' said Rose, seeking to soften the blow to Hossein, 'she's so weak. We can't say for absolute certain she knew who Looper was. Or that she didn't know you, Wyngate. Deep down. She knows more than she lets on.'

'Please can I see her?' Morris begged. 'There must be something I can do.'

'There is nothing to be done,' Rose replied calmly. 'Nature will take its course.'

And with that she led Anagupta upstairs to the bedroom.

They heard the imperious ring behind this statement of unexceptional fact. What she meant, of course, was that nothing *would* be done. She was at the end of her tether, after many false alarms. Frau Katie had weakened and rallied before. There was a tension now in Rose. When she sat or when she stood, you saw her flexed like a sabre. There was a glint in her eyes, there was something about the hunch of her shoulders when she had sat staring out through the window into the darkness of Antaeus Street. She was facing up to becoming the guardian of Frau Katie's future and would see to it that nature took its course. Dimly Looper now began to perceive how someone driven to distraction by the lingering and painful death of a person they have nursed day and night over a long period, might begin to look with furtive desperation at the pillow, at the plastic bag, dream of the necessary pills, pray for the friendly doctor who understood . . . Rose was at this stage. Rose was a dangerous woman.

But they were all aware of that and never more so than at this moment in which they contemplated Rose's furious determination to see this thing through. For they all felt, afterwards, she would want to see them off. But it was the normally unobservant Mona May who drew their attention to something which frightened the Hottentots quite terribly.

89

'Where has Coree's cane disappeared to?'

They all stared at the strip of lighter wood above the bar where the cane had been.

'Perhaps Frau Katie took it herself,' Gerrie suggested desperately.

'Nonsense,' said Elize. 'Why on earth should she take it down from the wall? Besides it was screwed on. Look, you can see the holes still. Can you imagine Frau Katie using a screwdriver?'

The idea was ridiculous.

The Hottentots realised that Rose must have taken the cane. What could she want with it? It was a sign, they knew that. But what did it mean?

Even as her mother lay dying some crucial change was taking place. They had heard her talking of the place 'paying its way'. They had seen her bring the man Julius Bafney from Gimpel Fils the merchant bankers, right into the Hottentot Room and show him around. While they sat there, drinking at the bar, they heard her apologising to him for the 'somewhat pungent odour', by which of course she meant the mixture of wax floor polish, the homemade African beer with its sour yeasty aroma much enjoyed by Wyngate Hossein and occasionally the Soweto Knights, as well as the characteristic bouquet of tobacco, alcohol and what Rose called, opening a window as she did so and smiling sideways at the dark young man from Gimpel Fils, 'a lot of late-night perspiration'. If the Hottentots had any doubts about Rose's determination to destroy the place once her mother went, those doubts faded when they watched her show the banker over the property. Julius Bafney wore large round gold-rimmed glasses, and carried a thin gold pen with which he took notes. He said: 'Oh quite', and 'absolutely right' very frequently while Rose led the way, with the energy and forward thrust of an armoured car.

The banker Bafney was that curious mixture of avarice and propriety the City of London breeds. Young, slim, devoted to the service of the usury, who regarded profit – which he did not understand and did not possess the words to define (despising those who tried to do so) – with the mystical reverence the medieval peasant felt for the secrets of God, that is to say he yearned for it with heart and testicles. For him investment was the sacred current between worshipper and godhead, and the fructification of an investment was the divine promise made flesh, the incarnation of God

90

made executive. He wore rather sharp black shoes and a dove-grey, double-breasted suit. One fragile stem of his dark glasses fell from his breast pocket like a broken straw. Looper had also met Mr Plotz, the builder, 'Refurbishers since 1879', and he had no doubt that radical changes were being planned. He had also made it his business to glance over the plans which Rose kept locked in a steel filing cabinet in her bedroom. Locks had never presented Looper with problems.

As the end drew nearer, the others made it clear they expected Looper to intercede with Rose. They pinned everything on him. They knew nothing of her affair with him. Or of the secret engagement. But if they had done so, Looper knew they would have been delighted. He felt that if by cutting him up into slices and feeding him to English Rose would have kept her sweet, they would not have hesitated.

He told the Hottentots: 'English Rose wants you to stay on. She has no plans to drive you away.'

Gerrie spoke for them all when he said: 'The trouble is that she may not leave us much alternative. I'm glad about what you say, Caleb. It means she isn't planning to shut up shop, or sell up and get out of Antaeus Street. But does she care about the spirit of the Room?'

'Of course she doesn't.' Hossein shook his head at such *naïveté*. 'Let's keep it open. That is all we can ask. She doesn't need a religious commitment.'

'As long as she isn't planning to turn it into a discothèque or a dancing club,' said Elize.

'I'm afraid none of you understand the ferocious onward drive of English Rose,' said Buffy. 'She's a radical reformer. She wants the Room in whatever new manifestation it emerges, to be modern, successful and profitable. She will wish it to run on time, on budget and along business management lines which I, for one, will find repugnant. The being, the character of the Room, is precisely that it provides a haven for the odd lot we are. Frau Katie's genius was to see that we are all antediluvian oddballs who can never go home. She not only understands, she approves! English Rose hates us for both reasons. Our exile and her mother's approval.'

'I wouldn't say "hates",' Looper interjected. 'She assured me she wants you to stay on. All of you. She gave me the assurance. She expected me to pass it along to you.'

Looper's study of the plans had not revealed very much. They were rudimentary and contained specifications which presumably the builder could read. But one phrase caught his eye: 'computerised laser bank/console'. There also seemed to be a lot of lights . . .

'She hates her mother. Of course she hates us,' said Elize. 'The only person she doesn't hate is Looper. I don't know why.'

'You don't usually hate what you're planning to eat,' said Gerrie.

'I feel redundancy creeping on. I could never live under the new regime,' Buffy said.

'Give her a chance,' Morrison pleaded.

'Let me explain something,' Looper said. 'Rose is more a phenomenon than a person. Like a forest fire. A force of nature. You don't "give a chance" to a force of nature. You just have to hope that it misses your house.'

'What will you do?' Mr Govender asked.

'Nothing, until I know Frau Katie's gone. Then I'll see. I'll be lost without Frau Katie.'

'If it's anything like I think, this place won't be worth visiting,' Elize declared. 'And I shan't come if it goes fancy.'

'Nor I,' Buffy swore, raising his right hand.

'Now, I don't think it will necessarily be that bad,' said Morris. 'I really don't believe that Rose hates us.'

But of course they knew she did. She detested everything about them. From Mona May's home baking to Gerrie's floor polish.

Mona May spent long hours training. When not training she baked. When she baked she became a farmer's daughter again: milk tart, plum pudding, fly cemetery and *koeksusters* appeared in the Room. Rose found these South African delicacies quite repugnant. The *koeksusters*, golden, twisted and dripping with oil, she found most repulsive of all. Such things evoked her contempt. She hated Hossein's cheap Texan cigarettes with their peppery aroma and, even worse, the foul cheap brands he had grown used to in the townships, which even now someone found a way of sending him from South Africa, she could not abide. The sticks of dried salted meat, the cans of South African beer, the little bags of witch-doctor's bones they threw for fun, all these she regarded as the props and toys of a childish band who simply could not forget what they had left behind them and could not let go.

'Remember what she said to the Knights?' Elize asked.

92

A few weeks before when Frau Katie was already weakening quickly, the Soweto Knights arrived late one night after giving a concert, arrayed in leopard skins, their bodies shining with oil. Rose attempted to throw them out. Indeed she would have done so but for the sudden, unexpected, magnificent appearance of Frau Katie at the top of the stairs, risen from her sick-bed, tiny, emaciated and furious, declaring that the Knights looked 'quite beautiful' and ordering Gerrie to supply them with drinks throughout the rest of the evening, 'on my account'. Rose had shrieked at them. 'This is Britain, you know! We are living in *Bri-tain!*' The way she said this gave it a harsh, metallic sound, as if she were really saying that they were 'at war!'. Then punching the air she had shrieked again and run from the room. The only time he had seen her lose control.

The Hottentots knew what she felt. They knew that she considered them feckless, dirty, unreliable, undependable, lazy, child-like, wasteful, treacherous and utterly out of place in the new world she was planning. As individuals they resented her opinion of them but as members of the tribe they understood how she felt, they were not of her world which they regarded with fear, derision and dismay. Frau Katie's imminent death and the threat posed by Rose, worried them. What were they to do for a home now that the only home they knew was to be swept away? It had been Frau Katie's guiding principle that only those who in a very special sense could never go home were permitted to belong to the true tribe. And in a sense, Frau Katie's decision of who truly fitted the category of unalterable exiles was more final than the government's decrees that had driven them from South Africa in the first place. What she saw was something in them which related to her life and she measured their distance from home against her own, far more radical, exile. Those who met her secret conditions were taken into the tribe. Of course there had been other tribes, for Frau Katie had been in charge for many years. In the good old days the tribe was richer, larger, stronger. Frau Katie sometimes spoke of those times, of former members, of Theron who'd gone back to Kenya to mine tin; of the Vargas who were lost in the Congo; of the beautiful Maisie Tromp who, against all good advice, emigrated to Paraguay. That was no answer. That was no way home, Frau Katie declared. Home was the Hottentot.

Looper had not asked to come to England in the early seventies and what he found there left him dismayed. On first acquaintance the natives seemed to be of two sorts: there were those who said things like: 'That's just not on' and there were others who said: 'Sod off'. The first lot seemed obsessed with the economic crisis which as far as he could see dominated all. The second lot had nothing to say about the crisis, they merely suffered from it. In the papers read by the first lot the news was dominated by headlines which trumpeted fiscal catastrophe; *Pound Up a Penny!* the front page shrieked. Up or down, that was the world to the first lot. *Trade Balance Drops!* and *Payments Crisis Looms!* . . . The other lot were occasionally allowed on television to relate the effects of this down-turn and complained of having to send back the hired colour set because they couldn't keep up the payments. The politicians, whose parties seemed indistinguishable, he named Grim, Grin and Chin. They insulted one another with expert, if rather weary, thrusts. Few people seemed to know about South Africa and those that did seemed right behind the way it was run. The frequent response on hearing that Looper was a South African was to congratulate him on his country's firm policies and to complain that there were far too many of 'them' in Britain. Indeed the unshaded racialism of the native English left Looper quite weak with embarrassment.

The things that really seemed to work were the army, the police and the monarchy.

Frau Katie explained: 'Why? Because they are where the power is! Or let's say, these have it and show it. Some have it. Others suffer under it. Nobody talks about it, because they deny the idea that those with power can make them do things. They close their eyes and pretend they're doing what they like when they're really doing what others tell them. My daughter Rose understands this. Born to rule – but when have you heard her talk of force? But the fact is those in control want more control. Politicians, bankers, pressure groups . . . they all want more! Only they are too careful to say so. Too English. They are at war with the small people. They insist on directing them hither and thither, up dale and down hill. But they prefer to say nothing about it. Do they do it for profit? Or for their own good? Who cares – if you have to do what they say, anyway? In my country they just stopped pretending when young Adolf, alias Schicklgruber, took over. Germans were always too impatient! But the tendency is the same everywhere. Some must

94

rule – the swine! Our government wanted control because it was good for the Party. Here it is good for democracy – isn't it Caleb? Same result. At home we were expected to obey. People here have a much harder job; they are expected to agree.'

Looper felt at first that perhaps he should get out of London. London wasn't Britain after all. Perhaps he should explore more widely. He ventured into the interior. The country seemed very run down. In general people seemed depressed. They tended to wear car coats and go on long drives on cold days. He saw them parked in lay-bys beside the national motorways, calmly drinking tea and eating sandwiches at folding tables while juggernauts howled past. They seemed to be waiting for something. He met a man who told him that his granny went around with an empty bag in the hopes that one day someone would want to give her something for nothing. Ever deeper into the country he ventured. The provinces were eerie. The little houses – everything seemed so little – were sad and forlorn, especially in the flatter bits of the country. And very small. After no time at all he would arrive at the sea and thus was reminded that Britain is an island. He fell into a rage. The bastards had marooned him! Thereafter he did not go into the countryside again.

Years of exposure to the attrition of European life had not weakened the African within him. It had not turned him into an Englishman, it had not given him a taste for smart ties and French restaurants. Now, this sort of temptation was always the fear of those back at the Office. Insidious attractions and dangerous seduction lay 'out there', whether by people or places or things, in Geneva, Brussels or London, which might persuade the susceptible to go the other way, to turn. It had happened. There had been the celebrated case of Gerald Raubenheimer thought to be totally committed and thoroughly incorruptible until he eloped with a young man in a visiting Spanish dancing troupe and published his memoirs – 'I was a South African Superspy!' – in a sensational German scandal sheet and was now said to be living in seclusion with his lover somewhere in the Pyrenees. And then there was the notorious case of Ria – an agent employed in the office of the Military Attaché at the Embassy who at a diplomatic reception one night had fallen in love with a handsome young Russian weapons analyst with whom she had returned to the Soviet Union amid

95

enormous publicity, and claimed to find the place 'just like home'. In the case of Looper his long exposure to Europe had merely served to emphasise his foreignness. He knew he was not at home. He recognised, but did not succumb to, the densely layered pleasures of services and infrastructure, that rich, long-established vertical network of goods, opportunities, order and organisation which is Europe's chief attraction for the exile, a venerable mansion of convenient devices which has ruined many a soul wishing to live in that fine house without realising that it was built on generations of bones, that ghosts howled underfoot, that it was a little space wherein lived many people capable of such terrible blood-lettings that even the dead jostled each other underground and vied with the living for space.

The Office which transferred 'staff' abroad knew these operating risks. There was no way of avoiding them. Certain people had to be left in place, left for a long time, sometimes for years, with little or no supervision, before being called into play. The chances were during that long wait that they might be absorbed, take on the colour of the society in which they found themselves, play the game so well that they came to prefer the new life to the old. This was not Looper's case.

What had taken place in Looper was not conversion to some new cause but rather the ruination of hope. What finished him was not the place in which he lived, but the country he had left. It had become clear to some who gathered in the Hottentot Room, irrespective of their political opinions, that their country was violently torn, increasingly Balkanised into pseudo-states, principalities, Bantustans, casinostans, reserves, resettlement camps, tribal fiefdoms, Coloured ghettos, Indian townships, Chinese suburbs, white fortresses, black locations. The old order, dominant for so long, held together by a single-minded ferocity, was collapsing. The dominant tribe was losing its grip and the competitors were circling and jostling for position. They sensed a kill. It had ever been so, from the ruthless genocide of the Zulu king, Chaka, to the stultifying granite years of the white Führer, Verwoerd. The history of South Africa was the history of the rule of one strong force and when that fell into decay, the other tribes fought for supremacy. It was not the efforts of international communism that were pushing the country towards the abyss, nor was it the forces of Wyngate Hossein and organisations such as Via Afrika or Mr Govender's

Congress of Allied Democrats, and it was not the blood, stones and petrol bombs of rioters in the townships. The country was doing it to itself. The idea that a new administration would flame into being from the ashes of the old regime and govern a unified state stretching from the Limpopo to the Cape, from the Atlantic to the Indian Ocean – that was romantic nonsense. There was no single country any longer. The unity that existed now was a unity of hatred felt by the majority for the present incumbents. When they went what would be left, Looper wondered – except our hatred for each other?

In any event, the question of return depended upon a firm notion of the meaning of the word 'home'. Looper's sense of the word had deteriorated over the years. He increasingly saw his home as one of the lost cities of Africa, along with those vanished settlements that lived now only in legends, land of Punt, of Kush and of Zanj, and the tissues of truth and myth woven from hill forts, tiger skins, bronze and diamonds. Looper no longer cared whether or not such places ever existed. It was far easier for him to believe in Monomatapa the fabulous golden kingdom, in Zimbabwe and old Azania. One day cities such as Cape Town, Pretoria and Tzaneen would seem no less distant, legendary and fantastical.

'Stop!' the station master had ordered all those years ago, as the child Looper pushed his bicycle across the bridge. The Bridge designated for black people. 'Are you a white boy? Or a black boy?'

'A white boy.'

'Go back! This is the black bridge. Go back and cross by the right one.'

But of course he had not done so all those years ago and now he had no intention of doing so. Back in the place he came from they would not be pleased. Doubtless they were planning to fetch him.

If, increasingly, the idea of home deteriorated and dissolved in Looper's mind, he knew time was running out in London. He understood, and even thought he appreciated, the densely packed, interlocking values and references of European life. It was so tightly textured, it was the world of the hive, thickly structured, compartmentalised, organised, rich in the subtle recognitions of status, meaning, wealth, power. Life in Europe spread not upwards but sideways and was tightly knit. Whether through inbreeding or a long memory, European history had produced creatures highly sensitive to the most subtle gestures, to hints, guesses, allusions.

97

Hypersensitive beings, alert to the most delicate shifts in the social climate. Their emotions were wonderfully responsive to the least touch. Like sea anemones – touch them and they flinched into sonnets and paintings and symphonies. Of course, in Europe, there was a certain upward striving, there was ambition, the drive for success, but these things depended for their full satisfaction not on the display of money or power but on the far more important reward of the awareness of others, the knowledge that when you struck just the right note all around you others began vibrating like tuning forks.

The new world was different. There you aimed high, you built tall, and why not? You went up, for what other direction was there? Well, there was down. But that was something the Europeans knew nothing of, that long downward precipitation, that long fall, the plunge into the gulf of indifference. Where Looper came from, people were not anchored by history or by the heavy dead or by the pressures of population. There was no special virtue in staying put, or in knowing your place and anyway there was usually very little difference to be detected between one place and the next. In regions like Africa the geological scale was so much greater; you had to travel much further before you noticed the difference. History in Africa was no compulsive force, it held nothing together. Who knew what it had been doing before you arrived and started counting? Human ambitions seemed less important, human aptitudes less than impressive. The time scale you encountered there had done without you for so long – and would do so so long after you went. It would not be measured. If you stopped counting, it would not care.

The pressures brought to bear upon Looper during his early years in London varied considerably. For some months after his deportation from South Africa he had been left alone. He settled into an official flat in Sea Lion Mews. Thereafter he was subject to a succession of secret meetings in scruffy pubs situated on roundabouts in distant North London suburbs, where men handed him envelopes filled with banknotes, requested his signature, sometimes in triplicate, drank quantities of beer, seemed incapable of either holding their liquor or keeping their distinctive South African voices down, and complained about London prices. Looper described himself as a reporter. He rejected Rose's attempts to describe him as a journalist and shrugged aside the more jocular suggestions from the Hottentots that he was a newshound or a media man. Rose consequently admired him for his modesty and his colleagues for his lack of pretension.

In both cases they were wrong. Looper was merely being accurate. A reporter was indeed his sole function, though perhaps not in the sense that his fellow Hottentots understood. His assignments were those which suited his profession: he was asked for photographs of certain participants in political demonstrations and protests. He was given highly sophisticated equipment in order to do so and was trained in what was called the 'three camera trick'. In this device two ordinary cameras are draped over the shoulders while a third hangs on the chest and possesses a special lens capable of providing clear pictures from eighteen inches to infinity, the idea being that one used the fake cameras to distract attention while shooting with the third. He was given, as well, pens which were really radio transmitters and receivers; Samsonite briefcases crammed with dials and buzzers with which to sweep his room for eavesdropping devices; he was given electronic bugs for tapping the conversations of others; magnetic bugs, television bugs, and even exact replicas of entire instruments, the idea being the straightforward replacement of the suspect's phone with its twin. He was encouraged to join his local union branch and various associations of foreign correspondents for the purpose of identifying hostile personnel, and picking up hard gossip concerning the publicity machines of exiled liberation groups in London.

He was expected as well to read nearly two dozen magazines and newspapers for what was called 'security leaks', and as a means of identifying enemies of the Republic. He was also asked to read all new books with South African themes for the same reason, on the pretence that he intended reviewing them. On occasion he was actually asked to review them as well. There were also the requests for information which arrived from time to time. These were bald documents:

Andreotti, Mavis (an old friend). White, female. Now a social worker in Islington. Married, 1972, to Roland Andreotti, member of South African Communist Party; former student radical; height 5 foot 6 inches; brown eyes, dark haired, identifying marks, triangular pattern of moles beneath left breast. Academic record, Witwatersrand University – campus reports indi-

99

cate recruitment to Via Afrika 1962, moved to London via Bots-
·wana, 1974. Leftwing councillor: author of *White Madams and
Black Boys*, *The Politics of Sex Across the Colour Bar*, and *Gold
– a Marxist Dilemma*. Address, 4 Daduza Avenue, N19.
Reported to have taken a lover prominent in the Tory Monday
Club. Confirm and, if possible, expand.

Looper discovered that he was horribly unsuited to this detailed
work. To begin with he always messed up his three cameras at
demonstrations and found when he developed the film that he had
pictures of distant views of the dome of St Paul's or huge single
ears looking like hairy whirlpools. The electronic gear which he
was given baffled him and the instructions were frequently written
in Chinese or Hebrew. On visits to the houses or bedsits of suspects
he never found time to replace an electric plug with the one which
contained the bug, and the thought of carrying an entire telephone
on a mission seemed ridiculous. He found he was spending hours
each morning leafing through the pile of magazines which crashed
on to his mat at breakfast time and the books he had requested for
review took the remaining hours of the day. He calculated that he
could quite easily have spent his days reading and his nights writing
reports, had he chosen. The Association of Foreign Correspondents
he had been ordered to join was another depressing failure. The
journalists talked of sex, money and sport and the banality of the
'hard gossip' which he was supposed to ferret out was relieved only
when the quantity of liquor they had consumed rendered them
comatose.

It wasn't long before Looper discovered that there was a good
demand for second-hand surveillance equipment and he began
selling electronic gadgets and using the money to supplement the
very poor salary he was paid by his distant masters. He cancelled
his subscriptions to papers and magazines, finding that the bulk of
the information they supplied was usually carried in much pithier
form in any good daily paper, and the review copies of suspect
books he sold to a bookshop in Hampstead for a pittance. The
owner lurked behind a bead curtain at the rear of the shop and had
the slightly shifty look of a man receiving stolen goods. He told
Looper sadly, dropping a little silver in his palm, that there was 'no
money in Africa'.

The so-called 'expansion' reports on the enemies of the country abroad required rather more careful handling. Looper found that most exiles of long standing who had put down roots in the new community either by taking a job or a lover or a degree were consumed by fury, despair, scepticism and homesickness and the type so very soon revealed itself that he found it possible to compile his expansion reports without ever meeting the target. In fact he came to prefer this method of fulfilling his brief to the sad encounter with disconsolate souls who endured their wintry exiles in Ealing or Glasgow or the West Midlands and read in every report of township riots and hand-grenade attacks signs that the end was now surely at hand and the revolution would not be long delayed. Those hopeful, hopeless souls who toasted that hope each New Year's Eve with full glasses and the cry: 'Next year in Pretoria!' Those who went on marches, attended meetings and refused to buy South African peaches, who slowly began to lose their South African accents, saw their children growing up with the pink complexions and the doubtful dentures of the English; saw their once colossal hope receding like an ocean liner over the horizon, found to their secret shame that they no longer talked of death, blood and revolution and the big things which in South African politics were regarded as customary, natural and desirable, but began to talk gradually, but incessantly, of mortgages, the weather, the Royal family, and the exchange rate of sterling against the holiday currencies ... No, Looper preferred to avoid such of his countrymen whenever possible and so he took to writing his reports without reference to the person concerned. These he invested with great affection and sympathy, and considerable invention.

Mavis Andreotti [-he wrote-] is most unhappy in her job and finds to her discomfort, as do many South Africans abroad, that they are not the political firebrands they were considered to be at home. Once abroad they discover themselves to be no more than vague Liberals. The shock to the system is severe. Mavis is unable to relate to her fellow leftwing councillors and try as she does to embrace the militancy of her feminist sisters on behalf of the handicapped and their demands for council-controlled sperm banks to service aspiring lesbian mothers, she is far from happy. Her single concrete success has been to persuade her council to rename the local crèche after Chief Albert Lutuli, the winner of the Nobel peace prize. Even there she has been opposed by those lobbying for the

101

commemoration of some more radical figure. Her writing has ceased, with no work appearing since the small pamphlet, 'White Madam in Search of Gold – A South African Sexual Odyssey' – and this was printed only in small quantities and despite its sensational title enjoyed poor sales. Note: on the question of identifying marks, it is worth observing that there are four and not three moles beneath her left breast and that these resemble a parallelogram. She is no longer attached to a member of the Tory Monday Club, who has deserted her and returned to his wife in Surrey. Subject is a spent force, more to be pitied than feared ... Suggest file closed.

These and similar reports Looper sent to the Office, and heard no more. He presumed they satisfied requirements. He felt much relieved to get rid of the electronic equipment which so encumbered his little flat in Sea Lion Mews and was grateful for the small sums he earned from the sale of the bugging devices, the cameras and the unreadable books. Nobody ever asked him what became of it all. He concluded that this lavish outlay on the trappings of espionage was controlled by someone with more money than sense. He suspected a committee in some back room in Pretoria authorised these expensive fripperies. That no one followed up on either the productivity of the equipment, or on the reading programme or even on the requests for expansion reports, did not really surprise him.

He understood that two South African characteristics were at work here. The first was a desire to go through the motions, which in South Africa was usually as important, if not more important, than doing the thing itself. Perhaps it is always this way when a lack of talent or industry is linked to great wealth because then it is possible to buy whatever your own society cannot, or sometimes it is not permitted, or merely disdains to, produce for itself. Thus, for example, the desire for opera means that an opera house is built along lines adapted from foreign models. Singers are imported and a director and an orchestra. Local talents will be employed to make the whole thing run, a local painter will design the sets and a local electrician will henceforth be known as Director of Lighting. The newspapers will begin talking of a thriving operatic tradition. Thus when titles are being distributed, local people will line up to wear them. But as far as the actual work is concerned another force will be found, or bought. An air of transience hangs over the entire operation. The idea that anyone should do such things seriously as a way of life, always and forever, is quite foreign to the white South African temperament. The idea that someone should embark on the arduous apprenticeship of the soprano, or devote years of one's life to the study of stage lighting, is regarded as distinctly odd and rather undesirable. The mere thought of long hours of seemingly unproductive work is enough to deter even the most ambitious. For work is a mystery to the heirs of a society deeply damaged by the slave-owning mentality which, from the very earliest days of white settlement in the Cape of Good Hope, when imports of foreign slaves and the subjugation of the local Hottentots soon led to an enslaved workforce larger than the community of white masters, has been the most notable feature of the European settlement of Southern Africa. There you had a single principle on which white rule had been built. It was not, as was sometimes suggested, a sacred covenant between God and his white tribe – it was rather the divine, if passive, belief that somebody else did the work.

The second point which led to the South African fascination with expensive equipment had been the recent surge towards modernity. For many years the country had been a kind of white Albania of Africa which held to the rigid party line with ruthless, joyless tenacity – rejecting everything from television to Sunday fishing as sinful. These Calvinist idealogues regarded the lures of the outside world, and even the most gentle liberal challenges from within, with the same mixture of horror and anger with which their forefathers had viewed the call for the emancipation of the slaves. The Voortrekkers had turned away from the call and trekked into the wilderness where the corruptions of the world would not reflect their divine right to their god-given acre – and enough cheap labour to keep it weeded and watered. But there came the days when their modern descendants realised that they had reached the outward limits of that trek and so turned and confronted the world. Almost overnight the country moved from resisting the lures of Satan, to swallowing them, hook, line and sinker. It went in for computers, it formed think-tanks, television became the rage, it revamped its intelligence service, gave its policemen public relations classes and adopted the euphemisms of military establishments the world over. Army spokesmen no longer threatened to 'smash the heads' of 'invading terrorists', but promised instead that 'hostile incursions would be monitored and dealt with and that marauding elements in the operational areas would be neutralised'. Methods of dealing with indigenous insurgents were eagerly and widely studied and elevated into a minor science. To the euphemisms of the Pentagon was wedded a sudden desire for new technology. Like the passion of an elderly bachelor for his young mistress, it was all the keener for having come so late.

South African intelligence abroad, if London was anything to go by, was extremely well funded, energetically pursued and noticeably inept. There was for instance the behaviour of the diplomatic counsellor, Nico van der Merwe, known to be responsible for the control of several agents in the capital. That knowledge derived from the fact that van der Merwe was forever becoming drunk at diplomatic receptions and boasting of his intelligence contacts. However, if the work was inefficient, it was diligently pursued and there was a lot of it. So much equipment purchased, so many agents, so many reports, so many people required to follow and bug and read letters, search through suitcases, supply photographs, that Looper suspected that of course it was not his results which impressed the authorities but the sheer volume of work going on. There had also been the extraordinary service he had rendered in restoring and duplicating the treasured photographs in Gladys Hossein's family album.

Yes, it was almost certain that back at the Office Looper was very highly thought of and very popular indeed. He had provided a cache of hugely valuable material. It was, to use the metaphor the Office really preferred, an away win of astonishing brilliance. All the more so since he had done it without any instructions from home. It was for this reason that they were certainly determined to get Looper back.

CHAPTER 8

The Soweto Knights arrived in tribal finery. They were dressed in a variety of pelts and carried their drums. Oscar, Sipho and Zeke were a most striking trio of poets. They had left South Africa after the Soweto riots of 1976. Wild young firebrands then. Now, some ten years on, the fires were not burning quite so brightly. Oscar was short and plump with a curly black beard. Sipho (who had changed his name from Stanley) was broad and tall. Zeke had a yellowish skin and a wide grin and his nickname was 'Bushman'.

'Thanks for telling us the queen was so bad. I mean *thanks* a lot,' Zeke said.

'We phoned your place in Balham about a dozen times,' Gerrie pointed out. 'But they couldn't help. Why don't you leave an address when you go out?'

'We told them at our place. We were playing that bloody dump in Richmond,' Sipho replied. 'Can we go see Frau Katie now?'

'It's Mona May's turn next,' Elize declared, 'as soon as Anagupta's finished.'

The young athlete's shoulders shook inside her pink tracksuit. The laces of her trainers had worked loose, Elize had to take her hand and lead her towards the stairs. 'No, no. I've never seen a dying woman before,' said Mona, 'and I've never seen a dead one either. Look, I'm sorry to be a coward, hey. Won't you look for me?'

'So, why don't you tell these people at your place to tell people when they phone the right place to find you?' Gerrie persisted in questioning the Knights with heavy truculence. 'If you're in Richmond then why don't they say so? Anyway Richmond's not such a terrible place. I've been there.'

'Why don't you stick your thick Boer head in the fridge?' Zeke suggested.

'Who you calling a Boer? You stupid Kaffir!' replied Gerrie.

Rose returned with Anagupta. Her mother was in a coma. She shuddered at the sight of the Knights. 'Must you wear those skins?'

'It's feet of snow out there,' said Sipho.

105

'We'll go if Mona's too scared,' Oscar offered, draining his beer.

Rose examined them with icy despair, these black boys in their leopard skins and monkey-paw amulets drinking lager at the bar.

'I'm not sure you're dressed for the sick-bed of a very ill patient,' Rose said. 'Come on, Mona. Elize can go with you, if you like.'

'We could keep vigil by her bed,' Oscar suggested. 'I don't like the thought of her lying up there all on her own without someone from the tribe near her.'

'Why don't you keep vigil with us down here?' suggested Wyngate Hossein.

'Great,' said Sipho. 'You all get to see Frau Katie and to say goodbye, but we can sit on our butts down here and wait. That's right for you, old man. One law for the big brass, another for the kiddies. Where were you in '76?'

This was an old jibe. Hossein clenched his jaw, but all he said was: 'Seventy-six was a long time ago.'

The reference was to the famous riots in Soweto, riots which had been organised (if that word can be applied to a largely spontaneous uprising of school-children) by students like Oscar, Zeke and Sipho. It had been an outburst so sudden and so violent that it had for a time overwhelmed the white authorities and astonished the more organised black opposition groups. Later, Hossein's Via Afrika movement had earned much scorn and derision in the townships by claiming to have instigated and sponsored this extraordinary revolt against white rule. Over the years, this revisionist view had gained ground and now most people, not least the same radical black exile groups themselves as well as the South African government, had come to believe that the historic uprising had indeed been directed by the old men overseas. This view was more comfortable for those who simply could not believe that a bunch of kids could terrify the guardians of apartheid. Whichever way you looked at it, the old men had been far away in '76. And that was the thrust of Sipho's taunt. It suggested that Wyngate and his kind were redundant, that in '76 they had been out of town, out of reach, out of date. It implied that the black exiles, as well as the South African government, were geriatric adversaries who had been squaring up to each other for years without ever throwing a blow when suddenly a bunch of kids had taken to the streets and everything had changed utterly.

Of course that wasn't true either. Wyngate Hossein was neither out of touch nor over the hill. True, he had not been there in '76 but he'd given his life to the struggle against racialism. He'd spent many years in jail and his leadership of Via Afrika had given to that body a degree of professionalism it had not possessed before. There was, too, the fact that Hossein at least knew who he was; he had always been and was still very much in the front line of the war against apartheid.

Yet Hossein was undoubtedly vulnerable and the young men sensed it.

Whatever method had been used to alert Gladys Hossein to her husband's affair with Biddy Hogan, the effects had been devastating. Hossein had not been back to the Hottentot Room in weeks and when he did eventually return it was clear that he had been badly shaken. The way he kept glancing nervously over the shoulder reminded those who knew him in the old days of the way they drank in some illicit boozer or shebeen, fearing the arrival of the police on a raid. It was comic and faintly alarming to see how someone could be forced back into the old insecurities of his youth.

And yet with Frau Katie's worsening illness, to some extent this was happening to all of them. Lestrade's pronouncements took on an increasingly philosophical rotundity. Elize became the nurse she had once been and conferred with the doctor treating Frau Katie. Gerrie the barman talked rather hopelessly of going back to a gym and getting fit. Mr Govender worried about the growing number of violent attacks by Africans upon Indians in the continuing riots now a widespread and almost daily occurrence back home.

'They even attacked the house of Gandhi's son! I mean, Wyngate, where will it end? We're not going to have the old battles fought over again. We're not going to fight each other when it's the regime which is the enemy. Why must it be this way in Africa?' Mr Govender mourned. 'Whenever there's trouble Asians are attacked. When it's revolution, Indians die.'

'We will take steps,' Hossein assured him. 'When we're on the ground.'

The amicable relations between Wyngate Hossein and Mr Govender were misleading. The Via Afrika Movement to which Hossein belonged was bitterly opposed to Mr Govender's Congress of Allied Democrats. Generally speaking this division reflected their different political backers – Via Afrika was considered pro-Soviet while the Congress of Allied Democrats had been Maoist. Because

107

of the greater consistency of Soviet support, Via Afrika was widely regarded as one of the leading liberation groups. Increasingly, Mr Govender found solace in the bosoms of his daughters. The lovely silent Anagupta had buried her head in his neck and appeared to have gone to sleep.

'Isn't it wonderful,' Mr Govendor remarked fondly, 'how children can sleep through the worst crisis?'

Frau Katie had always understood the unfairness of his position. 'You depend on Mr Mao and then bang! He's dead. It was the same for us in the thirties with Hindenburg.'

But whatever their political disagreements, Hossein and Govender got on well around the bar at the Hottentot and they both disliked the Indian killings which took place in Natal. It was said by some that this was only to be expected. Assaulting Indians was a sport as natural to the Zulus as finger wrestling to the Boers. If Mr Govender had personal objections to the practice, Wyngate Hossein had sound political reasons for condemning it. The Zulus were the preponderant tribal grouping and Wyngate was himself a Zulu. He preferred it to be forgotten and no longer mentioned it. Instead he reminded people that his wife Gladys was a Zulu. This had two useful effects. By emphasising his wife's tribal grouping with phrases such as 'Of course, Gladys is the Zulu in our family', people forgot his own tribal designation. Then, too, Gladys was such a sweet, gentle person that she provided a most convincing case for the argument that not all Zulus were bloodthirsty warriors dreaming of war and glory.

Morrison was shocked at the reports of the bloodshed in the clashes between Africans and Asians: 'I would hope someone will come between them.'

Mr Govender and Hossein would have done nothing of the sort. It was not the bloodletting they objected to as such, it was the political damage such inter-racial rioting did to the cause of liberation and the comfort it gave to the 'Berta' regime. Had Hossein's party been in power they would have shot the ringleaders. Mr Govender's party would have shot the lot. What the Soweto Knights would have done nobody knew.

The children of Soweto, the young warriors of '76, as represented by the Knights, had undergone a far more noticeable transformation, for they had become the rather solid young men of Balham. By day they worked on building sites to earn some money. At

108

night they played the drums in clubs and pubs. They were lonely, cold, homesick and getting rather plump.

Even so, the insult stung. Such pricks and barbs are the mettle of South African politics. Morrison knew this and fearing a row he tried to calm things: 'This is hardly the time to be resurrecting old quarrels.'

'Hold your mouth,' said Oscar, showing, as he always did in heated confrontations, that even after years in England he still thought in Afrikaans.

Lestrade sniggered.

'What's the joke?' Oscar demanded.

Rose came silently into the room leading the sobbing Mona May. The others were horribly embarrassed. They could not bear that Rose should see them attacking each other. And they detested the thought that they should have given her a chance to scorn and deride them. Elize ministered to the weeping high-jumper. What a fountain that girl was!

They need not have worried. She understood nothing of their embarrassment. She did not despise them any more than she'd always done. In fact it could be said that in her mother's last hours, Rose felt a kind of irritable affection for the members of the Hottentot Room. What were they like? she asked herself, sitting at the window and staring into the darkness of Antaeus Street. They were like the Irish, she decided. There was the same fierce insistence on fighting old quarrels, always blowing on the embers of ancient feuds to keep them warm, always stirring the pot of history. There was also something Continental about them (one could hardly call it European without confusing things completely), something Latin, say, their emotions were so quickly aroused. Above all, they were so childish. She could quite understand how the first visitors to Africa had managed to dazzle the natives with baubles – a few glass beads, a bit of iron for their spearheads, copper for their bangles, a little tobacco, a few bottles of brandy and these creatures would barter their lives, souls, children, cows, sheep, kraals . . . That had been all right at the time, she supposed, out there in Africa. But times had changed and, for the Hottentots, so had the place. These refugees, these helpless exiles owed it to themselves and to the country which had given them asylum, to Europe if you liked, to become more aware of who and where they were. They needed to stiffen up, to think more clearly, to face their situation

109

honestly, to stop pretending that the Hottentot Room was home, a refuge from the world. The Hottentot Room was a house in Earls Court, London, England, and the day was fast approaching when they would realise that it was nothing more than that.

'Come on then,' she said to the Knights.

If they could only see how silly they looked! Sipho wore a brown cardigan beneath his leopard skin and Zeke was wearing a pair of brown hiking boots without socks. Worst of all, Oscar had on a pair of white PVC wellingtons. All wore woollen gloves without fingers. Rose had once seen a group of Hare Krishna monks in Oxford Street who were wearing loud sportsjackets over their flimsy robes. The Knights, she decided, looked even sillier.

The clock showed three-fifteen.

'Could I ask you not to *clump* your way upstairs?' Rose asked the Knights.

Mona continued to sob, her head on Elize's shoulder. 'I want to go home!'

'What's stopping you?' Buffy Lestrade demanded brutally. 'When did you want anything else? Why did you come to Britain in the first place?'

'She came to jump,' said Gerrie. 'She used her British connection.'

'There are another quarter million like her. English South Africans with British passports. They'll be over in their thousands when the balloon goes up,' said Mr Govender, kissing Anagupta on the earlobe. She stirred in her sleep, curled against him like a cat. 'It'll be the Ugandan Asians all over again.'

'Or the Vietnamese boat people,' said Morrison, 'drifting upon the flood of history.'

Elize said quietly: 'I'll drop the next person who picks on her.'

Mona's family background was interesting. The Mays were among the first English settlers in South Africa. They had struggled to root themselves in a hostile environment of the Eastern Cape borders, threatened both by warlike blacks and taciturn Dutch – they were left, in the words of an early observer, Thomas Pringle, 'quite isolated among the Dutch-African boers, on this remote and exposed part of the frontier'. Not only had the descendants of these early settlers inherited their toughness and resilient spirit, they had also inherited their passports. Mona May had never even been to Cape Town when she climbed on an aeroplane literally straight off her father's farm, and flew to Britain where she was issued with a passport without a murmur, all because her great-grandfather had found South Africa lent itself to the kind of confidence trickery he had practised rather unsuccessfully in London a hundred years before. Her reputation as a high-jumper of genius made her an interesting proposition. She showed her quality by jumping for Britain all over Europe, in Australia and America, and winning a good deal of the time. The papers loved her. MONA MASSACRES MOSCOW, they announced. The fact that she had trained with the springboks on her father's farm intrigued the British press: 'Mowgli Mona', they named her; 'Mona Doolittle' was another variation. While Mona jumped for Britain things were fine. The problems arose when she opened her mouth. It was not that she had much to say, but what she had to say caused a storm. What she said most frequently was: 'I want to go home.' Not only did she want to go, she went – and with considerable frequency, pleading death in the family. One newspaper commented on the plague that had struck down the May family, carrying off a member a month. Then Mona said she missed her pet springbok Hendrik who had taught her to jump. This won her enormous sympathy from the animal-loving British. A fund was immediately launched with the aim of 'Bringing Hendrik to Britain'. Unfortunately Mona rather spoilt the effect of this by rejecting the fund and its intention with scorn. She would, she said, see Hendrik at the abattoir before she allowed him to languish in some damp and dismal safari park. One member of the May family adrift in England was quite enough, thank you very much. The animosity this revealed towards her adopted country pained many of her friends and supporters though, in fact, it was not particularly surprising since the Mays, despite their English surname had always been among the fiercest of the anti-British brigade (a prejudice which probably dated from their ancestor's early brush with the forces of law and order many years before). Mona in fact spoke very little English. Her unwillingness to give interviews and her taciturn remarks when she did talk to the press were put down to 'shyness'. In fact this lack of communication was a godsend as her managers discovered, when in an unguarded moment Mona told a reporter who asked her what she thought of the police shooting people in the black townships in South Africa, that she hadn't thought about it but if the police were shooting people then she was quite sure they had their reasons . . .

111

It was widely agreed that meeting Elize had been the saving of Mona who would otherwise have returned home to yet another funeral and never jumped for Britain again. Instead they had met one evening in the Hottentot Room. Later she visited the Room for the politics, the gossip and the food, and cried on Frau Katie's shoulder. There she met Elize who had come in hot and tired and depressed after taking part in a march against apartheid organised by Jewish Lesbians Against Racialism and where she had been knocked about by several bobbies outside the South African embassy, an experience which had left her depressed and rather homesick at the same time. Elize and Mona spoke in Afrikaans of the beauties of the Cape. Thereafter they were inseparable.

Oscar, Zeke and Sipho returned looking sad and frightened. Frau Katie was asleep, Oscar said, and had shown no sign of knowing they were there. Sleeping with a faint smile on her face, said Sipho, as if she was enjoying some private joke. The Hottentots knew that smile, strange, secretive, so tiny that if you didn't see it coming you might miss it because it was gone before you got a good look at it. In spite of themselves they smiled to think of her smiling.

'Well, may I go up to her now?' Morrison asked.

'You've been,' said Rose.

Morrison looked shamefaced. 'If you don't mind, I'd like to say a prayer by her bedside.'

Gerrie the barman untied his white apron and hung it on the wall. 'I think I'll polish the floor,' he said. He took off his shoes and rolled up his trousers.

'Not now, surely,' Elize protested. 'You've done it once already tonight.'

The sight of him on his knees, a flat harsh-bristled brush in each hand, barefoot, the lamplight a pallid gleam on his chalk-white calves, his toes dug into the floorboards, scrubbing away, prompted the traditional comments from the Knights. 'Put more elbow into it,' Oscar suggested. Sipho enquired of Zeke if he didn't think that houseboys had a personal odour problem 'that rings bells at the back of your nose?'. Zeke replied that he looked forward to the day when the revolution at home ensured that every black family had one of these wonderful Boer labour-saving devices.

Gerrie didn't respond, as he usually could be relied on to do. Instead he went on resolutely polishing away, moving brushes in brisk inwardly-turning circles. Perhaps it was the very parochialism of these jibing comments passed by the Knights that got to Rose, although it ought surely not to have done so. Who can say what final straw broke Rose? After all, they were just killing time. And so of course was Gerrie and so were the others and so was Rose. Then again, perhaps it was the peppery waxy smell of the Cobra white wax floor polish which seemed so odd and disconcerting at around three in the morning. It had nothing of that reassuring quality or element which one associated with the days gone by, with some sunny weekday morning beneath a brilliant blue highveld sky as the genial houseboy of one's youth set about the floor boards of the living room with brush and polish, whistling as he worked. Of course it had never been like that. But that was the way one chose to remember it. However, there in the Hottentot Room the smell was more of fear than heartbreak, more sadness than rage, and Gerrie's brushes scrubbed away. Even this might not have been enough to set her off, but Morrison fell to his knees and began to pray. And if this weren't enough, Buffy Lestrade crooned into his vodka of love everlasting: *Unsere Liebe sie trennet sich nicht!* from Frau Katie's favourite Brahms. Certainly all this got under Rose's skin. She might otherwise have gone directly upstairs to her mother, and everything would have been different. Even so, she was trying to ignore Lestrade's hateful Brahms, when Mona May spoke up:

'Anyway, whether she's asleep or in a coma, I think it's lovely. Wonderful. That she should just be lying there in her bed with her husband, the General, looking at her out of his frame with his smart uniform and all and I think it's horrible, just *horrible*, that they should have been broken up by that damn stupid war and that she had to come over here, to this place, and to leave her husband behind, and her house, and her life, and her clothes, and everything ... Maybe even her dog!' and Mona gave a great, shouting sob.

'Now, now. They couldn't help it,' Elize said rushing to her and embracing the girl. 'It was the war. And we don't know that there was a dog. I'm sure there was no dog,' and here she cast an appealing glance at Rose, begging her to confirm this fact.

Rose stared back, white-faced, her lips working. She seemed to be trying to say something.

'She was young. Young as I am,' sobbed Mona.

'There was no option.' Looper spoke now for the first time. 'Frau Katie was known to be Jewish and it was more than her life was worth to stay in Berlin. It was an impossible situation. They were killing Jews.'

'She was only a little Jewish. Nobody needed to know,' Mona objected.

'Oh come on, come on,' said Sipho abruptly. 'You know better than that. Where do you come from, Mona? A *little* Jewish! Listen, a little Jewish is like Coloured back home. And you know and I know that little is enough.'

'Leave her alone!' commanded Elize.

'More than enough,' Sipho repeated.

'Who you weeping for?' Oscar asked. 'Why you weeping at all? You know the story. It's our story. Where we come from it's what happens to everyone who's a little bit not white, or a lot not white, or wholly body and soul not white. The country lives by what the war did to Frau Katie. It's our traditional way of life. So weep for yourself, your country, your people. But don't cry for Frau Katie. She don't need your water. Frau Katie knows – okay. That's enough! Frau Katie knows. She's with us!' and he jabbed his thumb in his chest.

Elize picked up Mr Govender's glass of Perrier water and flung it at Oscar. It missed, bounced off the bar with a great looping spray of water and shattered on the floor. Gerrie glanced over his shoulder at the broken fragments, then he went on polishing.

Morrison had slipped from the bar and was edging towards the door where Rose stood, transfixed, with her hand on the door knob. Looper understood his plan. If Rose should leave the door and move back into the room then, with all the commotion going on, Morrison would slip upstairs and say his prayer at Frau Katie's bedside. He was driven now by the demon spirituality which would not let him rest until he had brought grace and comfort to the dying lady. This demon whispered in his ear, whipped him and tempted him with the threat and the promise of his soul for hers. Once a priest, always a priest, whispered the tempter. Remember that one gift it is death to hide. And then it added, this holy devil, that yes, even if she *were* unconscious, or in a coma, the lady would still need his blessing and profit by it, and dropping its voice so he could hardly be sure he heard it, the demon said that, besides, if she were unconscious it would do her no harm, she would have no objection and it might just conceivably do him some good. Morrison stood swaying slightly in his effort to appear relaxed, fixing his burning eyes on Rose who stood between him and his mission . . .

Perhaps prayers are answered. For Rose had begun very slowly to move. She released the door handle and turned slowly back into the room. She held up her hand as if for silence. Looper watched Morrison begin to edge around her very, very slowly. Then Rose screamed.

Morrison and everyone else, except Gerrie, stopped dead. Gerrie continued to polish the floor and Rose's words were underscored by the dry scrape of his brushes and the shuffle of his bony knees on the floorboards. And whenever that extraordinary speech was recollected in future years by those of the Hottentots who remained sane enough, or brave enough, or fool enough, to remember it, the memory of her words was accompanied in their ears, and their nostrils and their brains by the rhythm of Gerrie's brushes and the sharp, peppery fragrance of the white wax floor polish.

Rose spoke through clenched teeth: 'You're such fools! You understand nothing about my mother, *nothing*! According to your precious story, my mother was once Mrs General von Sturz and lived very happily in Berlin until one day her husband happened to discover that his dear wife had Jewish blood. Then, the legend goes, being a noble fellow he tried to save her. Out of love he divorced her, tried to arrange for her to flee from Germany. He was a good German. My mother was also a good German. She went underground in Berlin. She became a U-boat. She stayed because she loved her husband. Certainly because she loved her city and, of course, her country. But, in the end, after many close scrapes evading the Gestapo, she had to flee and came to England. Observe: each of you has your own reasons for bringing her here. No doubt Buffy believes she was driven from Germany because the Nazis ate meat and factory-farm chickens. No doubt they also blinded them with corrosive chemicals in the interests of producing new cosmetics and performed all the scientific bestialities which Buffy so disapproves of. I am sure that little Mona believes it was cruel fate that drove young lovers apart. Oscar, and the rest of you believe Frau Katie suffered from the same disease that injures you – you believe that a Nazi was just another kind of Boer. To Wyngate, I suspect, she is a symbol – mother of the revolution to come. I don't know what Mr Govender and his daughter think

115

about her. You, Elize, probably think of her as the victim of a kind of German tribalism!'

What rage possessed her! She began to move now towards them and then to the left and right as if circling, to and fro, backwards and forwards, making tiny lunges now and then, the way a sheepdog will when it patrols the flock. The Hottentots shuffled and backed away from her and huddled closer together. Morrison froze, his eyes on the door. Mona had stopped crying. Gerrie continued to polish the floor.

'You, Caleb, have carried on a pretend-romance with my mother. Your dream, your joke, has been that one day you would abscond together.'

'Elope,' Looper corrected in the interests of his own dignity.

Rose ignored him. 'In other words, you have all got your reasons and the preservation of those reasons is more important to you than the truth. Well, I am sorry to have to tell you that tonight is time for the truth. I'm sorry about your reasons too. But they're going to have to go out of the window. My mother was not, to begin with, a good German. Up until the moment that her Jewish blood was discovered, she was part of the ruling establishment in Germany. She never opposed what was going on, she never thought about what was going on. She was with it, she was in it. To all intents and purposes, though I'm not saying she joined the party, but to all outward appearances, she was a Nazi. She was wedded to the way of life as she saw it and knew it. When her Jewishness was discovered she was ejected from that society. So much for my mother. For the moment.

'Now to my father. He's said to have been a decent sort at heart. The General divorced my mother in order to get her out of Germany and save her life. Rubbish! My father divorced my mother because she stood in the way of his career. An officer in his position, on the way up, discovered he had a terrible liability. He had a Jewish wife! So he got rid of her. It must have been very inconvenient to him when the silly girl refused to go. He tried to help by getting her out of the country. Instead she went underground. All right. While she stayed well hidden she wasn't too much of a problem. But it was dangerous. She might have been caught at any time. She was a Jew. And Jews and other illegal termites hiding under the floorboards were hunted. Police hunted them. The Gestapo hunted them. Other Jews tried to catch them. General

116

von Sturz wanted his former wife out of the way. Maybe he knew that the hunters were getting close. Do you remember what happened? One day my father paid her a visit. You know the story. He left her with two mementoes of his visit. He gave her a child, and a gun. Of course you remember! And when he gave her the gun he said to her that, if the need arose, she would know what to do with it.'

'She would defend herself,' Elize spoke with enormous conviction. Glad to be saying it. Saying it strongly, speaking, and they all knew this, as if she were testifying for Frau Katie herself.

'And she did use it,' chimed Mona, emboldened by Elize's lead.

'Yes. She shot the Gestapo agent who followed her home,' Mr Govender said.

'And she left him in the cupboard under the stairs in her apartment in Bleibtreustrasse,' said Wyngate Hossein.

'Where he's probably still to be found today,' said Oscar.

'The skeleton in the cupboard,' said Zeke.

Now Looper knew something was afoot. He saw from Rose's face that an announcement of some importance was about to break upon their heads. She was bursting. She could not hold the information back any longer. She moved close to them now. Her face was set hard, the eyes were round, wide and fiercely shining. Her blonde hair stood out from her head glinting, it had the hard look of iron. She seemed an avenging fury, armed, helmeted. Now was her moment.

'She would know what to do with it,' Rose repeated very slowly as if addressing a classroom of idiots. 'That was what gave it all away. You see my father handed her the pistol at a time when he knew my mother was at the end of her tether. Frightened, pregnant, facing the Gestapo – what was she expected to do with it?'

Now there was silence in the room except for the slide and scrape of Gerrie's brushes and even they began to slow down and eventually to stop. 'So that was it,' said Gerrie, sitting back on his haunches and shaking his head. 'Well, I'll be damned. She never did do what was expected of her, did she? Nope, never ever did.'

Hossein said, 'Right. Never did what they wanted. That's Frau Katie. She's a champion, your mother, the best.'

English Rose turned pale. 'No, no. I won't let it go this way. You're not going to turn this round into another fairy story about good and bad. You need to believe your illusions. I see that. You're

117

a people obsessed with simple divisions. You are people who live by the wall. Germans on one side, the Jews on the other. Whites on one side and the blacks on the other. Things are much more difficult than that in the real world. And much more hurtful. Just for once you're going to have to face up to that. My mother began with the Nazis. In all but name she was with them. If I put it into your terms, she was part of the white regime. Damn, my mother would have employed people like you.'

To this nobody said anything for a long moment. Just as Looper thought her point would cárry, Sipho said: 'And we would have worked for her, too.'

Rose saw the way things were going now. Even as she had been speaking they had been discounting what she said, rearranging her revelations to suit their cherished myths, their necessary fictions, their primitive Hottentot beliefs. She stepped forward now, lifting her hand as if she appealed for silence or respect or mercy. No one ever knew. Morrison meanwhile saw his chance and edged past her, opened the door, gained the stairs. He was moving up them two at a time when the shot thundered above their heads.

Looper was first up the stairs with Hossein behind him, brushing past Morrison who stood petrified. They entered the room together.

Frau Katie had chosen her moment. The disease had stalked her. She had let it come so close it must have thought it had her. Just as the agent from the Gestapo must have felt sure of her. Just as her husband must have felt sure of her when he gave her the pistol all those years ago. She had preserved until the very last her little joke. Looper wondered at her extraordinary coolness. She would have been holding the gun all the time he had been in the room. Probably in her hand, ready under the bedclothes. That was what she had been doing, planning her escape. 'Keep your eye on me,' she had said.

Frau Katie had fired the pistol into her right temple. The force of the shot had knocked her out of bed. There was a smell of gunpowder and singed linen where the blast had burnt the pillow. Hossein swore quietly to himself, 'She used the pistol. She used the General's gun.'

Looper phoned the police. Then he and Wyngate Hossein returned to the bar. They said nothing. The others understood what had happened. Elize sat on the sofa beside Rose with her arm

118

around her. Rose gazed blankly at the floor. Anagupta wept uncontrollably – the only sound they ever heard her make. Mona May clung to Oscar. Lestrade drank his vodka like an automaton. On his knees by the stairs where the shot had stopped him in his tracks. Morrison was praying some endless prayer they could not understand. Gerrie packed away his brushes and polish. Then his face crumpled: 'Shit,' he said, 'oh shit!'

No one noticed Biddy Hogan arrive. No one paid any attention. She marched up to the bar and placed Looper's air ticket on the counter and said loudly: 'I think, Mr Looper, that you owe us an explanation.'

CHAPTER 9

Looper drove alone in the old rusting Mercedes to the crematorium in North London. Rose was preoccupied with the feast to follow and said she would take a cab. It seemed inappropriate, somehow, to attend your mother's funeral in a taxi but Rose told him not to be so old-fashioned. The day was icy. Frau Katie had always been ferocious on the question of spring: 'If there's one thing worse than the English winter, it is the treachery of the English spring.' Naturally, English Rose took another view. 'Oh, to be in England, now that April's here . . .' Rose murmured, echoing the poet Browning. Frau Katie pointed out that Browning had taken care to write those lines a long way from England, where 'they go about like ghosts in mists of damp grey smoke'. Yet Rose persisted and found in spring crocuses, snowdrops and days growing lighter, longer, warmer. For her part, Frau Katie discerned bronchitis, broken bones and the lugubrious long-suffering demeanour of those she had persisted in calling the 'sodden natives'.

Katie's funeral then, took place on an icy April Friday with small, knee-high whirlwinds chivvying the dead leaves this way and that with a childish, petulant air, as if determined not to let them rest, scattering them with a sharp blast, waiting for them to land again only to send them cartwheeling away with a dry tinkle, like the sound of a stick on railings, or faint, disdainful applause from a distant room. A day of the worst sort. One of those end of winter days that denies the calendar and turns its small grey face against loose thoughts of the green and bounding spring, dismisses with grim, frosty relish any sentimental nonsense about the longed-for warmth to come. Funeral weather.

At times like this Looper felt his exile most keenly, felt he understood how foreign he was. Coming from the south, from the other side of the globe, you knew that whatever intellectual adjustment you made to living in the cold north, however cleverly you adapted your colouring, your clothing, your camouflage, you were not at home. You knew this in your marrow, in your water. However warmly you were dressed, whatever harsh re-education programme you gave your eyes, forbidding them their natural expectation of a distant horizon, and a wider, higher sky, you remained an impersonator, a savage in sensible clothing. You might learn to cook, speak, dress like one of the natives, you might give a most passable imitation of being a European, but then the late winter breeze lifted your trouser leg and exposed you for the fraud you were.

Rose had said eleven o'clock but Looper, who did not know North London, had left himself plenty of time for getting lost, which he had done driving around Hampstead Heath. He asked the way of a woman in a cerise tracksuit who gave him directions while padding effortlessly beside his car. A shadow crossed her face when she heard his question and he sympathised with her. It seemed somehow vaguely indecent to ask someone so full of health and beauty the way to a funeral. Here was someone who clearly lived on nuts and high-fibre grains, who observed a meatless diet, who neither drank nor smoked and refrained from all activities likely to damage the heart, the arteries, the liver, the lungs and doubtless even the cervix which, Looper knew, had of late also become a suspect. It seemed a dreadful imposition to ask such a question of a person so clearly determined to stride into her hundreds. The jogger wore a small pink ribbon in her blonde hair. A fine pearling of sweat glinted softly along her upper lip. Her colour was a full pink, healthy, and her trot rhythmical and steady. Looper deeply regretted his question. It was indecent, as if he had insisted on reminding some prosperous German American Jew, who had long ago left all those horrors behind him, of the days of the Gestapo. As if he were discussing some thoroughly unnatural sex act with a nun. He wanted to apologise. There is no God but muscle tone, Looper sang to himself. Who are you Caleb Looper to put yourself in the path of such striding perfection? But he need not have worried about offending her. The athlete's directions were precise and unafraid, as if he were unfortunately bound for a country of which she had heard something but had no intention of visiting. The heart, remember, Looper repeated to himself in passable imitation of the flat Capetownian vowels of Christiaan Barnard – is only a pump.

Tall, dark and dripping trees surrounded the crematorium, cypresses or yews, perhaps – Looper couldn't remember which was which. Many more cars than the Hottentots could run to stood outside the front gates of the Victorian Gothic building, and a

121

huge and gleaming hearse waited like some official limousine of a visiting dignitary. Doubtless a service was in progress. Perhaps several cremations were taking place at the same time. He was sure that the ovens were never idle. Cremations, undertaking, all the mortuary arts, these did not suffer from seasonal fluctuations, recessions or downturns in the market, factors which Rose and people like her, held to be the foundations, shaky but holy, of the world – 'as we know it today'. This was a favourite phrase of Rose's and by it she meant, quite simply, business. Then, she would add, lest he suspected her of sounding too materialistic, 'I am simply a tiller of the fields, observing market forces just as any peasant studies the weather for its effect on his crops.' Now that was typical of English Rose, that wholly inappropriate image. She thought neither of weather, nor of peasants, nor of crops. But he understood what she wanted to say. Rose did not care much for words but for what could be done with them. Although this argument had not yet taken place, Looper was already surveying his position.

'Do you know one business that isn't prey to market forces, Rose?'

'None at all, my dear.'

'I think of death. Death isn't affected by the market. It's suffered by others while we look on, until our turn comes. Its crop never fails. It's steady. Those involved are not dependent on the market. It is a nonsense, death. When it comes to other people we can't feel it or touch it. When it comes for us we can't tell the others. Death is a private property but the owner has no interest when it goes on the market. Doctors, undertakers, hearse drivers, oven minders, grave diggers must find things pretty steady. Unwilling, if assured, supply. No demand in any sense of the word we understand. Very little competition . . . Occasional excess, in times of cold, or plague, or natural disasters. But no shrinkage ever.'

But of course Rose would not be so easily lectured. 'Confused. Poetic but confused. Of course there is supply. And demand. And competition – if you knew where to look. Always is, if you know where to look. The living, you see, those who remain or, if you prefer, the next of kin, *they* make the demands on the suppliers of goods and services. They budget and haggle. You find them shopping around for coffins. If they know what's good for them. They'll protest if undertakers arbitrarily raise their prices. At least I would, I can tell you . . . I'd go down the road to someone else.'

Had she shopped around for her mother's funeral? Had she tested the market? Of course in this argument he was yet to have, Looper would object that after a death the relatives of the deceased might be prostrate with grief and unable or unwilling to quibble over costs. Then Rose would retort, with weary good humour, with the bright and alarming sparkle in her blue eyes. 'You always underestimate people's fighting spirit, don't you, Caleb? People are tougher than you think, especially in pursuit of their rights. At least, that's my experience . . .'

It's always her experience. Her experiences were limitless, which was surprising in a simple tiller of the fields. Some tiller! Atilla of the fields more likely . . . That made him smile. He stood outside the mock Gothic portal of the crematorium, muttering to himself and smiling broadly.

This in itself would have been sufficiently inappropriate in a man who has spent much of his life studiously avoiding attention. Looper didn't care. He had passed a point where he felt any attempt to safeguard himself was probably wasted. While he remained in England he was a target. If his cover wasn't entirely gone, it had great holes in it. That much had been apparent in the tumultuous events of two nights before, when Biddy Hogan arrived at the Hottentot Room clutching Looper's air ticket to Johannesburg and demanding an explanation.

When Biddy Hogan produced his air ticket and silence fell on the Hottentot Room he had been prevented from answering her by Morrison, who spoke from his kneeling position: 'That's impossible. Caleb can't go back to Johannesburg. He's a deported person.'

Biddy protested, 'Exactly.'

Hossein, Mr Govender and Lestrade stared at the ticket on the bar with wonder and consternation. Gerrie the barman reached out a finger and prodded it as if it was some kind of snake that might leap up and bite him. Mona left the encircling arms of Oscar and began to ask a question then stopped after glancing at Elize who was gazing at Looper with a look of horror. Elize knew, of course, that was why she pulled Mona to her so desperately. Of course she would have known. Elize had endured the lesson that treachery is the oxygen of revolutionary politics and she now gazed at Looper with a look of sheer terror. Death, her eyes said. Another death so soon! For that was what must follow the production of the ticket. Her arm was still around Rose who was chalk-faced, seeing nothing. Then Elize closed her eyes and said no to another death so soon.

Hossein should have seen it. Perhaps he did. Perhaps they all did but their minds were so full of what had happened that Biddy's shining eyes urging them to win the prize by saying the correct answer out loud did not have the proper effect. The death of Frau Katie still reverberated inside them like the echo of a giant explosion. Hossein suspected something. He even sensed something was terribly wrong. But he was emotionally shattered. He was utterly incapable of thinking, only of feeling, and the emotions are a shifting ground, no matter how powerfully our feet are planted, no matter how loudly and confidently we speak, posture, parade, the sands we stand on are being washed away every second.

Lestrade asked the question which sent Hossein so wildly off course. 'Where did you find it?'

Biddy answered, with a dramatic, accusing finger, 'In Caleb's room.'

It should have been enough. There should have been no more to say, Looper stood utterly naked, horribly exposed. There was nothing he could say to avert the realisation welling up in all the others. But, then, at the last moment, he did not have to. Hossein did it for him.

'What were you doing in his room?' Hossein asked.

Love led Hossein astray. Desire, if you like, jealousy certainly. Human loyalties afflict exiles most keenly, whatever political glue happens to hold them together. It was precisely personal relations that made the group of people who constituted Frau Katie's Hottentots interesting to one another. It was their interest in each other, their mutual support and hopes, their genuine, warm camaraderie that kept them together. These feelings made exile on a remote island tolerable. It was this that Biddy had overlooked. She had imagined that the ticket provided proof. It was documentary evidence of Looper's treachery. His intentions would be read in it. Here her great skill at close analysis of texts for discussion led her astray. So certain was Biddy of winning her case that she was quite unaware of the horror and bitterness affecting her audience. They were holding each other up and here she was trying to topple them in her wild gruff manner. Further evidence of her wrecking tendencies came in Hossein's question, and they turned not on Looper

124

but on Biddy Hogan with a request for an explanation of what seemed to be her infidelity. They understood immediately from Hossein's question what his relationship with Biddy had been. And they understood, from her admission of her close contact with Looper, that some sort of deceptive triangular relationship had been going on beneath their noses. They didn't know what it was but they wanted to find out.

Biddy saw it in their faces. She saw Rose in Elize's arms. She noticed the strain in their faces. Then saw properly for the first time that something very strange had happened. Outside a siren shattered the silence of Antaeus Street. Biddy grew cold. She looked away from the crumpled ticket on the counter. She was in the wrong place at the wrong time. She had made a bad mistake. Biddy glared. 'Go to hell!' She began to back away to the door.

Hossein nodded. He slipped off the bar stool, turned and began to leave the room. With a cry Biddy ran after him. He shook her off.

'Whatever it is, I don't want to know. Not now.'

'But Wyngate, you don't understand!'

Then the police arrived. And the ambulance. Looper picked up the air ticket and put it in his pocket. No one mentioned it. For the moment at least there was nothing to say.

He stood in the cold spring breeze in a pale fawn Italian woollen suit with dark square buttons and double vents. It was such an inappropriate choice, a summer suit, as the icy breezes soon proved. But he could have done nothing else. He had moved in with English Rose on the night of Frau Katie's death, judging it unwise to return to his flat. He was glad of her bed for the first time. It was a temporary measure. He knew the Office would have people out looking for him and he suspected, too, that Biddy Hogan would soon make another attempt to get Hossein to understand her suspicions. Suggestions from Rose always made him perverse and she had insisted that he wear black. More important for Looper had been Frau Katie's promise that some day soon she would dance with him in Paradise. Dark suits would not go down very well in Paradise and at whatever celestial soirée Frau Katie had intended to show him off, Looper was determined to look the part. But he was cold. He was suffering not only for his perversity but because he had made the blithe miscalculation so common in exiles whose

125

pores tell them that because the sun is shining it must be warm. Whereas the fact of the matter is that in Europe the sun will shine in the coldest winter, indeed the sun is more likely to shine in winter. Looper had lived abroad for long enough to know this. But he always made the mistake. You knew where you were in Africa – which was nowhere. It wasn't hostile to human affairs, it simply did not care about them. The continent might well have been the cradle of *Homo sapiens* but having hatched the creature it wanted no more of him. It did not interfere with him but it did not care either whether he lived or died. Mother Africa possessed no maternal instincts. Africans learnt to live with this huge disinterest, with this massive indifference.

Europe was quite different. There you were allowed a place in the landscape; things had a human scale. There were tests of course. But in a way you *were* the test. The question was always to see how you performed against the odds; how you shaped up to seasonal fluctuations, how you survived the challenges thrown at you. In Europe, nature wished to see one get on in life, to prosper, indeed so strong was this desire that you were dead if you didn't. Capricious weather patterns and lying seasons. Brief perfidious spring, some uncertain weeks of summer and endless winter . . . No wonder, thought Looper in the yard of the crematorium, that the aboriginal Europeans sacrificed to the gods to woo summer back again, to bring the dark winter to an end. No wonder that these ancient people gave themselves over to astrological tyranny, to priests who were a form of murderous weather men, who decreed the building of great stone circles from which the movements of the heavens could be tracked, mapped, timed, predicted. Rocky observatories that ran on blood and fear. You danced, you prayed, you observed, you waited and you watched for things to improve. The English obsession with the weather was surely an echo of the time when such forecasting was literally a matter of life or death. Who was to say, as the cold and dark winter gave way to grey and icy spring, that this would ever end? Who was to say that summer would ever come again? There was, too, in England, a special quality to the cold. Of course there were many places where the temperature as measured on the thermometer dropped very much lower and degrees of frost unheard of in England were reported. But we are talking here of cold that is wet and grey and gets under the overcoat, under the nails, behind the eyes, which gathers in the joints, between the bones, a cold which brings vicious falls of snow in spring, pelting out of clear sky to strangle the daffodils, a cold which gives that lugubrious and characteristically damp texture to the English soul. Real cold, as opposed to the spurious dips in temperature associated with places such as Moscow and Iceland; the hopeless chill only lost souls know but cannot flee.

The hearse arrived, followed by several cars containing the mourners. Rose was accompanied in her taxi by Morrison who was at his most discreet and sober, and on leaving the car he walked a pace or two behind her, like a royal consort, or a private detective, in rich dark suit and muted tie. Morrison rose naturally to such occasions. They were, after all, professional events for the ex-priest who had conducted his share of burials in the days when he was a parish priest on that distant African mission. Though of course in those days, being a Catholic priest, he would never have taken such services in a crematorium. None the less, the demeanour was doubtless the same whatever the method for the disposal of the remains. Rose wore a black fur coat, black boots and a black pillar-box hat into which her blonde hair was swept and gathered. A small veil fell across her face. She wore no make-up and Looper noticed that she had taken off all her rings. Was this some strange idea of hers for stressing the solemnity of her mourning? Rose had never shown the slightest indication of a religious belief but she had a flair for the appropriate gesture. She extended a pale hand. Looper seized it and shook it vigorously because he could think of nothing else to do. Rising in him, though he managed somehow to contain it, was the wild urge to congratulate her.

Seeing Rose reminded him of Frau Katie as she had once been, bright and golden, a calm, assured beauty which had been wonderfully preserved, well into her seventies. And then there had been the old lady of the last few months, bedridden, when the disease had taken so firm a hold that she could no longer pretend to be resisting it, or as if now that the struggle had entered the terminal stage she had decided the best thing to do was to lie very still, to save her energy for the final struggle.

'If I lie very quiet like this, Caleb, I can hear it. It is searching for me just the way the soldiers were searching for me in the Dworski house.'

The Dworski house had been one of her final hiding places in Berlin. The Dworskis had themselves been Jews and had been

127

discovered. Frau Katie stayed on for some time after they had been taken to the camps. Her luck, even then, had been good. Once again, as her illness grew worse, she told him, she felt her pursuers getting close. Frau Katie tapped her nose very slowly and nodded. 'Yes, but don't worry, I have a plan for that. And of course the General will help.'

Rose greeted him very coldly. 'Caleb, you might have worn a dark suit, as I suggested.'

'I'm sorry. I can't associate your mother with darkness.'

'It's not a question of what you feel; it's to do with dressing for the occasion.'

'I'm wearing a black tie.' He touched the article concerned.

'A black tie with a light fawn suit gives you a vaguely military look as if you belonged to some semi-secret force.'

'She's right, Caleb,' said Morrison. 'You look like a steward at some not very respectable political rally, or the gatekeeper at an agricultural show.'

Wyngate Hossein and his wife, Gladys, arrived accompanied by Mona May and Elize, to whom they had given a lift. Elize swathed in black and utterly distraught. Her attachment to Frau Katie had been total. Frau Katie had represented for her the very image of a survivor. Her death was a terrible loss. She tottered like a blind woman leaning on Mona's shoulder. Mona wore a checked grey suit with bulky shoulders and flat shoes that gave her the somewhat disconcerting look of an English country-woman attending a village fair. The suit was rather too big, undoubtedly borrowed and probably belonged to Elize. Gerrie the barman, looking slightly sinister in dark suit and tie and wearing a pair of dark glasses, wandered up. His forehead, where the steel plate lodged, was lumpy and heavily cratered. It was the first time Looper had ever seen the barman in daylight.

'I lent Caleb that tie. It's one of my bar ties. I told him it wouldn't do on its own, not for a funeral.'

Gerrie's suit was old and musty, when you saw it close up you realised it was too small for his beefy frame. He breathed the air of his bar, of beer and whisky, of the wooden slats on the floor behind the counter where the booze splashed, of the leather stools and the metallic, slightly salty scent of the ageing banknotes pinned above the bar, of copper polish, floor wax and tears.

Looper became sharply and sadly aware of the futility of their presence in that place on that cold morning. Better, surely, to be back in the Room behind Gerrie's bar. Their presence in this draughty place did no one any good. Of course he knew they were all required at Frau Katie's cremation. And it was more than the demands of her daughter that brought him there. Death demanded its witnesses. If they had stayed behind then they would never have been able to confirm that Frau Katie had truly been laid to rest. If they had stayed behind in the Room, they might always have been haunted by the possibility that the old lady would appear at the top of the stairs and shout for champagne. They came so it would be easier, later, to lay her ghost. Looper knew that they would be haunted anyway by that possible hallucination, for the recently bereaved are always watching and listening for some achingly familiar sign or sound which signals the lost soul's return from the grave. They were there in North London for their own sakes, to see the end of the old lady, so that when they returned to Antaeus Street, stunned and anguished at the manner of her leaving, yet feeling her all-pervasive presence in the Club over which she had presided for forty years, when they heard, late at night and deep in their cups, the Morse code of her stick on the floorboards, that gnarled and knotty weapon of polished oak with which Frau Katie cut and slashed her way through entanglements which blocked her shuffling progress from bathroom to stairhead, that is to say the shoes, articles of clothing, chairs, electrical cords which generally lay scattered in her path, then they would know it was all in their imagination. When they heard the triumphant cry as she reached the head of the stairs, arms uplifted, stick jabbing at the ceiling: 'Champagne, Gerrie. Flutes for Frau Katie and all her friends!' They would know it was all make-believe. Frau Katie's invitation to the flutes had been for many their first introduction to instruments which did not play music but held in their slender conical perfection the pale, winking wine. The memories of Frau Katie would press hard and fast on all of them. The Room and its air were thick with her. Air which English Rose would be quick to clear.

For of course Frau Katie had been incorrigible, impossible and hopeless; unconnected with the real world or her real position in it. This was what had enraged her daughter and delighted her friends and followers. To see Frau Katie entertaining a young man, recently released from a South African prison, with champagne

129

and tiny squares of toast and pâté and telling him of the five o'clock tea dances that took place beneath the palms on the roof garden of the Eden Hotel in Budapeststrasse, '. . . in the old days, darling. Always and only in the old days – of course, it may interest you to know that the men always wore suits and the ladies cotton print frocks and hats of course. Hats. Most important was the hat. Do you know, when they danced the woman often looked taller than the man? Yes, it's true. You may be as amused as you like. In fact this is what is called an optical illusion. You see, the ladies wore very high heels in those days and together, the heels and the hats, made them to seem to tower over their partners. But only to seem, darling, only to seem. For naturally in Berlin, in the days of which we speak, the men were of course taller than the women – it was an order!' This last sally would be accompanied by a wink and a shriek and an unsteady nudging toast to the bewildered refugee who had perhaps flown in that morning after three months of solitary confinement, had never set foot out of Africa before, and now having fled the over-scrupulous attentions of the police, lucky to be alive, found himself in some corner of gigantic London confronted by a warm, witty madwoman who poured fine champagne into a crystal glass, so oddly shaped, a heavy base and long elegant stem, the flute above intricately incised with grapes and vines, found himself listening to tales of old Berlin interspersed with toasts to their mutual health and curses upon their tormentors and pursuers who were stigmatised, variously, as 'childkillers', or 'the walking disease', and frequently (this term was used with deep and somehow fearful weariness) as 'the old, old story'.

And yet, somehow, they liked her. There was this quality about Frau Katie which so immediately impressed those who were thrown, propelled, into her company. There was this slightly shocking sense of collision, a strange resonance. It was a percussive experience when you met Frau Katie the first time; but not unpleasant. And one which grew on you very quickly. With her square shoulders, carefully tinted hair, copper when still her own, shamelessly fiery in the later artificial arrangements, curling above a wide forehead and bright green eyes. Until the end she had been beautiful, with a strange bronze sheen to her skin and an eager vibrant presence which had about it somehow the quality of a struck gong. 'My dear, I know how you feel! How lost in the world you must be. Flung from your home into this great city. I know how it is. You feel like a country pumpkin when you come from here to there . . .'

And so the young black refugees from the violent townships, who stared at her with large eyes, found the champagne strange to the taste perhaps but the lady herself was familiar. She spoke wildly, incomprehensibly at times, but what she said had in it something of the quality of great poetry. She spoke to their hearts and they shivered and understood. Sometimes they found this happened before they knew what she was talking about; they touched her and she rang true. Perched on her air cushion, seated on the hooded porter's chair of red leather, straight-backed, serene and smiling, she loomed over the new arrivals who only learnt some time later, if they were accepted as regular Hottentots, about the real reasons for her seeming height, that she appeared to sit so tall owing to Debussy's complaint. And it was only when they discovered what she meant by Debussy's complaint that they comprehended how ill she was.

Yet somehow, until the last, she gave the impression that she was the one who felt sorry for them. They were the people under threat. Scattered by the power of the master-race – corrupted by the ways of their governors, displaced, decimated and, yes, diminishing year by year. She showed them her African curios; she pointed to the Hottentot cane behind the bar and she told them the story of Coree, the Hottentot captain.

'They brought him to London because at the time they were crazy about freaks. To them the Hottentots were freaks. They smelt high, they rubbed grease all over themselves, the women had enormous buttocks, the men had only one ball – like Goebbels. Or was it Goering? What's more, they were bad workers. Bad slaves. Bad news. With qualifications of that order they weren't going to manage AEG! So what good were they? Well fortunately, I say *fortunately*, they were good with cows. Otherwise, *kaput!* – they go the same way as their cousins, the Bushmen. They would be shot. Like vermin. You know how the Nazis felt about the Jews? And about the gypsies? And about the lunatics? Well – imagine a tribe of mad Jewish gypsies and you've got the Bushmen in the eyes of the master race. As to the Hottentots – well, they looked on them as a step up – the equivalent, say, of mentally ill Jews. They also got wiped out, naturally – only it took a little longer. No wonder these English liked freaks. They were so rare! And here they had in this Coree, a Hottentot captain. They snatched him off the shore, I

131

guess, and shipped him over. They give him a nice cane, and a free trip and teach him some English and say O K my boy, here you're in London, so give us a smile – and what does he do? Does he fall at their feet? Does he drop his trousers and show them his testicle? No, he says he wants to go home! Show him the greatest city in the world and this stinking, greasy Hottentot says no thanks! Teach him the English tongue and he asks to be excused! No wonder they took their cane back. And deported him. I bought the cane in Bermondsey Market in '46 for nineteen and sixpence – old money. There it hangs on the wall. Let it be a lesson to all of us . . .'

Towards the end she shrank noticeably and had difficulty balancing on the air cushion. Finally she no longer appeared at all in the Room but lay upstairs in her bed, occasionally banging on the floor with her stick around ten or eleven at night when she knew the bar would be crowded – to the annoyance of Rose who complained that this dislodged sections of the papery stucco on the old ceiling. 'She'll bring the roof down,' Rose complained.

Seated around the bar the Hottentots said nothing. They merely picked bits of plaster out of their drinks when the ceiling shook. They didn't mind. After all, the knocks on the ceiling were just Frau Katie's way of saying hello. She was keeping in touch, letting them know that 'the old story' had not finished for her yet. To Looper she confessed that the illness had fallen below expectation. 'It is such an unmusical complaint, my dear.'

When they entered the Chapel, Rose who was on Looper's arm, hissed angrily when she caught sight of the Soweto Knights and Lestrade, who had brought them. Lestrade was wearing a black and white checked suit, dark green socks and brown sandals. Doubtless his old academic uniform. Zeke, Oscar and Sipho were wearing what passes in Europe, and probably at their poetry sessions, as authentic tribal costume. In fact it was an eclectic assortment. The West Indian influence showed in their hats. Sipho wore a knitted woollen hat shaped like a tea-cosy, Zeke wore what looked like a plump woollen saucer, the pudgy rims of which extended out well beyond his ears and the complicated knitted pattern was made of chevrons of green and orange. Oscar was bareheaded but he wore immensely large round leather earrings of the sort ricksha boys were wearing on the Natal coast many years before. Sipho was swathed in some sort of long white Arabic-

132

looking robe, the square collar picked out in crimson. Oscar wore a blanket around his shoulders and, most incongruously, spotted the white PVC gumboots. Zeke wore monkey skins and carried a Zulu cowhide shield and throwing stick. Most astonishingly of all, perhaps, he was barefooted. In that cold weather the others looked on with amazement. He was also bare-bellied. And this was unfortunate since of all the Soweto Knights Zeke's figure showed the most ample evidence of the effects of an English diet of bread and beer. He looked, on that icy spring morning, the very picture of one of those petty black potentates which Victorian artists visiting Africa delighted in depicting for their editors and their admiring, gullible public.

'Oh God,' said Rose between clenched teeth. 'What if they've brought their drums? Buffy swore to me that he wouldn't let them bring their drums.'

The coffin was made of some dark and gleaming wood and covered in an enormous wreath of daffodils. It lay to the left of the charming young Anglican priest who took the service and as he spoke he occasionally turned to it as if someone inside was listening to him. He spoke of Frau Katie as one now 'sealed in Christ'. He referred to her as 'Mrs Brahm'. This made her sound very English. Of course Rose knew what she was doing. Looper understood he was present at the making of history. The large gleaming coffin was far too big for the waif Frau Katie had become in the end when a breath of wind would have blown her away. The prayer was inappropriate. 'Sealed in Christ'? And the girl from Berlin who had grown up considering herself a good German Lutheran, Katerina Brahm, later the wife of the up-and-coming young career soldier, Erich von Sturz, destined, if things had gone as they should, to become Frau General von Sturz, had instead discovered herself to be, against all expectation, all reason, all unavailing protest, a Jew. And it was as a Jew with her baby that Katerina Abrahamsohn had fled from Berlin and come to London where she had been neither German nor Jewish but had entered a long and triumphant reign as the queen of the Hottentots, and had now become at last, again, a Christian. Indeed, a stranger at the funeral would imagine that Rose's mother had died quietly, a pleasant English lady of advanced years. Rose's long dream had finally come true. Her mother had been rehabilitated. At long last, things were being done properly.

133

There followed a reading of 'The Lord Is My Shepherd'. Cards were provided with prayers, psalms and hymns to suit the occasion. The mourners cleared their throats and shifted uncomfortably. The choice of psalms was another incongruity. Frau Katie had in her nothing of the woollen docility which is the received image of the sheep, nor could it be said that she possessed the slightest touch of the rural or the rustic which we associated with the shepherd. Frau Katie had despised the countryside and the English countryside in particular.

'Too unhealthy,' she pronounced. 'I was once in Suffolk' (she called it 'Suffork', making it sound like a penitentiary). 'This was around '42, when Schwitters was interned. You know the artist, Schwitters? – he was interned as an enemy alien. I thought, oi-oi Katie they'll want you next, so I took my baby and fled to London.' She directed her beautifully flared nostrils towards the hiss and fume of Earls Court Road, declaring: 'One needs to be able to breathe after all . . .'

Looper's predecessor, the Hungarian Jew Krepl, had said to him on his posting to London all those years ago: 'You're lucky. One day they'll call you home and you'll go. You'll have a home to go to. This won't last for ever.'

He had arrived in London, a raw recruit, to replace Krepl. Krepl had been an 'export agent'. Looper was described as a 'journalist', a useful, unrevealing, spuriously informative description evoking sympathetic responses in most people.

'Journalists are the mendicant friars of our times,' his controller, Brigadier Langman told him. 'They travel the world attending the most intimate ceremonies of life and death, the conclaves of terrorists, the elections of popes. They're there when the condemned man is poisoned. They're there when the new pope is born in a puff of smoke. Where everybody else except warders and cardinals are refused entry, the journalist may pass. As the clerical orders infiltrated the medieval world, so the media people are all over the modern world. There is nowhere, repeat *nowhere* they cannot get with the right ticket. Someone once said that whatever begins in mysticism ends in politics. Nowadays, one begins in politics, and ends in television. Once you spoke certain things only to the priest. Now you tell it only to a reporter, to a journalist, to a TV camera. Just as in the old days you fought off sin, now you fight the flab.

134

Just as in the old days you worked for heaven, now you go to the gym and exercise for life. Once you went to church and confessed your sins. Now you go to the papers. You're lucky in your assignment abroad, Looper,' Langman told him, 'our people, with whom you will have to deal, are great talkers. They like company, they're lonely, they drink more than they should and they tell you everything. Krepl says that one of his big problems in London was always stopping them telling him things. They want to chew your ear off. And Krepl's just a businessman! For a fellow in your position, they'll come running. They'll be giving you their memoirs!'

Langman's high position in the service into which Looper was recruited was an indication of the very bizarre world of clandestine operations in South Africa. It was known, for instance, that Langman who was in charge of all foreign business had never been abroad himself. It was known, too, that he was tough, shrewd and, the whisper said, ruthless. It was also known that he headed up the Service. For one thing he made no secret about his job and only the Official Secrets Act prevented the publication of this information. Langman was odd, to a further degree, in that he appeared obsessed with self-publicity. He lost no opportunity to give anonymous interviews to the press about everything from the price of gold to the war against foreign subversives. He appeared in the papers always as a 'top security source'. Only a week before Looper left, so suddenly and unexpectedly for London, Langman, on his way home from the opera, came across a group of police surrounding a building which housed the German consul in which a demented young male student held the consul hostage and was demanding a supply of consecrated hosts and communion wine together with safe passage to Israel. Langman, in full evening dress, took charge and talked the raving youth into a kind of temporary sanity, promising that there would be no shootings or beatings if he were to come down quietly. Indeed, the police present on the streets downstairs turned their batons and rubber bullets on the huge crowds that had choked the streets around the consulate frantic for a glimpse of the chief actors of the siege – such a thing until then having been available only in the cinema. Langman promised the boy access to a rabbi and medical treatment. Eventually the terrified German consul was released and led from the building by Langman who appeared in the papers, described the

135

next day as a 'highly placed security official who may not be named . . .'

Looper walked down Tottenham Court Road with Krepl on his first day in London. Krepl, short, squat, with immensely powerful neck and the face of an angry frog. Krepl smiling his bleak smile and shrugging with the weary resignation of a wrecked millionaire, which indeed he was rumoured to have been in the pre-war, pre-Nazi days back in Hungary, smiled as one would who has looked ·on great riches as the most natural possession in the world and snapped his fingers at the thought of home and how easily home can disappear. Short stubby fingers with square nails and bushes of wiry, greying hair above the knuckles. They turned into Charing Cross Road. The big yellow flag above Foyles bookshop hung motionless.

'In Hungary in 1944,' said Krepl suddenly, '15,000 Jews wandered the roads and the government pretended to be unaware of them. From 1943 it had been mandatory to wear the yellow star so people could hardly have been unaware of who these vagrants were; they were Jews thrown on the streets because of pogroms. Hungary, like Poland, Czechoslovakia and Germany carried out many pogroms. For some reason, in our family, we stayed at home and thought it wouldn't happen to us. We helped the wanderers of course, where we could. We helped them with food, shelter, papers. Star called to star. We didn't know we were giving from a diminishing store. The cupboard was almost bare. We would have done better to have locked our houses and joined the wanderers. Got out was what we should have done, and kept moving. Instead we were kind, clever . . . for we were resourceful. That was the worst of all, our resourcefulness. When the bread ran out we baked our own; when they stopped our meat we bribed the fishmonger, when they arrested him we kept a pig, or a goat. Goats were especially prized. Families dreamed of their own goat. We drew the curtains on Friday evenings and lit the Sabbath candles. Prayed that the Red Army would arrive in Hungary before the Germans. Lord send us the Russians, we prayed. But the Nazis got there first. And what did we do?'

They passed Leicester Square tube station where the afternoon headlines declared: 'Minister in Bongo-Bongo Storm'. What these Bongos might have been was not clear to Looper. He had heard of bongo drums of course. But that seemed an unlikely explanation.

136

Then there had been that song, popular years ago: 'Bongo, Bongo, Bongo, I don't want to leave the Congo / Oh, oh, oh, oh, oh, oh, no .../' Somehow the word had an African ring to it which intrigued him. But equally this did not seem to be the moment to ask Krepl for an explanation. There was clearly much to learn about British life.

Krepl paused. A stocky figure in a crumpled jacket and expensive but very old grey flannels. An odd, rather pathetic, old-fashioned figure just about right for retirement. Krepl. Was that really a Hungarian name? Behind him was a cinema entrance where a poster advertised *The Bird Fancier*. A woman with a large bosom and a stern expression nursed on her lap a golden bird cage. Inside the cage, sitting forlornly on the swing, was a man in spectacles and a grey suit. 'She sneered at him, tamed him, fattened him ...' the poster announced.

'Sex in the modern world,' Krepl observed, regarding the lady and her catch, his head cocked, 'is another word for power. Priding ourselves on our freedom to say whatever we like about sex, we conceal the fact that this has provided us with a code for talking secretly about something else entirely. Power is really what excites us. That is the dirty secret. That is the dirty talk. Power is what you want to do to other people. And since the war, I refer to the last of course, we have known what we can do to other people. We deny this knowledge. But we know. We know. When the Germans came to our village we didn't fight. We didn't object. We didn't even run. I'll tell you what we did – we *organised*. That's what we did. We organised our destruction. First, the Germans took Jewish hostages and they told us to collect a ransom for them. So we did. Then they said we should form a committee to register all the Jews in the town. So we formed a committee and we tidied up all those untidy Jews into some sort of order. We told ourselves – it's better this way. We organise ourselves and then the Germans don't do it for us. We thought we had to do it, you see. The Germans we saw not merely as Germans, but as being very modern. That's a point people don't realise. They forget that now. Nazism was the latest thing! It was modern, efficient, look-ahead. It was the future. And it had arrived!'

Krepl was no longer seeing Looper. He was many miles away and many years back. The pale blue eyes blinking with the concentration of focusing backwards and inwards on images hooked from his memory. Behind him a huge hoarding advertised the play, *No Sex Please We're British*. The head of Krepl with its bulging eyes and its high round cheekbones and its froggy mouth and its pulsing, vein-laced powerful neck was so placed that it obscured the centre of the poster and this had the effect of showing an eager lover diving into Krepl's right ear while a girl with long hair flying, clutching a towel to her bosom, emerged from his left. 'Outrageous!' said the headlines, 'Uproarious ... I laughed till I choked', said the *Sun*.

'When the Committee had labelled all the Jews, the Germans said "thank you very much" and marched us all to the ghetto, which in our case was the old brick factory outside the town. Please will you march, they said. We marched. After all, they were the clever, crisp, successful Germans. Who were *we*? We were silly old-fashioned people. We went patiently. But we stayed resourceful. We bribed the Hungarian soldiers who guarded us in the brick factory. Cigarettes in exchange for soap. Silver jewellery for a spade to dig a deeper latrine. Love for bread. The women saved small amounts of drinking water for washing clothes. Our inventiveness was terrible. Nothing got us down. Some of us thought, well, maybe, having made this move, we'll be all right now. Maybe because we co-operated with the Germans some of their modernity would rub off on us. Maybe, we thought, we're catching up with history. Mind you, history wasn't saying so. History was playing a very tight game. It held its cards to its chest. Later we found out that history had passed on. History had written us off. Let me tell you that in the brick factory that was our new ghetto and prison, the children played in the old ovens.' Krepl shook his head wonderingly. They were now passing the South African embassy. Its bulk loomed over Trafalgar Square. Neither man so much as glanced at it.

'Now you're going home?' Looper asked uncertainly.

'No, I'm not going home. I'm going back. I can't go home. I left home a long time ago when the Germans took us away from our house. When they marched us to the brick factory. My mother got the Germans mad because she insisted on locking the front door. "Against what?" the soldiers demanded as they pushed us down the path. "Robbers?" And they laughed. Like I say, we had fallen out with history. It had lost interest in us. At that time if you interviewed history on our behalf, it said: "No comment".'

They took a tube from Piccadilly to Earls Court. 'There's a little something I wish you to see,' Krepl said. 'We have a tradition for the retiring man to pass this thing on to his successor. It's in the nature of a gift.' They walked along the tawdry length of Earls Court Road with its travel agents, late night grocers and fast food outlets. At times they were ankle deep in discarded polystyrene hamburger boxes and paper napkins. A couple of blocks along Earls Court Road they turned right into Antaeus Street. 'Being in the journalistic line, writing and all that, you're bound to meet more of the exiles than I did in the export business,' said Krepl. 'The exiles of course, as exiles do everywhere, long for home. Which is as it should be. One day some of them will go home and it will be waiting for them. There's a little club I know where a strange assortment of our countrymen and women hang out.' Halfway down Antaeus Street Krepl paused outside a nondescript house indistinguishable from its neighbours in that undistinguished terrace. 'It doesn't look much. But you must learn to get over that. A lot of places here look like hell from the outside. And when the place gets you down, remember it's not for ever. One day they'll invite you to view the head of Trajan – and that will be that.'

'The head of Trajan?'

Krepl laughed, 'You'll see one day.'

'Will you be pleased to leave?'

Krepl shrugged. 'Not many people knew me here and no one will know me back there. I'll just fade away. It suits me. I shan't be sad to get back. But it's not the same as going home. Home for me was when my mother insisted on locking the door though the soldiers laughed and told her she had nothing worth stealing. I can still see the door, I can hear the key turn.'

'And your family?'

'My family I haven't seen since we took the train.'

Looper must have shown his puzzlement because Krepl smiled understandingly. 'Before your time. Thank God. Completely foreign to you. You see we spent our time in the camp I told you about, in the old brickyard, waiting for the trains. Every day came the rumour: "Today the trains are coming!" The trains were supposed to take us away to work camps, that's what they told us. Sure, some of us had our doubts, but doubts we did not need at that time. We yearned for the trains. Each day in that stinking place when they didn't come we asked: where are the trains? We

139

might have been impatient travellers going to the seaside. At last they told us to pack up what we had and address our parcels to Work Camp 600, Germany. "Write clearly," they told us, "your luggage will follow on the next train, we don't want you to lose it, do we?" Well, I mean what do you expect? We were impressed! In spite of ourselves, we were impressed. Such efficiency! This was the German way, we said. Certainly they knew how to organise themselves. No wonder they were winning the war. And fancy – they even knew where in enormous Germany this Camp 600 was to be found. They must have had a huge map, we told ourselves, and all our stuff would speed along there on the steel rails of German efficiency. It's funny, isn't it? You can laugh. You'll forgive me if I don't. But you go ahead if you like. What else can one do? Consider: few of us had ever taken a train journey; many of us had never left our homes before and none of us had the faintest idea of what awaited us at the end of the line. But we wanted the trains. We wanted to get aboard and go some place. Those who had doubts kept them to themselves. Maybe they felt otherwise they'd spoil the holiday spirit with which we waited for the trains . . .'

After the war he stayed in Hungary. It had been the Russian invasion that pushed him out. 'Fifty-six was too much.'

'May I ask, then, how someone who had seen as much as you could sign up in this line?'

Krepl looked at him as if he was quite mad. 'But, my boy, this is quite different. This is child's play. You can't compare this with our way of things.'

'Like to bet?'

Krepl grew irritable. 'Listen, I was there. Europe then was bad. This – this is kid's stuff. A job! Granted, it helps if you hate fascists, communists and all that. But strictly nine to five, all the same. Little league! And you? How did you come to take the pledge?'

'A philosopher at University talked me into it. Back in the mid-sixties.'

'Worst sort. You'll meet one at the Hottentot. Lestrade's the name – Byron Francis Elisha, if you can believe it.'

'I can. He taught me once.'

'Damn coincidence! But he wasn't the one who pulled you over?'

'Not really. There aren't many philosophers back home. Mine was pretty, a logician.'

'Ah well,' said Krepl, as if this explained a great deal. 'A logician, and pretty! Who could resist?'

'She put up a good case and then she gave me a glimpse of the mallet.'

Krepl shrugged. 'A glimpse is all it takes.'

Looper's recruitment had been very much in his mind since he arrived in Britain if only because he had virtually forgotten about it until two uniformed policemen with heads like the thick ends of baseball bats marched him on to the flight for London and he realised Cerise Mendel was calling in the agreement made years before.

Looper had been eighteen when Cerise Mendel took him to coffee in the student canteen and coolly announced in one breath that certain friends of hers in official circles had an interest in him and that she had a small proposition to make. The success of the approach in persuading Looper lay both in the charm of the messenger who sat demurely over her lemon tea and the fact that no commitment was to be asked of him for a long time, possibly for many years. What was on offer was long-term credit, a credit which, if not entirely without strings, was one to which strings would only be attached at some dim and distant future date. It was a scheme, said Cerise Mendel, slipping naturally into the language of the hire-purchase firm which her father ran, under which he 'paid nothing now'. Acceptance of what the logician called this 'attractive commission' would not in any way prevent him from developing his own political ideas, even if those ideas conflicted with government policies. He would remain a free agent. It was merely that one day he might be called on to give to his country that assistance which, as a patriot, he might have felt obliged to render whether he was asked or not. The question that was being put to him was whether, if he saw his country threatened with destruction by alien, foreign forces, he could be depended upon to help. Certain of her friends, said Cerise Mendel, wished to partially formalise (here she wrinkled up her pretty nose at this less than logical proposition) in advance, the free and spontaneous patriotic gesture which they expected him to make in any event should the pressure they feared come to pass.

Looper was impressed that she had taken him out to tea. He was dazzled by the clarity with which she put her proposal. He was painfully aware that he did not have enough money to pay for her tea. It was true that she had invited him, but as they were sitting in the student canteen he felt obliged to keep his end up. Yet he had no money. The tea would have cost fifty cents, a pittance in the heavily subsidised canteen. But fifty cents was his daily allowance. He used to buy rolls in the bakery before lectures started. The rolls were his lunch. He ate them with water. His breakfast and supper, which alternated, were taken in the room he rented. Everything was budgeted down to the last cent. His small income came from the waiter's job he took over the weekends.

He had lived in this cheerless, spartan fashion ever since he left home after the great war with his father. Looper's father, small and moustachioed with a distinct streak of cruelty, obsessed with personal hygiene, with side whiskers and black thickets of ear hair and the grin of an irritable catfish, was a man obsessed with personal hygiene. His special field, as a mining inspector, had been the operations of rock under great stress, and, after cleanliness, his great passion was scuba diving.

'He spends half his life in the water closet and the other half under water or down a mine,' he remembered his mother saying to him long ago. 'Sometimes I think this world is just not good enough for him to breathe in . . .' Then his mother died – and it had seemed to his childish way of thinking that her death had been a form of protest. Her way of walking out. After she died, the years of trench warfare began. One sunny Saturday afternoon Looper had tried to shoot his father with a harpoon gun and then wept like a baby with frustration when the gun jammed. His father had retaliated by hitting his son with an oxygen canister and thereafter locked himself in the lavatory.

There followed the division, the rented room, the waiter's job and near penury. Looper's father, perverse as ever, continued to pay his son's university fees because, as he said, he knew he could not pay them himself. Caleb's degree course still had over a year to run. 'You can twist on the rope. You get my money whether you like it or not,' was the way the inspector put it.

Looper had no option. But it hurt.

In her clear-sighted way, the logician Mendel saw exactly how much it hurt. She saw why it hurt. Her offer could not have come at a better time and the terms were so good. Money now, independence, nothing to pay for the foreseeable future. One in the eye for his father.

If that was all it would have been simple, and bad enough. But there was one other thing. Mendel mentioned it 'only in passing'. Her apologetic tone suggested she hated to detain him in so small a matter. But there were, it seemed, a few rather strange facts about Looper's family. Certain researches which had been conducted into the provenance of a number of old Cape families showed that the Loopers, far from being descendants of English settlers, were not in fact the heirs of the union between Guy Looper, descendant of 'the fighting Loopers of Surrey', as Looper's father claimed, they were descended from some Dutch liaison with a Hottentot woman known from the historical records simply as Elsa of the Cape. Indeed, it was likely that the very name 'Looper', which sounded European, probably derived from the Dutch name for the Hottentot bands who scavenged the coasts of the Cape of Good Hope and were called 'Strandlopers', literally 'Beach Walkers'.

Looper knew what it meant. The family line was polluted by Hottentot blood, the family was, in effect, Coloured. This presented Looper with lethal information he could have used to destroy his father. People went mad and killed themselves when faced by such knowledge. But Looper could not use it against the inspector of mines. There was his mother's memory to be considered. Mendel assured him that the research was carried out in order to protect the information once it had been gathered. The families concerned ranged from the highest to the lowest in the land. The information was top secret and would remain so. He had her word for that.

'Of course I don't mind, not for myself,' he said.

'Of course not.'

She understood the position perfectly. She also understood the exquisite irony that Looper should now take upon himself the responsibility for protecting his father, whom he hated, from this fatal knowledge. Of course she was too discreet to say anything. Looper could feel her sympathy and he was grateful. The deal was clinched in mutually appreciative silence. And she paid for the tea. Somehow he could not find it in him to protest.

The ironies multiplied and abounded in the years that followed. The effect of Looper's university course upon him was to politicise and radicalise him. On leaving university Looper became a political journalist covering treason trials, riots, uprisings, massacres and strikes. He was detained, beaten, arrested on a number of occasions, and served sentences for refusing to reveal his sources. He was well known to radical opposition groups and heartily detested by the

143

government. He was widely regarded as an uncompromising, articulate enemy of the policies of racial separation and an unsparing critic of the rich idiocies of constitutional and mystical segregation. He was recognised as an unflinching liberal crusader. And so he was.

When the authorities, in an ingenious ploy only recently dreamed up, gave to themselves the power of revoking the South African citizenship of anyone holding dual nationality, then Looper's father's fake British citizenship proved very useful indeed. A meeting with Langman restored his memories of his promise to the logical Miss Mendel.

Looper was shattered to learn that his father held British nationality. He said it was rubbish. Brigadier Langman laughed and showed him the papers. The inspector of mines was a British citizen.

'But he is utterly committed to this country. He is a fanatical supporter of the government. He despises Britain!'

Langman had laughed again. 'What's that got to do with it? There are thousands like him. They're more patriotic than I am, but they hang on to their insurance.'

'But I don't have British nationality.'

'It doesn't matter. You're eligible and that's enough for us to withdraw your citizenship and deport you. It's neat, isn't it? And the most perfect cover.'

His head spinning, Looper was bundled on to a plane for London. A radical journalist expelled for his crusading battle against racialism. It was undoubtedly very neat.

So it was with the satisfaction of one carrying on a good tradition that Krepl pointed to the heavy iron sign of the naked Hottentot woman which hung outside the front door of 31 Antaeus Street.

'What you need are friends,' said Krepl. 'The very best friends can be useful. I know of nowhere more friendly than this little Club of mine. It's a kind of home from home for people from Africa. You'll like it. And, as you say yourself, you already know someone in the Room – the ex-philosopher Lestrade. Isn't it strange that people like us always seem to find ourselves among friends? It's a small world.'

Looper thanked him.

'Not necessary. This goes back many years. Every new man the

Office sends over gets introduced to the Hottentot Room. Shall we go in? It's run by an old lady who went through the mill, like I did. She's lovely, Frau Katie. She was the wife of a general once. You'll love her.'

CHAPTER 10

At some secret signal, a touch of a button, a movement of a hand, Frau Katie's coffin was borne away on well-oiled runners through the heavy, dark red curtains. Could the unseen operator of this slow, smooth exit perhaps arrest the process if he chose? Could he bring the coffin back through the curtains for another appearance? Of course not. There were no curtain calls here. When you were seen on this small stage in front of an audience of grieving friends it was positively your last appearance. Certainly there was something about this final rite that reminded Looper of some dark première, the closest that most people would ever come to tasting stardom. There was about the occasion something of the air of tingling expectancy associated with the show business, with first nights and command performances. The big cars drew up loaded with flowers; awaiting them were the expectant crowds, the solemn hush, the emotion, the straining forward for a glimpse of the star, the blaze of glory. Of course it was true that there was a more grisly side to this last starring role – but then was there not always a bleaker side to show business the sensible theatre-goer wished to know nothing about? Who really wanted to see the truth behind the make-up? Why speak of the reality behind the coffin varnish, the gleaming brass fripperies, the bouquets, the big cars? Who wished to concern himself with the prosaic, dull and frightening details of the job taking place on the other side of the curtain. On this side of the curtain, there was art alive in all its waxy perfection. What was there on the other side of the curtain but the stoking of the furnace, the bone crushers, the raking over of the coals? It was understandable that the audience never bothered with life behind the curtain, because in fact there was no life behind the curtain; everything you looked for in a star existed on the stage, in the appearance, in the role – done to the very life.

It was over. They stood up to leave. Then quite unexpectedly the Soweto Knights began singing in strong, perfectly blended voices, the African hymn *Nkosi Sikelel'i Afrika*, God Bless Africa. The young priest looked startled and blushed a deep cherry pink. Gerrie

146

the barman joined in the singing and so did Wyngate Hossein in a rich baritone. Then all the Hottentots took it up. Looper who knew the tune but not the words hummed along. Mona the high-jumper sobbed noisily as the voices of the Soweto Knights resounded, anchored by Hossein's strong baritone and edged oddly, but pleasantly, by Gerrie's gruff backing and Looper's rusty hum, filling the church with the sweet, dark melody. Looper took out his handkerchief and wiped his eyes. Beside him, Rose sat tense, furious and dry-eyed as the hymn proceeded, the alternative national anthem of their country, sounding rich and defiantly inappropriate in the small, cold chapel as the Hottentots closed the Anglican service for a German-Jewish lady with an African song.

'If they start drumming now, I shall go mad,' said Rose between clenched teeth as the last notes died away.

'They haven't brought their drums,' Looper whispered.

But he was wrong. As it turned out, Mr Govender, who'd kept an eagle eye on the progress of the service had, upon a signal from Buffy Lestrade, fetched the instruments from his car. Now the drums began. A slow tattoo, a riffling, syncopated rhythm rising to a great crescendo that made the stained glass rattle and died away to a single, slow, throbbing beat that softened and then faded until all that could be heard was the stifled sobs of the high-jumper, little Mona May.

It was Rose, with dry eyes and a dangerous look, who led the mourners from the chapel. Outside the door, the first person Looper saw was the Zulu. He was dressed in his grey suit and was leaning against a motorcar beyond the fence watching him. He was smiling broadly. Looper stayed close to Rose. It made him feel rather queasy. The Zulu was a striking figure, broad, well over six foot, memorable. It was the way he smiled at the mourners that did it. You don't see such unabashed smiles at funerals. They must have been feeling very angry to put their man out front like this. Or confident. It was a message. The message declared he was running out of time. To remind him of this they had stood his replacement in front of his eyes. The appearance of the Zulu said that the Office was confident of his removal and return. It was only a matter of time. The Zulu did not wave.

'I wonder if that is another of my mother's friends, Caleb?' Rose asked.

'Certainly not,' said Looper. 'Shall we go?'

'Not yet. We must wait for the remains. Tell the others not to stay. They may return to Antaeus Street where they're cordially invited for tea, or something stronger. A few of my friends will also be stopping off. Go and ask for the ashes.'

Looper did as he was told, glad to escape the sardonic gaze of the Zulu.

Looper had not seen the Zulu since the invitation to view the head of Trajan, at which he had received news of his recall. He had been instructed to meet his replacement 'for briefing prior to departure' and to offer all the assistance in the normal way. It was in this tradition that Krepl assisted him when he had arrived in London.

After they left the British Museum, Looper had taken the Zulu to the Rag and Bone Club in Soho. Looper, who had been eyeing his air ticket the way a mouse eyes a snake, hoping for an ally in the new man, boldly told him that it was impossible to meet the deadline for departure.

The Zulu had rubbed his large square jaw and adjusted his midnight blue tie, he had fastidiously flicked dust from his good grey suit and sent a look around the club which suggested some scorn. 'I think they're expecting you. I don't think the welcome committee can be denied.'

'Yes, well, I have things to wind up. I don't like loose ends.'

The Zulu shrugged. 'Not for me to say, but I reckon the Office would rather you left things unwound.'

Looper had tried again. 'You're new here. You'll want your card marked.'

'Pardon?'

'London's a curious sort of place. Affairs get rather tangled.' Looper had begun to resent the Zulu's patronising air and his clear disapproval of the place to which he'd been brought. Looper rather liked the Rag and Bone Club. It was a handsome, comfortable watering hole with its olive green plush and dark panelling. Indeed, he thought it rather pleasant. But seen through Zulu eyes it was a dark, cramped and seedy little joint. Maybe I'm getting English eyes, Looper thought. Maybe I have been away for too long.

'What I mean is, you'll want some directions about how to find your way into the best circles. You'll want to be shown the landmarks.'

'The Office gave me a map.'

'Maybe. But the place names keep changing.'

The big man gave him an affable wink. 'What you mean to say is: how the hell is some raw African going to tell which way's up in this old town?'

'You took the words out of my mouth,' said Looper.

They drank gin. The Zulu wrinkled up his mouth in disgust. 'Good God! Do they call this a tot?'

He gave a grumbling chuckle and swirled the liquid contemptuously in the glass, blinking incredulously as if he couldn't quite believe what he saw. 'There've been changes back home. Big changes. Wait till you get back and you'll see for yourself. It's not the place you left. It's anybody's game now. No more rules about who does what. *Doing* is all that counts. I tell you, you wouldn't know the country. But you'll see for yourself. They plan to show you around in a big way. They're on the run, see? And they need the odd victory to cheer them. To cock a snook at the world. They're going to be really glad to see you. You're quite something. You're one of their prime stars and they can't wait to wheel you out and tell the world what you've done. Bet you'll enjoy that, Caleb. You're really going to love that. And why not? You deserve it. You won't mind if I tell you that certain wrinkles of yours are hailed by one and all. Classics! The family album business. Well that was a coup. A real coup. A coup of mammoth proportions! You'll be pleased to be getting a glimpse of home again. You deserve it all right. Tell me something – this place get you down?'

Looper said that the place did, from time to time, get him down.

'It's the natives, I suppose?' The Zulu looked sympathetic.

'They take some getting used to. They're an odd lot, I get the feeling they're happiest when they're dressing up and pretending to be elsewhere. Somewhere else in time – if you see what I mean. Any time but today. I get the feeling they're not really happy about today. They're really only happy in uniform. I think they get depressed in long periods of peacetime.'

The Zulu nodded. 'It seems so. I get the impression that they're a very warlike people. Always fighting. I think the only news we ever got from here was strikes and riots. Not that home sweet home is a vale of peace. Which is another thing you'll discover has changed. But our problems are, well, *natural*. You could say we deserve them. But people here seem to be looking for trouble. They

149

can be pretty savage when they get abroad, too.'

'They've always been savage abroad. Going abroad to fight foreigners is part of their history.'

'Maybe it's a trick of the light,' said the Zulu, 'but what strikes me after about two minutes here is that they're a queer, dark lot. Dark as in colour, I mean, not skin.' This was his little joke. 'Dark hair, dark eyes, dark looks . . .'

'I suppose they're a very mixed sort of race. The aboriginals, pure Britons, they've long gone. There have been intrusions and invasions by Romans, Celts, Vikings, Normans – mixing in with the aboriginals and it gives them the look that you refer to. Down south they tend to lighten. I'm told that, if anything, the Welsh are even darker.'

'Half-breeds,' said the Zulu with conviction.

'Well, not half. Say a quarter, or a fifth, or maybe even one-eighth breeds. That would be more like it.'

'And gloomy,' said the Zulu and he shook his heavy head. 'The weather has something to do with it, too. It's done nothing but pee since I arrived.'

'That's because it's early spring,' said Looper.

'You know it's a funny thing, but arriving here among these English and seeing them *en masse* for the first time, I couldn't believe that they were the same people we whipped at Isandhlwana all those years ago.'

The Zulu's eyes sparkled. He was back in Natal, on the mountain called 'The Little Hand', or, more picturesquely, 'The Third Stomach Of A Cow', because that is what it looks like. He was recalling one of the great disasters of British military history when the Zulus, under their General, Cetawayo, wiped out an entire army.

Looper knew just by looking that the locals were not going to present this man with many problems. Why should they? He'd passed some stiff tests to get here. He was a black man who'd worked his way up in the service. He'd won an overseas posting. If the powers in the land imagined that by recruiting such people they were scoring points it could just be that they were going blind. It could be that they'd wake up one day to find guys like this had taken over. None the less he had an idea why the people back home were signing on men like the Zulu. Pragmatism was the spur. And desperation. Those who ran the factory found they just didn't have enough hands to go round. To work the machine, once upon

150

a time, you had to be white, over twenty-one, dedicated to the Party and to the preservation of western Christian civilisation and believe that the Afrikaners were God's anointed. Nowadays anyone could mind the machine, as long as they were willing to keep shooting. This policy of desperation went by the name of progress. The Zulu was working the system. Looper wondered about the manner of recruitment. Had he been taken on board by some equivalent of the pretty logician who once spoke to him? Or did they have black recruiters now? And did his appointment to London suggest that the white component in the resistance movements overseas was diminishing to the point where white appointments such as his own were no longer necessary, or practical? There was something in the way that the Zulu looked at Looper that suggested how marginal he had become. The big man looked at him like he was some old coat he had just found in a cupboard. It was a sad, fond look. The coat had been useful once but now it was threadbare, rather cheap, unfashionable and far too small. A place would have to be found for the old coat.

The Zulu ordered champagne. He offered a toast: 'To Cetawayo!'

Looper had one last delaying tactic. 'You'll want to join the Hottentots. Now that's something that I can arrange. You see there's never any guarantee that you'll get in. But you need a sponsor in any event. I've been a member for years.'

'No thanks, boss.'

'It's traditional. Everybody new gets introduced.'

'I hate traditions.'

'Look, you don't know what you're saying. You talk about the famous photograph album. Let me tell you there would have been no album without the Hottentot Room. You'll want to join, I promise you. So I'll have a talk to a few people there and see what I can do. There's no question of my going home yet. They're very finnicky, the Hottentots, about who they accept.'

The Zulu threw back the last of the champagne and laughed. 'Thanks all the same but I don't need it. I hope you won't take it to heart when I tell you that I prefer to run my own comb through this town. What must I do with these Hottentots of yours? No, man, thanks all the same but leave me out of it. I'll get along just fine. I don't need your Hottentots. 'S far as I'm concerned, Hottentots are extinct.'

151

CHAPTER 11

Frau Katie's ashes had been presented to them in a cardboard pail, the sort of box that might have held ice-cream.

Rose had commanded him to keep it on his lap while she drove the Mercedes back to Antaeus Street. When he'd objected she'd told him crisply: 'We can hardly put it in the boot. And it will roll about on the back seat.' So he had sat cradling the earthly remains of Frau Katie while Rose negotiated the heavy London traffic. Looper could not hold back his tears. One would have imagined, thought Looper, seeing the weeping man beside his dry-eyed chauffeur, that he had lost his mother. His tears fell with a flat sound on the box.

When they entered the Hottentot Room the others, crowded around the bar, fell back with a little murmur which might have been grief or superstitious awe when they saw what Looper was carrying, or possibly even relief. Clearly everyone wanted a drink but they had held back until the chief mourner arrived. Rose had threatened Gerrie severely on this score.

Rose strode to the bar. Looper walked behind her carrying the ashes. He would have liked to have taken the box upstairs to Frau Katie's old bedroom but Rose had other ideas. 'Let her stay down here, Caleb. Let her preside over her old friends one last time.'

Looper was rather shaken by this.

Such uncommon kindliness towards her mother was most unsettling. A signal to Gerrie the barman set the liquor flowing. Under Looper's directions Gerrie placed the box on a high shelf behind the bar, high enough to be sure that her mother, as Rose put it, was out of harm's way. By which Looper understood her to mean that she was unlikely to be knocked over. On the left of the box of ashes was an ancient mid-fifties tourist map showing the vastness of Lake Nyasa, all of 380 miles long and depicted in oily greens and violent blues. The lake steamer, the *Ilala* (620 tons) was shown setting out on a ten-day trip from Monkey Bay around the lake – bookings were invited. Excellent accommodation was offered at the Monkey Bay Hotel. The high ground north and east of the northern end of the lake was pronounced suitable for European settlement. The only dangers appeared to be violent south-easterly winds which whipped up heavy seas between June and September. To the right of the box of ashes was a copper plaque showing elephants drinking at a water hole.

Both of these depictions of Africa were utterly false and yet each in its way made a statement about the continent with which no one would quarrel. There had once been a Protectorate of Nyasaland just as it was true that elephants once wandered through the continent at will, visiting water holes where they found them. It was true, as well, that the cardboard box reposing on the shelf, situated between Lake Nyasa and the elephants drinking, contained the remains of a once beautiful woman with a thick Berlin accent and strange ideas about Africans, who had loved a small group of them – and had been for them their great queen. But when you thought about it, these statements mocked the observer all the more cruelly for being apparently true, for providing this workable approximation of reality. For these statements would never comfort the bereaved, even though they might pretend to do so. These images of the deceased were simulacra. The lake, the elephants, the box of ashes on the shelf – these were symbols intended to arrest time, they represented a punitive raid on the past, a kind of petty revenge on the appallingly treacherous nature of time, on the damned slippage of things. Looked at in this light, perhaps the items up there on the shelf were just about bearable. But Looper did not care to look at them in this light. He persisted in demanding that he be shown the truth and the truth blinded him with anger. Was it possible to drink a beer at the Monkey Bay Hotel as you waited for the next steamer? If not, the advertisement on the map lied. To hell with that gaudy rag! And where were such elephants to be found today with their gleaming rumps, looking, in their strange copper mani-festation as if they had been carved out of a livid Cheshire cheese? And where was the water hole? And, anyway, when had water been so free in Africa? What was that strange square box doing up there on the shelf behind the bar? Oh yes, it might claim to house the mortal remains of a great lady. But he repudiated that claim. What sat up there on the shelf were cheap trinkets, tourist mementoes, some very bad copper, vulgar splotches of colour and a cheap, ugly, cardboard box.

Suddenly the Room was more crowded than he had ever seen it

153

before. The curtains were drawn back, the front door left wide open for the first time anyone could remember, the windows were thrown wide and the gusts of fresh, rather cold, air blew in.

And still the strangers kept coming. Rose clearly had asked people who were either personal friends of hers or, he suspected, people she considered potential customers for whatever establishment was going to rise from the ashes of the Hottentot. She was deep in conversation with the banker Bafney from Gimpel Fils, splendid in gold glasses and a dark blue suit who tossed back his thick black hair when he laughed and twirled his glass delightedly as Rose gave him one of her animated briefings, frequently brandishing a clenched fist, chopping the air with her other hand, or stabbing it with her chin so that her head rocked on the strong broad spring of her neck and her blonde hair swirled about her face.

'Drinking?' Gerrie asked Looper.

'All the time.'

'That's the spirit. I get the feeling that this is like those funerals that they have for heads of state. You know when all the other government ministers get together, an occasion for state business.'

Gerrie had a point, Rose's guests now far outnumbered the Hottentots. They were unhappy, out of place and unable to protest at Frau Katie's funeral feast. Their outlandish, or excessively neat or shabby, clothes set them apart and they tried to compensate for the embarrassment and the unease they felt by pretending to feelings of superiority; by talking loudly in Afrikaans, by lounging rather showily around the bar, noses in the air, casting disdainful looks at the *arriviste* cronies of English Rose who had gate-crashed, it seemed to them, this solemn event and who were clearly intent on turning it into an occasion horribly out of keeping with the loss they felt. The Hottentots felt, indeed Gerrie had said, that Rose's attitude in inviting these people here was like spitting on their grief. But of course Rose's friends did not care. It was unlikely they had even been told the reason they had been invited to the Hottentot Room. Or, if they had been told that Frau Katie was dead, they were determined not to let it spoil the spirit of the occasion which was clearly one of joyful celebration – whether of Rose's endurance, or of her future plans wasn't clear, but a kind of coming-out party, certainly. Frau Katie's tribe might huddle about the bar, might look down their noses as much as they liked, might bang loudly on

154

the counter and demand refills from Gerrie the barman and ignore the waitresses who circulated with trays of champagne. Buffy Lestrade might pull himself up to his full height and puff himself out to his most impressive rotundity, allowing the light to bounce off his great forehead which showed a most high and disdainful gleam, Mr Govender might sip Perrier, pulling at his golden wrist chain, presenting a lean, elegant, expensive demeanour, buffed to a steely gleam, proudly glinting beside the beautiful Anagupta. Elize from Zimbabwe might stand there with her aggressive, wide-legged, lock-kneed stance, a glass of whisky in her fist, blowing smoke angrily out of the side of her mouth and throwing challenging looks at the strangers, but it did no good. The strangers did not see or care.

Well, perhaps that was not entirely accurate. Who would fail to notice Anagupta, so beautiful, so silent and so young? And then of course they knew Mona May, because she was so famous. On a number of occasions she saw Rose pointing her out, but fortunately any conversation with the celebrity in their midst was not possible. For when Mona opened her mouth it proved fatal. Mona's voice was one which gives to the South African accent, already suspect for flat monotonous vowels and droning pronunciation, its rather dull reputation. In Mona's case it was rather worse than usual since she spoke that flat twanging English characteristic of the border country into which the first English settlers were decanted in the previous century as a buffer against marauding black tribes. When Mona spoke, although the mouth was open for speech, the words were released through the nose. Those words were: 'Ar-thinkertsbleddimeen. Andertsdahnrahtcrooltoo.' By this the Hottentots understood her to complain at the idea of giving a swanky party to mark Frau Katie's death was both mean and cruel, and they agreed with her, though they wished Mona would not persist in stating the obvious and flinched inwardly at the rawness of her accent, the high, driving whine of it. Of course with an accent like that, Rose could do little more than grieve inwardly that such a talented person had such a miaowing mode of expression and felt quite unable to introduce her to her friends.

What her friends thought of the Soweto Knights in their diverse finery was more difficult to imagine. Looper saw several people point to Oscar's white PVC boots. To some extent, of course, they might have seen the Knights as living examples of the rather odd

155

African connections which Rose's old mother had maintained for unfathomable reasons. Then again it was possible that English Rose's friends took them for West Indians, with their knitted caps and plaited hair and wondered to themselves, quite possibly, whether they smoked marijuana all day and fought with the police by night. In any event they undoubtedly thought of them as exotic, slightly dangerous creatures and attributed to Rose's mother some special skill at handling them. Looper imagined this to be of the same order as the respect one accords to a lion tamer, or snake charmer. That is to say respect tinged with a certain sceptical amusement. For, after all, may not seemingly fierce circus lions be elderly, toothless and thoroughly domesticated? And surely the snake that emerges from the basket was long ago stripped of its poison fangs? And, by the same token, even if these were drug-struck rioters, perhaps they had mothers they were kind to, and helped old ladies across the street? Then again, perhaps not. A slight, faint doubt clung to their scepticism like a trace of garlic on a kitchen knife. So the Soweto Knights, and others among Frau Katie's Hottentots, became interesting in that they contained within themselves a wider range of possibilities than Rose's friends were accustomed to find in one room at any one time. There was too the connection with Africa, and the continent retained, in the English mind at least, something of its former magic and mystery. And so these old, slightly odd friends of Rose's eccentric old mother (for that is already how they were being seen) provided a little bit of foreign colour on that grey afternoon. There was the fat man wound in white sheets who talked loudly and burst into snatches of German songs about love and darkness and the silent lark: *Und die Lerche sie schweiget nun auch* – Buffy lamented ... but no one had the first idea what he was saying. There also was the very imposing African with the distinguished looks. This was Wyngate Hossein – though no one could have put a name to him, solid and distinguished in his dark suit, with his grizzled grey hair. Long gone were the days when the thin, nervous, recently released prisoner from a South African gaol arrived in London and found himself sipping champagne with Frau Katie until, overcome by alcohol and freedom, he had passed out and slept on a red plush bench beneath the tartan rug she kept for such occasions. Now, he looked so assured. He might have been an ex-Prime Minister of Nigeria deposed in some forgotten coup, who had lived to see his deposers

156

swept on to the rubbish tip of history, survived them all and now did rather nicely as a consultant to some City firm with interests in the Third World. It was doubtful whether Rose's guests gave Gerrie the barman more than a curious glance. He might have made himself more noticeable, and therefore more objectionable, by polishing the floor had not Rose confiscated his brushes and his Cobra wax polish and he had to content himself between pouring drinks by flicking dust from the copper elephants at the water hole and polishing the ostrich eggs with his bar cloth, mumbling tearfully to himself as he did so. It was most unlikely that Rose's guests saw Looper at all – he was a man adept at not being noticed. At least, not until Rose drew him forward into the centre of the room and presented him with the Hottentot cane.

Coree's cane! Rose presented it with a flourish and a beaming smile. She had not wrapped it but she had tied a silver ribbon around its copper grip. With icy fingers he untied the ribbon. Rose's friends, thinking this some special ceremony, a reward for long service or some special family feast applauded politely and some of them shouted Skoal! and Cheers! The Hottentots looked on with pale faces and huge, astonished eyes.

'Rose. This is Coree's cane.'

'I know. But it's yours now.'

Looper looked at the name inscribed on the copper grip. 'Caleb Looper!' So that's where it had been. Sitting at the engraver's where his name replaced Coree's.

'I can't take, it Rose. You don't understand what this means.'

'Of course you can take it. It's yours now.'

'No, no. Look, I can't take it. It belongs to the Room. It's historically valuable, you see. It's the cane colonial governors gave to the Hottentot captains who, who . . .'

'I know perfectly well what it is,' said Rose. 'I live here, remember?' She laughed happily and several of her guests joined her. 'But it's yours now. We want you to keep it.'

'We?'

'Yes. Mummy and me. It was Mummy's last wish – or almost her last wish. "Give him the cane," she said. "Give Caleb Coree's cane. He deserves it." So it's yours, now.' And Rose clapped her hands and the others joined in the official round of applause.

Looper had no doubt that this was true. The supreme ambivalence of those words identified them immediately as having come from Frau Katie. No one else would put things in quite that way. It made him tingle to think of it. It was like receiving a message from the dead. Indeed, he would know what the cane meant. He would know that it meant servitude, the bended knee before the colonial master, the promise to be a good boy. Those were the things it meant. When she left that message for him Frau Katie had undoubtedly been up to something. He glanced at the cardboard box on the shelf behind Gerrie. She was still up to something. He went over to the bar.

'You keep this safe for me?' He handed the cane to Gerrie.

'Sure. It'll be here when you want it.' Gerrie placed it beneath the bar.

'And I think I'll have a whisky.'

Gerrie shook his head and muttered to himself in some internal debate while he poured the drink.

'A lot of new faces in here. Her guests. A new breed. You know she's been dying to make changes. What I want to know is what's the pace, man? What's the time scale?'

Looper hesitated. Succinct brutality seemed the kindest option. 'Yesterday belonged to Frau Katie. Today is ours. Tomorrow belongs to English Rose.'

'Caleb, time's cheap for kids like you. But me, I'm pushing sixty. I came to this place way back when. Frau Katie, she took me in. Gives me a job. Make yourself at home, my darling, she says. I've been barman of the Hottentot ever since. It's more than a job. It's me.' Gerrie lowered ice cubes into the glass with terrible precision. 'What am I going to do? I mean it's not the same for me as it is for you, or Wyngate, or Elize, or any of these people who's over here because they're in exile from the government in South Africa, who they're at war with and planning to bring down as soon as bloody possible so they can all go home and be heroes of the people. I'm here because of an accident. In South Africa I lived in the Karoo. I'm like one of those Russians who come out West for a tractor show, take one look at the lights in Regent Street and disappear. They're not going back to Siberia where all you do is sit around waiting for the snow to melt. You got me, Caleb? In the Karoo you sit around waiting for the rain. That doesn't happen either. I don't have any other life. I don't want any other life. But Frau Katie's gone. God rest her soul. And we're left with Rose.'

'She'll always need a barman.'

158

'Don't give me that shit. Rose doesn't like the Hottentots. She hates them. And how am I going to get on with these friends of hers? I tell you they'll be all over us! C'mon, Caleb – can't you do something?'

'Why me?'

'You got the cane.'

'Yes. But I didn't ask for it. I don't want it.'

Gerrie's answer was a broad wink.

'Why did you do that?'

Gerrie dropped his voice and spoke without moving his lips, in the manner of a ventriloquist. 'We all know Rose is engaged to you.' His tone conveyed both the scandalous nature of this insight as well as the sympathy he felt.

'Who told you that?'

Gerrie's answer surprised Looper even more completely than the information that the others knew about his secret affair with Rose.

'Frau Katie.'

It took all his professional skill to keep his calm, half-interested manner intact. 'And what did she say?'

'Said there was more of herself in her daughter than English Rose suspected. Said that she also once settled on the wrong fellow and look where it had got her ... Said Rose felt for you the way the goose felt for the fox.'

This information was delivered between tense, unmoving jaws, with many little knowing grimaces and rapid elevations of the eyebrows intended to show Gerrie's shock, fellow-feeling as well as a rather wicked masculine approval of what he regarded as an affair all to Looper's benefit. Gerrie concluded his performance with a highspeed thumbs-up.

Looper wandered away from the bar in a daze, Gerrie's words flying about his head like uncaged birds.

The sight of English Rose presenting Looper with Coree's cane had had the most extraordinary effect on the Hottentots. No doubt drink and grief and rage had also played their part, but they were beginning to behave very strangely. Flamboyantly. Obviously they wished to draw attention to their behaviour.

Wyngate Hossein approached him and in a very hostile manner began to describe to Looper the heroic resistance by people in the South African townships which, he said, showed the revolution had begun. He spoke loudly, in terms which suggested this was

159

some kind of test, that he was probing Looper's integrity, as if he were daring him to show his good faith, to declare himself and so expunge the memory of Biddy and the production of the airline ticket. Though whether Hossein wished Looper to extinguish the memory or wished to wipe it out himself was not clear. He urged Looper to print the good news of the revolution in all his stories, for all the right papers. Progressive journalists, like Looper, had been given the privilege of announcing the new order. Looper thanked him and said he would do what he could. Hossein said that the great townships like Soweto were rapidly making themselves ungovernable. They were killing black stooges and collaborators in their midst and turning the townships into no-go areas for whites. The next step would be barricades, arms training and concerted forward action into white cities. Looper listened politely. He had recently read the reports reaching him from the Office, which described the present troubles as disruptive but containable, and the inhabitants as being engaged in a petty civil war amongst themselves and quite without the means or even the will to assert themselves with any military effect. They posed no threat except, perhaps, to themselves. And to talk of serious insurrection, belonged, concluded the report, 'to the vapid imaginings of desperate, elderly political exiles in England and elsewhere . . .'

Now Gerrie challenged Mona over the question of her British passport. Hossein chimed in: 'Yes, that's right. If you hang on, you will soon compete proudly under the flag of your own country.'

Mona thanked him but said that she hoped that day was not far off because high-jumpers had a limited career and were old by the age of twenty-one. While she had the legs she would jump. And to illustrate this she began jumping on the spot. It was an exercise she did, she told Gerrie, and she could keep it up for hours. She would leap up shooting out her legs in opposite directions in a kind of scissor movement.

Now the Soweto Knights rounded on Hossein. Zeke demanded that Hossein give credit to the kids who started the revolution and stop trying to hijack it. Hossein refused to discuss the matter. Oscar asked Looper if he ever reviewed African cultural events and gave him a complimentary ticket to their forthcoming concert at the Commonwealth Institute. Looper thanked him but said he only really covered political news.

'Our poetry and our music are political,' said Zeke.

160

'Our poetry is our struggle. Our art is liberation.'

'I hope you don't think,' said Sipho, the baritone of the group, 'that we speak our poetry. We don't speak nothing! We drum!'

Oscar said: 'That old man, Hossein, asked us to join the cultural section of his organisation. I told him that we'd get about as far playing for his cultural section as we would playing with ourselves. The cultural section of Via Afrika is full of old aunties playing calabashes with nice scarves around their heads, singing about cows and fetching water from the hill. That sort of thing is even older than Hossein.'

As if to rub in their points, the Knights then disappeared only to return a few minutes later, stripped down to nothing at all but thin and rather meaty loincloths, their naked bodies glistening with grease. Before the horrified Rose was able to stop them, they had arranged their drums and begun to play. Mr Govender immediately asked Gladys Hossein to dance. The Knights began singing, a dark rich harmony. Mr Govender and Gladys did a kind of tribal shuffle. Rose's guests looked on astonished and entranced. Little Mona May was still doing her scissor-like exercises beside the bar. Gerrie must have asked her to stop and Elize had taken objection because the next moment she and the bartender were sparring none too gently with each other. And one or two of the more nervous of Rose's friends screamed quietly at the sight of a man and a woman apparently boxing.

It was then that Biddy Hogan made her entrance. Her face was dead white, her eyes burning. Eyes that searched for Hossein. Looper began to move to head her off. Biddy had a wild, grief-stricken look which worried him. She'd come for a show-down, there was no doubt of that. The room was by then very crowded and Biddy was at the far end and it took a few moments before she caught sight of Hossein up at the bar talking to Mona who listened to him while continuing to spring backwards and forwards. Looper leaned over to Hossein.

'I rather think someone's looking for you.'

Hossein saw Biddy squeezing her way towards him. Placing his glass on the counter and glancing over to where his wife was still dancing with Mr Govender, Hossein set off in the opposite direction. Now Looper began working his way towards Biddy, who as yet was still unaware that her quarry was making his way around the room in the opposite direction. He felt if he could get to her he might at least block her path, he might point out that Gladys Hossein was here, he might even wave this fact at her like a crucifix before a vampire in the hopes of slowing her down. As Looper shouldered his way through the crowd he passed for a while within the gravitational field of Buffy Lestrade and heard his resonant voice.

'We intend to inject the egg with a harmless purple dye. Not every egg, naturally, but random eggs. And we intend to mark foods the same way, cake mixes, certain breads, pasta and so on. The warning will read: "Beware egg cholesterol!" '

Even for the short period he was near him Looper found Buffy increasingly and alarmingly irritating. He wanted to seize a bowl of white sugar and spoon it into his drink. He wished to throw the portly ex-philosopher on to the ground and force butter down his throat and wash it down with cream.

Lestrade was now saying: 'We intend also to demonstrate at professional sports meetings. Exercise is increasingly available to an elite who seduce the general public into spectatorism; the few stay fit, while the many sit around waiting and watching while their arteries silt up . . .'

Someone touched his shoulder. It was Morrison. 'I wanted to say goodbye.'

'I just might be leaving with you.'

'No, no. I don't mean this –' Morrison indicated the room. 'I am thinking of going to that place where companions are forbidden. Death or the contemplative life in a monastery become more attractive daily.'

Biddy had now seen Hossein's manoeuvre and instead of trying to circle around the outside of the room she changed direction and began to cut through the centre of the crowd. Looper was in the right position. He had only to wait now. He was in her path.

'Well, Caleb. What do you say?' Here Morrison showed signs of his former clerical vocation by adapting his careful listener posture, the head turned aside, one broadly curving ear facing the penitent, waiting to track his confession like a radar dish. When Looper made no reply, being too absorbed in calculating Biddy's slow progress, Morrison said, 'I do like to see Mr Govender and Mrs Hossein dancing. It's a fitting image of the union of the two liberation groups, Via Afrika and the Congress of Allied Democrats that so many of us have prayed for for so long. A pretty picture,

162

don't you think? Then last night,' Morrison continued, now well into this vein of moral uplift, 'I dreamed I was back in collar again, on my old patch in the Zululand hills. Then I woke up, of course, and knew there was no going back. Frau Katie's failure taught me that. You can't do it, can you? The poor woman was so sure she was going home one day. Now is the time to act, isn't it? While we still can.'

Looper grew hot and angry at the mention of the word 'failure'. He said cruelly, 'You couldn't go back, anyway. Defrocked priests are out for good. Like debarred attorneys.'

Morris looked reproachful. 'In the first place I was permitted to leave the priesthood by Rome itself. I was not defrocked. Secondly priests are no longer defrocked. *Tertius* – priests don't any longer wear frocks: they are more likely to be found in tracksuits. The era of the frocked priest is over. Not even nuns may be said to be frocked these days. Good heavens!' – Morrison was staring across the room towards the door. 'It looks to me as if Hossein's leaving already. But he's going without Gladys!'

Gladys herself reached that conclusion just as her husband disappeared through the door. She threw up her hand as if to call him back when she saw Biddy Hogan and the words died on her lips. Biddy, having gained the middle of the room and seeing Hossein disappearing through the door, gave a despairing shriek and plunged after him. Throughout it all the Knights kept drumming.

Because that night the curtains of the Hottentot Room were open, having been drawn on Rose's instructions, very few of the others had not noticed Hossein's departure, hotly pursued by Biddy. None of Rose's friends found it more than a trifle amusing. But it had an effect on the Hottentots. Quite apart from reducing Gladys Hossein to a shaking, shivering fury, it put an end to their display, their defiant misbehaviour intended to remind English Rose that they were, after all, Hottentots still.

At the window Looper watched Hossein reach his car at a trot. His nerves had clearly been shot to pieces; he was fleeing the wrath of a deserted mistress though Looper very much doubted that it was love that Biddy wished to discuss with him. Perhaps Hossein thought he was getting away as his car pulled off from the kerb, but Biddy was not to be thwarted. Without hesitating she flung herself on the bonnet, her arms outstretched across the windscreen, oblivious to the amazed stares of passers-by. Hossein kept going, he speeded up, he began to weave from side to side trying to throw her off but Biddy was tightly fixed, a windscreen wiper in one hand and the driving mirror in the other, her chin resting on the windscreen ledge she lay stretched out full-length across the bonnet of the car, her legs wide apart, riding it, resisting Hossein's desperate attempts to dislodge her. It must have been terrifying for him, trying to drive while Biddy's face rested inches away from his, her jaw clenched. Looper came away from the window. There was no way Hossein could drive like that. He would have to stop the car before it reached the end of Antaeus Street. This time Biddy had won. This time he would hear her out.

Looper actually asked to stay on that night with Rose. She took it as a compliment, as a small victory. She smiled graciously, happily and agreed willingly. But of course there was now no longer any opportunity for Looper to go home. His flat would be far too dangerous a place. But he had with him all he needed, his papers and money. As Frau Katie had liked to remark, better never to leave home without your papers because who ever said that you were going back?

Rose stood broad and strong against the window as she undressed. Beside her Looper felt thin and ill. She stood quite naked and crossed to him with a purposeful tread. Looper shivered beneath the sheet. Rose clung to him. Arms around his neck, legs about his waist. This is how the victim drowns the rescuer, he thought. Later she slept. He listened to her, in her sleep contentedly reeling off figures. Large, warm and comfortable, like some ocean liner come safely to berth, whose work is now done, Rose rumbled warmly and gently.

At four o'clock he got up quietly and dressed. From the window he could see quite clearly a number of men sitting in a car across the road. There were undoubtedly other men outside his flat. Were they Hossein's? Or were they from the Office? Or had word got around to such an extent that Mr Govender had sent a few of his boys over? No matter. It was possible to leave the house by the back door and that was what he would do, allowing the watchers to stay in peace. Downstairs the Hottentot Room smelled of beer and old cigarettes. Moonlight practised a pale resuscitation upon the street vendors of Old Berlin and it polished the ostrich eggs. Behind the bar counter Looper found the Hottentot cane. Carefully, deliberately, he broke it into several pieces and left it on the bar. Behind the bar, too, he found the store of old plastic shopping bags garnered by Gerrie on his weekly shopping trips to the big stores of the West End. He found a large carrier bag with good handles. Upon her high shelf, where Rose had placed her, Frau Katie was waiting for him.

CHAPTER 12

In the chilly dawn of Friday morning he waited on Earls Court
station. The underground at this time was warm, dusty, silent,
empty, and people moved like sleepwalkers. On his knees was the
plastic bag he had pulled from the box beneath the bar counter.
Now, in the sharp neon light overhead, he saw it came from Liberty,
the West End shop, a favourite destination on Frau Katie's great
shopping expeditions in the rusty Mercedes. The bag was deep
purple, with the famous name in familiar, elegant script. Purple for
kings, purple for power. Looper was once again reminded that he
was inadequately dressed. He had not eaten since the funeral feast
and then only a hasty sandwich snatched from a passing platter,
borne aloft by the pert waitresses in black and white who had
circulated amid the swirling crowds of guests, rich and fragrant
strangers who were something to English Rose and nothing at all
to the Hottentots, who clung to the bar like drowning souls, feeling
and looking like the poor relations they were, fading wallflowers at
a superior party, or elderly retainers at the sale of a great estate.

But of it all he felt worst about the presentation of the cane. For
what had it been but an attempt to shame him? And by shaming
him, to drive him towards a course of action foreseen, as so much
had been foreseen, by that old vixen, Frau Katie. Caleb deserves
the cane indeed! He saw it now. He had been set up. The affair
with Rose which seemed to go against the grain because surely the
old lady was too jealous to want to share him, even that had been
calculated. What had seemed contrary was anything but so. Frau
Katie had encouraged the liaison with her daughter because she
knew that once in it, Looper would have to break it. He would
have to run. The old lady doubtless also suspected a great deal of
the truth about Looper's real occupation, just as she saw the probable fate of the Hottentots, who had made their last lunge for
freedom at her wake. They had attempted to outrage Rose and
alienate her guests, embarrass and disgust them with their heath-
enish, outlandish, savage customs and clothes and behaviour. The
naked drummers, the jumping girl ... but all it had done was to

irritate Rose very mildly and, he suspected, to intrigue and even amuse her friends. Yet only Looper had been given the cane. Only Looper could be relied upon to run and to take Frau Katie with him. Very clever. It was always hard to believe that the flower unfolded its scent and beauty not for the delight of the onlooker but to ensnare insects and propagate itself. But there it was. The cane had merely been the final element in the trap. The master stroke. Even now he blushed when he remembered his humiliation. His ears sang. Sitting on the bench in Earls Court station he buried his face in his hands and groaned with the shame of it.

Looper remembered when he had last seen something resembling Rose's funeral celebration. Christmas Day at home when the presents were assembled beneath the tree. Outside, the heat was laying siege to the house. The sun came beating in through the windows, dancing on the tinsel and warming the cotton wool snow so that you could smell it. The servants would be invited inside to receive their presents and take a glass of sherry or beer with the family. In they crept, hands clasped before them in an attitude of prayer, bowing their heads as if entering a cave, or coming through a doorway too low for them, or visiting some church, to sit on their haunches in their clean white cotton uniforms, pulling their pinafores up in front of their faces and making a deep obeisance when their cake of soap, or pair of sandals, or bolt of material was taken from beneath the tree, as if bowing down to an idol. They would stay on their haunches in the far side of the room while his father located and then read out the card addressed to them: 'For Evalina from the Master and the Missus and Caleb. A very happy Christmas . . .' and Evalina would scurry across the carpets still on her knees, or venture forward in a crouching trot, take the parcel with a little bob and scurry back to her place. This is how he felt he had looked as he scuffled across the floor to receive his present from English Rose: the cane of the Hottentot Captain, Coree, who had gone home because he hated London.

For the first time in years, decades perhaps, the curtains had been drawn in the Room and the thin, cold light fell on the lifetime collection of redundant banknotes, on bad copper, vivid prints of Germany, on the map of Tanganyika, and on the Hottentots themselves and showed all to be, what perhaps they had always been, a collection of useless bits and pieces, relics of vanished worlds. There had been a breeze in the room. A draught. Rose had also opened the windows. Never before could he remember the windows having been opened. Frau Katie forbade it. People were looking for her, she said, and so she took no chances.

The first train for Heathrow arrives at Earls Court station at six o'clock and at that time of the morning carries few passengers. It was convenient that Frau Katie's local station provided a direct service to the airport. More than that. It could have been foreseen, so well did it fall in with her plans, her dreams and, above all, with her jokes.

'My dear, dear Caleb. One day I'm going to take you away from all this . . .'

It was not that he was without good reasons for being on the move but the direction in which he was now proceeding was not his choice but hers. Looper sat among the early morning workmen in their donkey jackets, carrying their lunch pails and attracted no notice as the train gathered speed through the winding darkness. On his knees reposed his only luggage, the precious parcel wrapped and hidden in its royal purple with its elegant script. Frau Katie had had her little joke. Except, as in the case of Biddy Hogan's vests, it had turned out to be no joke at all. Looper carried with him the earthly remains of one who had been young Katerina Brahm, was later to become the well-respected Frau von Sturz, almost but never quite became Frau General Von Sturz, and finally turned into Frau Katie, the Hottentot queen. What he saw, when he looked in the bag, was something rather like an awful hat box, or conical ice-cream container or tub into which the crematorium placed the ashes. Looper felt a stab of rage. Surely they could have put them into an urn, a jar, a lead box or something rather more dignified than this wretched pot – or bucket, which was appropriate, at very best, for fried chicken or crystallised fruit. The workmen around him saw him peering into his bag and probably thought he was inspecting his lunch – such are the natural misunderstandings which occur on trains in the early morning. For who knows what people carry in plastic bags?

His angry, inner self proclaimed that he was free at last; he was doing precisely as he wished for the first time in his life. Looper was back on the railway bridge. He'd crossed by the bridge reserved for blacks and had changed colour. The station master examined him: 'Go back again across the bridge, sonny. Pushing your bike –

remember you're not allowed to ride it. Then you come across the other bridge and when you get to this side you'll be white again.' But now, as then, Looper wasn't crossing any bridge. He could see through the station master's raised arm the patch of blue sky. He put his head down and aimed for it . . .

Doubtless by now the story of his treachery was also spreading among the Hottentots. He retained a most vivid memory of Biddy Hogan sprawled across the windscreen of Hossein's car as he roared down Antaeus Street, swerving vigorously as he tried to dislodge the desperate girl. But Biddy stuck like a limpet. With her arms stretched wide across the windscreen, her ankles clamped on either side of the bonnet, her eyes huge and frightened, staring at him through the windscreen and her hair flying, she must have presented a terrifying sight to the man behind the wheel and of course obscured his vision. That's what she wanted. This time she would make him listen. Once Hossein had begun to think over Biddy's information the appalling implications would have sent him crazy. He would have remembered Looper with his wife Gladys. Looper with the photograph album. He would have been on the phone to Govender. By first light they would all be hunting him. Not forgetting the watchers from the Office, they would also be up early this morning. No one had got away before . . .

He remembered the others. The sad case of Rabinowitz who had simply fallen in love with Europe and thought to resolve his difficulties by fleeing to Eilat in Israel. Alas, in matters of security of the State everything is permitted, even among governments who loudly resolve to have nothing to do with one another, and so it required only a few Pretorian whispers to circulate in Jerusalem that Rabinowitz possessed particular secrets about certain collaborative efforts in nuclear matters and the poor man was flown back to Johannesburg in such haste that he arrived in Jan Smuts Airport still wearing the pair of denim shorts and rubber beach thongs he had bought only that morning on his way to the beach. Then there had been Loggerenberg who truly had turned, vanished without trace and people imagined really had got away, until one day he arrived home unconscious in a wooden crate marked 'Tractor Spares – This Side Up'. And who could forget the tragic story of pretty Lois Harwood who deserted for love? She had only wanted to marry the handsome French military attaché she had met at a diplomatic reception and remained true in her heart to the ideals of racial separation, multi-cultural education, the sacred rights of all ethnic communities to freedom and self-determination within their separate homelands, or spheres, be these communities black Xhosas or Sephardic Jews or white Calvinists or Irish Catholics ... And believed this as fervently upon her wedding day in Chalon-sur-Marne (reception to follow at the Hôtel d'Angleterre), as she had done on the first day of her recruitment. But even this had not saved her. A lady gained entrance to the room where the bride was being prepared, by claiming to be her godmother all the way from Afrique du Sud with a special little present for the lovely little bride, and bloodily delivered to Lois's pretty face a handful of razor blades embedded in a leather glove. Then there had been little Leo Papst who had genuinely converted to the other side in an electrifying volte-face and seemed for a while to have escaped, and got to Lusaka where he lived reasonably well until he made the mistake of opening his own letters one morning ...

All in all, the Office had a fiercesome reputation for dealing with what were called in the trade 'the wingers'. Office policy had always been that they either got you back or ruined you where you stood. In his case, Looper thought they probably wanted him back, or dead. Both would do, but they'd settle for either.

Looper felt nothing but contempt for his hunters. He was overwhelmed by distinterest. He was not recrossing any bridge. He was emigrating. Retiring. Moving on. Heading out. On the run. The single attachment he felt was to the parcel on his knees and since reason told him that it made no sense to feel emotionally attached to inanimate objects, to wit a tub of ashes wrapped in a plastic shopping bag, he told himself with a measure of permitted sentiment which he allocated to himself from his small fund of this scarce resource, that it was to Frau Katie's memory that he felt attached and that he planned to repay his debt of gratitude to his friend by doing for her what she had always promised to do for him – he was taking her away from all this. 'Keep your eye on me,' she had said. Absolutely.

He was lucky. He got the very last seat on the plane and the girl at the desk complimented him on his good fortune, explaining there was a big international travel conference taking place in Berlin and all flights were heavily booked. She hoped he didn't mind having to sit in the smokers' section.

An attendant placed his bag on the conveyor belt and watched it disappear through the plastic strip curtain of the X-ray machine. The girl sitting at the monitor watching the pictures promptly stopped the conveyor and scrutinised the skeleton image on the screen for some moments. Looper looked as well. It might have been a box of sand or baking powder. The ashes rose to a peak against one wall of the container. He must have been shaking it about. He would have to remember to carry the parcel on a level. It looked like one of those 'guess the beans in the bottle' games you got at village fetes. Looper did not know what he would say if he were asked to identify the contents of his parcel. Did one need permission to transport the ashes of someone abroad? I will show you fear in a handful of dust . . . Indeed. What about a bagful? However, the girl pushed the button and the conveyor trundled on. He seized the bag and ran for it.

Looper chose his position in the departure lounge very carefully. He sat with his back to the glass wall. Through it he could see the airliner waiting on the tarmac. He faced the door and examined his fellow passengers as they arrived. Travel agents, he decided, looked slightly bemused when travelling. The room filled quickly. The hostess made an announcement on the public address system: 'For reasons of security, passengers are allowed only one item of hand-luggage. If you have more than one item, please report to the check-in desk. Passengers arriving at the barrier with more than one piece of hand-luggage may find that they are not permitted to board the aircraft.' He watched a worried man remove his duty-free purchases from their bag, pushing packets of cigarettes and even a bottle of gin into his coat pocket. Looper peered into his single item of luggage, he tapped the lid of the container gently but firmly to level the contents and stood up with a feeling which he diagnosed, with some surprise, as one of contentment.

Looper sat between two passengers. On his left was an Asian dressed in an olive-green safari suit. On his right was a pretty red-haired girl who smelt of expensive perfume and tobacco. Looper declined the invitation from the air hostess to place his parcel on the overhead luggage rack and settled it between his feet. He wanted it where he could feel it. The Asian was clearly nervous. He kept glancing at the windows, tapping them with a knuckle as if testing their seal and durability. He sniffed the air as if it were strange and somehow dangerous. He shivered frequently and Looper could see

171

the goose-flesh on his bare forearms. Indeed the atmosphere in the plane was not one of happy expectation but of a kind of scepticism mixed with wary resignation. Looper had cause to reflect upon the fact that travel agents prefer other people to do their travelling for them.

'Do you happen to know the current exchange rate of the pound sterling?' the Asian asked suddenly.

Now it so happened that the question of exchange rates, and the value of the pound sterling in particular, was something which Looper never discussed if he could possibly help it. He regarded the obsession with the value of their currency as one of the most diseased aspects of English life. You dignified this disease with fine-sounding names such as 'balance of payments' or 'trade balance', or 'worries over inflation' or 'rate of exchange' or 'fiscal discipline', when in fact what you were talking about was up a penny, down a penny with all the yipping ferocity of a floor full of stockbrokers. This was a religion of the cash till which promised a heaven where all the tills rang up right and stayed that way for ever and ever. He had said as much to English Rose and had been chided by her for being prejudiced, boring and inaccurate. 'There are many, many more aspects to the English than that. Why – just consider Henry Moore and the music of Walton, and the very special green of an English spring and the gentleness and decency at the heart of the national character . . .' To which Looper, goaded beyond endurance, had retorted 'Henry Moore and Walton, my arse! A people driven insane by petty economics, that's what they are. A greyish, penny-pinching island of antheads. A nation enthralled by accountants.'

This contumely so angered Rose that she blushed a deep browny red and began to breathe heavily through her nose. She even clenched her pretty, broad hands into fists. But she said nothing. She valued her self-control. In this she remained and prided herself in remaining truly English. There was also the question, important to her, of remaining scrupulously fair. She was determined to respect his right to be as bloody-minded as he chose. However, she had inherited enough of her mother's German fire and vigour to resent bitterly the slur upon her people and to wish to shoot the perpetrator of these insults, or at least to assault him in some manner so painful as to make him wish, at the very least, that he had never been born. But all she said was, calmly, airily, yet glowing

the dull, muddy red which reveals real rage among the English –
'Well, I suppose you're entitled to your point of view, Caleb. But I
wonder how many would people agree with you?'

Faced now with the question posed by the nervous Asian passenger beside him, Looper replied brusquely, 'I'm afraid I know
nothing about the sterling exchange rate.'

His companion looked relieved. 'Then we are alike. Two
foreigners upon a foreign wing. Tell me, sir, this Berlin we are
going to – what is there exactly?' He must have been aware of
Looper's surprise, because he tried again. 'This place that is Berlin
– do you go there often? Are you off on holiday?'

Looper was at a loss. He did not warm to the assumption made
by his questioner that ignorance had suddenly made them kinsmen
– as if ignorance was a country from which they both hailed. And
besides, how could a man know so little of the world that he asked
such questions about Berlin?

The Indian must have seen his look of surprise as he hastened to
reassure him, 'I'm from Africa, you see. Kenya, in fact. So I know
nothing. It is my brother, Salim who should have come. Not me.
Would you ask the lady beside you to refrain from smoking?'

Looper tightened his ankles on either side of the container at his
feet. He explained that they were in a smoking section and nothing
could be done. When the hostess passed he called for gin. The
gesture was intended to alienate him from Salim's brother who, as
he had guessed, ordered orange juice.

'Tell me please, on the map, what comes behind East Germany?'
'Russia.'

The man now looked utterly wretched. 'Salim should have come
on this trip. He's always the one to travel. I keep shop and Salim
travels. That is how we operate in Nairobi. Now why does he decide
this time he's not coming? I can tell you. He looked at the map.'

The map! The picture became even more bizarre. There is in
Nairobi, Looper thought to himself, a travel agency which is run
by two brothers who make their living by sending people on tourist
packages out into the world. And yet only one of them looks at the
map. There is only one map at which one of them looks . . .

'Salim would have seen that behind East Germany is Russia.
When he heard this was where we were having the conference, he
did this. That's to say, he sent me.' Here he shook his head at
Salim's perfidy. But then he made a determined effort to wrench

173

himself out of his depression. 'So tell me, sir – what is there to see in this Berlin?'

'There is the Wall.'

'Wall?' Salim's brother looked disappointed, if not downright aggrieved.

'There's a wall built across the city of Berlin. The Wall was built by the authorities in the eastern part of the city to prevent their citizens from crossing into West Berlin. It is called the Freedom Wall. People trying to cross it are shot or blown up by mines. It is a great tourist attraction in Berlin.'

Salim's brother looked puzzled no longer. His head went up and his eyes gleamed. He seemed almost happy. 'I understand. It is like South Africa. East is east and west is west and never the twain shall meet.'

'Right. Each group has their independent homeland.'

'Their private bantustan,' said Salim's brother happily. 'It is rather like apartheid.'

'I would say so,' Looper agreed, 'only it is rather more advanced.'

The mists of ignorance and depression into which Salim's brother had wandered seemed to have vanished. He now exuded a confidence which Looper found insufferable. He patted Looper's knee reassuringly. 'Don't you worry. I know all about it. Doubtless there was a time when Berlin was one and people could mix as they liked from the west or the east, or to put it more correctly, I suppose I should say that in those days there was no west or east, there was only Berlin. No doubt it was then a happier place. A big, successful place?' He turned an eager eye on Looper as if he were on the scent of something and growing warmer.

'It was the capital of Germany. Nowadays East Berlin is the capital of East Germany but West Berlin is no longer the capital of West Germany.'

Salim's brother nodded enthusiastically, he had clearly entered a world in which he felt increasingly at home. 'Actually the Berlin capital we are now talking about existed in the past – let us say in a time before the Jews.'

Well, that was one way of putting it. Indeed, when you thought about it, the phrase 'before the Jews' had a force entirely lacking in the more conventional designation of 'before the war'. How much more sense it made to think of Germany before, and after, the Jews. It was a distinction which Frau Katie would have liked.

174

'Yes, you could say that.'

His companion inclined his head graciously. 'You see I understand perfectly. It's in my blood to understand such things. I am a Kenyan Asian.'

And he was right. Who was in a better position to understand Germany 'before the Jews' than a Kenyan Asian? It was an understanding that grew out of the chromosomes. Asians in Africa were pedlars and salesmen, the ones who bought and sold, worked impossible hours, sometimes prospered and were hated for it and sometimes starved along with the others and were hated for it anyway. Like the Jews they were tenacious, brave and foolishly clung to their host countries as if they really were home. Whatever the signs to the contrary. If a dictator of some state where they had thrived for generations decided one day to expel tens of thousands of them, and the country next door unleashed mobs to burn their shops, and a country further south suddenly mounted a pogrom and Asian families were incinerated in their beds, and the general who ran the country nearby spoke darkly of the need to purify the people of the foreign disease that inflicted his land and battened on the lifeblood of the African people ... then Mr Salim's brother did not draw the obvious conclusions. Indeed, his very remarkable and dangerous gift was for not drawing the logical conclusions and somehow managing to survive. To survive for at least some of the time and usually for longer than anyone might have thought possible. It was an ability to see the writing on the wall but not to read it. It was a quality African Asians shared with German Jews, in the time when Germany still had Jews. They called themselves Kenyan Asians, or African Indians, just as the Jews had once called themselves German Jews, or Jewish Germans. Germany had been the place where the full force of this contradiction was realised, where the presence in the country of these objectionable hybrids was increasingly resented, where they were found to be obscene and revolting contradictions. Now the Germans were a logical, methodical people. They found ways of resolving the contradiction. Afterwards, it became possible to talk of Germans in straightforward terms and of the Jews there was no longer any need to talk at all. In this sense Jews differed from Ugandan Asians, or Tanzanian Asians or Natal Asians – but only in this sense. For the moment at least, they were still there when people wanted to talk about them.

'And what are you, sir?'

175

'I am a South African,' Looper said.

Salim's brother bestowed on him a look of moist-eyed sympathy. 'Ah well, my friend – then I don't have to tell you anything about this. We have an understanding, we people who might disappear tomorrow.'

Thoughts of disappearance obviously reminded him of home and he remembered how far abroad in the world he was. A fellow who came from Kenya and shouldn't have been there at all. Salim's brother stared out of the window in gloomy silence.

On Looper's right the pretty redhead was deep in conversation with a man sitting across the aisle. A curly-haired, deeply serious American with dark hair. His face was pink. He perspired easily and his earnest sense of his own importance came off him in warm waves. He discussed business with the solemnity Looper imagined the medieval schoolmen had reserved for discussions on the angelic orders.

The meal arrived and Looper fell on it with gusto. Salim's brother, after prodding the ham angrily, sent it back and called for a vegetarian meal. Looper ordered another large gin. The purple plastic bag was wedged safetly between his feet. Purple for Trajan, for Roman patricians and for Lent – season of sackcloth and ashes, purple for Frau Katie, queen of the Hottentots.

Replete now and considerably more relaxed, Looper took a quick peek into his bag, and his heart stopped. For there, in the bottom of the bag and down the sides, he detected what were undoubtedly deposits and streaks of ash. His head between his knees Looper frantically checked the lid of the box, feeling along its sides for any sign of a split or fissure. Nothing. He was nonplussed. Then he noticed traces of ash on his trouser leg, and on his shoes.

'I hope my smoking doesn't bother you,' the redhead tapped his elbow. 'I'm afraid I've been spraying you with ash. This darn little hole in the armrest pretending to be an ashtray simply never works – does it? I'm terribly sorry.' She blew ash from his sleeve.

'It's quite all right. Really.' Looper flicked ash from his knee.

It was true. He was vastly relieved, even if this mingling of the ashes, secular and sacred, struck him as repugnant. He contented himself with folding the top of the bag tightly and placing his feet on the container for added security. The air hostess came by offering drinks. The suave couple on his right ordered champagne. Looper followed suit. Salim's brother asked for orange juice. He toyed with a lettuce leaf. His self-righteous attitude suggested that since Looper sat beside a woman who smoked, drank and flirted quite brazenly, he deserved all he got.

The girl and her colleague talked shop across the aisle. They had about them the lethargic hauteur of truly professional travellers who have been everywhere and seen everything. They spoke of huge sections of the planet over which certain agents had special rights and there was, in their description of these swathes of territory, a lack of emotion which probably characterised the board meetings of the great mercantile brotherhoods that once divided up the trading world between them. Like directors of the East India Company they disposed of entire continents, swapped notes on respective territorial holdings and announced global ambitions with the sort of authority he imagined Stalin, Churchill and Roosevelt displayed at Yalta, where they carved up the planet to suit themselves. But always he was aware that this was not just business talk. The girl talked this way because she knew it excited the man across the aisle.

'For a while it seemed certain that Morgas would take the Philippines. And I mean the entire thing. Lock, stock and barrel. No one was going to get the Philippines, except Morgas. The Philippines are opening as you know, in '87 . . .' The girl paused for effect. 'I had this straight from Keithie.'

'Oh well,' said the man, 'we all know Keithie. Keithie just has to talk.'

'Of course Keithie has to talk. But I think you must agree that in the matter of licences, Keithie is nobody's fool.'

'Oh, sure,' the American conceded. 'Keithie's nobody's fool. He learnt everything he knows about licences from Derek back in the old Long Island days. When Derek was at his peak. I'm talking of a time long before Suntour bought into London. Derek taught Keithie everything he knows about licensing and when Derek taught you, you stayed taught. As a matter of fact, Derek taught me ticketing.'

The effect of this news on the girl was electrifying. She straightened and turned on him shining eyes. 'Go on! Derek taught you ticketing?'

The man flushed darkly with pleasure.'Sure. He was dying at the time. You remember the business? Anyway, it didn't blunt his edge. Not a bit. When I go, I want to go like that.'

Looper could feel the temperature of the girl beginning to rise.

'I just can't believe it! I don't mind telling you, between us, that I happened to have dinner with Archie the other night. You know Archie from A and O, Malaysia? Well, Archie said to me that in his opinion if the Japanese had met Derek early on, we wouldn't have a single shop in the Middle East today. Not one. Incidentally, A and O have got something new on discounting. I know your people would like to see the projections. We could talk about it over dinner. That's if you plan to socialise in Berlin.'

He shook his head. 'Naw. Not really. I find if you do, you tend to get noticed. People say – "Ah, look. Isn't that Tommy and Jenny together?" And then they type you and kinda include you together in their thinking and I find that puts a drag on mobility. I value my mobility. I like to run free.'

Far from disappointing the girl, as Looper had imagined this apparent disclaimer would do, it only delighted her even more.

'Exactly! I was saying something very similar to Keithie over dinner last night. That's when he told me about Morgas and the Philippine story. It seems that they imagined they had it all rolled up and waiting for them in '87. In fact, Keithie says that what they don't know is that the Philippines means carrier trouble. The Philippines is no push-over.'

'You don't say,' said the American, pulling a little gold pencil and notebook out of his pocket and making short, fierce, stabbing notes. 'You don't say. Poor old Morgas. This could be worth a call. This could just be worth a call!'

Now he was really heating up. Clearly, the girl opposite was a considerable number. The thought of stealing a march on a competitor obviously excited him so much that if he could have done so, Looper felt sure, he would have fallen on the girl in a fit of gratitude and respect for her shrewd advice on the Morgas Philippines deal.

She was now well ahead of him. Each shift was gracefully launched. 'I still can't believe it. You actually worked with Derek in the old days.'

'Sure I did. Ticketing, stop-offs and excursions. We used to call it Derek's litany. Maybe you heard his famous story. He used it to illustrate his point. He was travelling home from the Far East with his partner, right? OK, next thing he knows his partner falls silent. Hell, it's some minutes later that Derek realises he's dead! Instead of calling over one of the crew, what does Derek do? He straps him

178

into his seat and turns his head to the window and then makes conversation – get this! – he makes small talk during the stop-overs! He does it, he says afterwards, because dammit it's cheaper to fly a corpse home in an airline seat than it is to land, pack him in a box and book him home in the hold!'

The girl clapped her hands, delighted at the story. 'I love it! Mind you, Derek must have cut it a bit fine. I mean he was on a Far East flight. In that climate, I imagine they begin to smell a bit after a time. It must have been a close thing.'

They were now leaning across the aisle, their faces almost touching.

'Maybe we ought to take this up later. I've got a pile of Derek stories. Where you staying?' And out came his little notebook and the thin gold pencil gleamed rich and hard.

'The Kempinski,' said the girl. 'Do you know it?'

'Know it! Hell, the Kempi's my canteen.'

It was at this point that Salim's brother spilled a cup of coffee across Looper's lap. It was a gesture of petty revenge, the action of an aggrieved man. The Indian was not in the least apologetic. Indeed he looked rather put out, staring at his empty cup as if it had a life of its own. He turned his mournful eyes on Looper who had risen abruptly from his seat as the scalding liquid penetrated his trousers and ran down his legs. Something in the Indian's eye told him that this was another thing for which he blamed Salim.

'My, but this really isn't your day,' said the pretty travel agent. 'First I spray you with ash and then this gentleman tries to boil you alive.' She took charge. Sending the hostess back and forward for wet towels and then insisting, though Looper protested, on drying him herself and getting down to wiping the excess coffee from the plastic bag between his feet. She was quick, expert, helpful and unstoppable. In no time at all Looper was wiped down to a state of manageable dampness and sat in his seat smelling very faintly of coffee.

'You also on this binge?' the American enquired.

The plane lost altitude as they entered East German air space and flew along the air-corridor. The ground below was clearly visible, cold, brown farmland here and there iced with snow.

'Why are we dropping and bumping?' cried Salim's brother.

'So the Russians can keep an eye on us and shoot us down if they feel the need,' said the girl cheerfully.

179

Looper explained that he was not in the travel business. He had decided on Berlin for a break.

'But where are you staying?' cried the girl.

It was with consternation that they heard him say that he was not staying anywhere in particular. 'I just fancied Berlin. I thought I'd look around when I arrived. I'm not planning to stay long. I'm visiting an old friend,' he concluded lamely.

And so it was that Looper came to find himself in a small room in the Hotel Pension Dolores in Fasanenstrasse just off the Kurfürstendamm. They had to pull plenty of strings to get him in. The experts had not been exaggerating when they said that there was not a single hotel bed free in Berlin that weekend.

The Pension Dolores in Fasanenstrasse possessed a marble staircase of grand and sweeping design, solid evidence of the gracious house it had once been, and might one day be again for clearly this was an expensive and desirable area and a number of the lovely broad-faced villas had been exquisitely restored and turned into galleries or antique shops. The Pension Dolores, however, had not been touched. In the entrance hall the black and white marble flagstones were broad and gleaming under a weak electric light. Between the balustrades of the grand staircase there were wrought-iron cornucopia, fat hampers of iron fruit ascending in stately grandeur towards the high ceiling from which a genial sun wearing spiky hair and a beaming smile gleamed down on all who entered by the great wooden door. The roof was supported by marble pillars, veined in greys and red which gave them a rich, bruised look. A brass banister rail led up the stairs, past medallions showing a wild-haired, wanton maiden leading a little boy by the hand across meadows and mountains towards . . . towards, what?

CHAPTER 13

Brazen city, city of soldiers, city build on sand, city of rivers and lakes set among pines, city of sex clubs, bars, booze, city of dead choirs singing from the stones, city drawn, quartered and thrown to the wolves, city painted like a whore's wagon on a battlefield, beaming its promise of light, warmth, music to the troops in their trenches . . .

On the afternoon of their arrival in Berlin Looper and Frau Katie took a walk down the Kurfürstendamm for old time's sake. A useful little map of the city on his bedside table in the Pension Dolores helped Looper to orientate himself. He had toyed with the notion of leaving her behind in his room but was seized by anxiety at the thought that she could be stolen. Anything might happen here. He could smell it – the scent of opportunity, aggression, the whiff of anything goes that you get only in truly big cities, the salty aroma of possibility. He could not possibly leave her behind. Not now. Not even in her home town.

Naturally Frau Katie had talked happily of the Kurfürstendamm, or the Koo'damm as she said it was called by Berliners. Doubtless there were stretches of it which she might have recognised still but much of it would have been strange to her, for Looper saw very quickly that the Ku'damm is where Berlin pretends. Pretends to be modern, pretends to be chic, pretends that things are back to normal, pretends that the city is part of the real West and not an isolated enclave in the middle of East Germany. Pretends, with its hamburger joints and steak houses and its sex films and its strolling ladies in their uniform of white boots and tight pants with their ritual offer of companionship to passing customers – to be as big and brash and as real as New York or Paris. Pretend also to a more gracious past. For here too are coffee houses and gilded cafés and glimpses of former glories, sedate and elegant memories of a larger, grander, more imperial place altogether. The curious thing about all this pretence, Looper realised, was that it seemed to work. How else to explain the feeling of energy and confidence in what should have been a blasted ruin of the place? How else to account for such vigorous life in an amputated limb? No doubt if she could have seen it she would have wept for all that had gone. But it shocked him to have to admit that even now it made the tawdry length of Earls Court with its damp grey listless decay seem even more depressing. How Frau Katie must have lamented her decline in the world when she moved into the house in Antaeus Street! Something of the old Berlin began to emerge when he turned off the Ku'damm and investigated the side streets. He soon identified what must once have been the traditional architecture: curved full fronts to the buildings, ornate, rather heavy perhaps, but charming even so. An extraordinary degree of solidity, a feeling that these houses, apartment blocks, corner shops had been built as if their owners were going to live forever. Plenty of iron work, big square blocks of stone, lots of decoration, curls and flourishes, cherubs, griffins, lions, heads of gods and babes peering from doorways and rooftops. Looper noticed after a time on some of the older buildings a strange rash, or gouging. Then suddenly he knew what this pox was: bullet holes, shell damage still unrepaired. He noticed too the many gaps between buildings where something had gone and not been replaced. The subsequent building history was not difficult to trace. After the bullets of the forties came the developments of the fifties: square, bland, functional. Old buildings that escaped demolition had been refaced in the plainest of styles, their curves and graces gone for good. Reface the old and rebuild in the wasteland – that must have been the programme after the war. Old Berlin, what parts of it were spared bomb and bullet, went down to the demolishers' ball. The new buildings turned their faces from extravagance and ornament. They reflected a desire for something different, for sobriety, hard work, new housing, amnesia, miracles, peace . . .

Back in the Kurfürstendamm he decided the broad boulevard had a Parisian feel. He had an idea that much in the city would have felt like Paris once. That feeling was all that was left. What you saw were hamburger joints, many Americans in and out of uniform in the bars and cafés, in chauffeured staff cars sliding by with flags flying. He also saw those whom he took to be native Berliners. Rather stocky women in bulky furs walking tiny dogs, well wrapped both, against the cold. Silent, solid husbands a pace behind. They were better wrapped than Looper, shivering con-

182

tinually in his thin shirt, light jersey and funeral suit. So he went shopping – why not? Scarf, gloves, a most uncharacteristic black and rather greasy-looking cap, rather like a sailor's cap, which hid his tough, gingery, springy hair, and a great black leather coat that hung well down below his knees. This was spending on some scale but the transformation was marked and he was not displeased with it. His progress down the Kurfürstendamm became all the more impressive in his new clothes, and his purple shopping bag. He looked almost at home. He decided that it was the bulk of the coat and the way that it hung below his knees. When he looked at himself in a shop window he recognised a distinctly 'German' look. He felt obscurely pleased that he had been able to create this impression with such comparative ease. It might bode well for the future.

The future for Looper concerned one thing only. He would find Friedrichstrasse and try to get as close to her old home as he could, if it any longer existed, and there in some manner not yet clear to him he would deposit his travelling companion.

Where the stocky women in the furs and their dogs were accompanied by husbands, they tended to use them as porters to carry their handbags. Dog, mistress, husband made up a little procession; the small dog led the lady, the lady led the husband and the husband walked one or two paces behind with the handbag, often holding it by the strap with both hands, pushing it out somewhat before the stomach as if it contained something precious and possibly dangerous, like the codes to start the missiles arcing into enemy territory. Looper passed a small bull-terrier leading a single lady who wore black trousers, a brown fur coat, and whose blonde hair was scraped back over large ears. She stood as if frozen on the pavement. Her little dog pulled on the lead one way, the lady faced in the other direction. A rather strange obelisk or pole rose out of the pavement, patterned with parallel diagonal stripes in black and white. The dog was straining towards the pole, drawing its leather lead tight. On this treeless boulevard there was no doubting that the dog was very much attracted to the pole. What did the dog think of the pole? Did it think it was an elegant tree? Did it think it was God? Dogs, too, must have their moments of doubt and anguish. Whatever it thought it was, it wanted to get to the pole. It strained towards the tall, chevroned totem pole built out of stripes of white-wash and shadows. But the dog's mistress

183

wasn't having that. A silent battle raged between them while each looked the other way and only the leather lead suggested the tension. The dog twitched its tail and glanced pleadingly at its mistress. 'I am only curious,' said the dog. 'Liar,' said the mistress.

Dog and mistress stood quite still as if painted, or photographed, as if there was nowhere else to go, as if in a strange way this was exactly where they belonged. Behind them was an enormous black and white photographic blow-up, tall as a wall and several yards wide, which showed a street scene from old Berlin. Perhaps it showed this very spot where the lady and the little dog engaged in frozen combat. The period depicted must have been very close in time to the days remembered in Frau Katie's falsely coloured, hand-tinted postcards and prints of old Berlin that hung in the bar of the Hottentot Room. In the foreground stood one of those curious circular structures, rather like a post box, but much taller, plastered with advertisements. For shattered nerves, it seemed Neocythan was the unbeatable remedy. On the right of the photograph was a newspaper stand, built of cast iron with a fringed awning and intricately decorated roof. Beside the news-stand was a little clock tower. The time was half-past ten. A few loungers in dark suits stood around enjoying the sunshine. A lady in a straw boater strolled past the news-stand and idly glanced at the periodicals displayed. Behind the clock tower a man stood on the kerbside with his hands in his pockets staring disconsolately into the street where one tram was just entering the picture on the right while another exited left and a boy, judging the gap in the traffic to a nicety, quickly pulled a handcart across the road, bending between the shafts. The lady in the fur coat with the little dog joined her fellow Berliners in the old photograph and, for a moment, Berlin then and now fused – froze like a frame when the moving camera stops. Then suddenly, with a jerk on the lead, the little dog and the lady sprang into life, the camera began rolling again and things fell apart. Likewise Looper, clutching his bag more tightly, moved on down the Kurfürstendamm passing the Café Kranzler, where young Katerina Brahm drank coffee with her husband-to-be, the handsome Erich von Sturz, all those years ago. But wait – there was another Café Kranzler in Friedrichstrasse. Today the café was closed and scaffolding almost obscured the name. The windows were boarded over. The place was being refurbished and the hoardings announced the coming of a new management. The

184

pictures that Frau Katie possessed of the Café Kranzler showed a very different scene. Frau Katie's Café Kranzler had Sarotti's next door. Above was the Schloss-Atelier and Art. Fischer, Maler. The clock on the little tower on the street corner opposite showed ten to one. Maybe it had been the other Café Kranzler.

His impressions of Berlin gained from Frau Katie's old photographs did not help very much in his attempt to familiarise himself with the new Berlin. He took out the little street map provided by the Pension Dolores and studied it. Unfortunately it provided a most inadequate guide to the topography and layout of the city though it made up with a great many invitations to such centres of pleasure as Big Sexyland in Martin Lutherstrasse. He was invited, as well, to a Paradise of Lust provided by 'beautiful leather men'; was cajoled to an Erotic Bath Show in the Stuttgarter Platz. He was surprised to see his own hotel, the Pension Dolores, listed and to find that visitors of sophisticated and discerning tastes were most welcome in the intimate and discreet Club Mon Coeur, which promised its clients a taste of *dem besonderen Etwas* – 'that certain something . . .'

He began to understand why it was that his friends from the Travel Convention had been able to get him a room in the Dolores, despite the fact that every hotel in town was full. The Pension Dolores did not depend for its income on its regular, overnight guests. 'You feel like a country pumpkin,' Frau Katie had reassured recently arrived refugees in London, 'when you come from here to there . . .' Well, Looper knew what she meant. Studying the advertisements made Looper depressed. How sad that vice should have been stripped of its power to corrupt, that now it offered itself cordially to holders of all major credit cards. The wages of sin were not death – but good business aided by better book-keeping.

He walked down the Kurfürstendamm as far as the Kaiser Wilhelm Memorial Church, which had been left a blasted stump. Looper guessed it was intended to serve as a grim reminder to the horrible destruction the city had seen. Beside it was a rather curious steel and glass tower illuminated from within by bright blue lights and signifying, no doubt, the spirit of survival. Looper turned and retraced his steps down the Kurfürstendamm until he came again to his starting point in Fasanenstrasse. Across the road he found himself outside the Kempinski Hotel. This is where his friends whom he had met on the plane were staying. It was very grand.

185

'The Kempi's my canteen,' the American travel agent had boasted. Some canteen. Opposite the hotel stood an unprepossessing, reddish building notable only for the fact that there was a guard posted before its gates. Closer inspection showed Looper that this was the Jewish Community Centre. However, it had not always been a Jewish community centre, for embedded in the wall was a scrap of something much older, a relic from another world, a piece of carved stone which, it seemed, was a remnant of the portion of the Old Synagogue burnt down before the war.

The scrap of portico from the Old Synagogue peered out at Looper from its stone prison. In Berlin, he decided, the stones sang. They had been hurt into song. Stung by bullets, blasted by bombs, wrecked by developers, the stones sent out their anguished messages. The people who had lived among these stones, when these stones were whole, when they had formed houses, churches, synagogues, had long gone and were quite untraceable now. Only the stones remained. Each stone a dead soul calling from the past. Like the sound of the wind on a dark night, loud and then softer, dying down almost to nothing and then springing up again, their song would not let up. It was a sound which might at times be almost human. Of course the song of the stones was no longer human. It spoke of a lost civilisation, a distant habitation calling from the icy reaches of space. This surely was the call Frau Katie heard as she lay dying, the cries of the lost ones, former friends, those who were once, and now were no longer. Those whom the disease had struck down were trying to make contact. But of course the distances in space into which the lost souls had disappeared were vast, the world which they now occupied was so distant that the messages took ages to reach us. They took so long that the listeners, like the callers themselves, would be dead by the time they arrived.

The guard in front of the Jewish Community Centre shifted uneasily and began to patrol the fence. He did not like the look of the man in the black leather coat with a peaked cap who stood in the golden lights of the Kempinski Hotel and stared at the Centre with dark eyes. The guard liked even less the purple plastic bag which the man clutched by the neck, knocking it rhythmically and reflectively with his knee in time to some deep, hidden music. The guard was relieved when the man in leather reluctantly went on his way. In Looper's ears the voices of the distant choir shrilled to protest this abandonment. Looper heard them not in his ears but in his marrow, and they faded as soon as he stepped back into the bright lights of the Kurfürstendamm with its noise and its traffic and its crowds.

Even with the aid of the bad little map to the whorehouses in downtown Berlin a determined visitor can find his way to Bleibtreustrasse. Somewhere in Bleibtreustrasse Frau Katie had lived in a cupboard. The area was charming, with eighteenth- and nineteenth-century houses. It was a pretty, painted, crowded, relaxed little street. In one of these houses, Frau Katie had hidden and here she had shot the man from the Gestapo and left him locked in her little room. This was the use to which she had put the Mauser which Erich von Sturz had given her because he believed that when the time came she would know what to do with it. What she had done was to shoot and kill an agent of the State – and very proud of it she had been, too. 'The English have a saying about skeletons in the cupboards. We Germans have real skeletons!'

But English Rose had distinguished the flaws in that story. Frau Katie had not told them the whole truth. Or rather, she had not told herself the whole truth. Erich von Sturz had not made the gift of the pistol to his wife so that she might protect herself, and its intended victim had not been the hapless Gestapo man. Looper guessed that it was indeed very likely that the police had been directed to put pressure on the frightened, pregnant girl by her former husband, as Rose had so persuasively contended. The policeman had been sent to Bleibtreustrasse by von Sturz in the expectation that the terrified girl would take the decent way out. Looper was struck by von Sturz's careful attention to detail. He recalled the extraordinary fact that some months before this, von Sturz had sought out his former wife and had expressed himself so attractively that she had yielded to him. What rank would von Sturz have held when this happened? He could not help thinking that a clear link existed between his rank and the seduction of his ex-wife. There was the very troubling fact that Frau Katie had yielded to her former husband. He was sure, sadly, depressingly, *sure*, that von Sturz's growing importance must have had something to do with it. Perhaps also she had felt that by this gesture she was reconsummating their marriage? Maybe this was her claim on von Sturz and in her desperation she had welcomed the pregnancy – maybe even intended the pregnancy!

For in Frau Katie's heart, right to the end, General von Sturz retained his pride of place. He had been loyal to her. He had tried to save her, just as he had tried to save Germany. His actions had always been of the most noble kind. He had saved her family. When the disaster of her real racial identity struck the his unsuspecting, young wife, he had put her safety before his happiness and insisted on a divorce. Thereafter he had watched over her and protected her in the period she spent on the run in Berlin. The General, as she often insisted, was a good German. If any further proof was needed there *was* his part in the assassination attempt on Hitler's life in July 1944 when the bomb placed in his bunker so nearly killed him. For his complicity von Sturz had paid with his life.

It was a convincing and moving story. Frau Katie believed it absolutely. But it was not true.

A fire engine, painted shocking pink, drove slowly down Bleibtreustrasse. Nobody turned to stare at it except the tourists. Judging by its leisurely pace it was not going to a fire. It had the look of a large, rather benign creature taking the air. Looper was tempted by the yellow and purple curlicues which adorned the front of the Café Bleibtreu and he would have gone in there for a coffee had he not discovered that diagonally opposite the Café Bleibtreu was the Café Untreu. That was much more like it. Looper thus rejected the Café Faithful and took coffee instead in the Café Faithless. It seemed to be appropriate.

And so it was that Looper sat over a cup of coffee, with his purple Liberty bag on the chair beside him. He found his father's unopened letter in his pocket. It was written on notepaper he did not recognise, from an address in Pretoria. The notepaper was sunflower yellow and carried the title of a political party which it seemed his father had joined, or founded. He could not be sure. The organisation was called the *Rassuiwer Nasionale Party*, the Pure-Blooded National Party; its emblem a circle of 7's placed toe to toe and its motto: *Wit Man Word Wakker!* – White Man Awake! A glance at the letter showed the former Inspector of Mines to be in good form:

> ... You will be interested to know that we have made good our pledge to support the police. In the lamentable absence of any clear lead from the government who everyday step closer to the integrationists, liberals and communists, our police

188

have the heavy reponsibility of defending civilised standards in our country. In order to show our deep appreciation of their bravery and self-sacrifice, three thousand members of the pure-blooded National Party took part in a candle-light March of Gratitude from the City Hall to the Central Police Station the other evening. The sight of three thousand people moving in utter silence through the streets amazed the sleepy burghers of Pretoria who rubbed their eyes to see us, and well they might! For the white man is on the march! Our capital was illuminated by our blazing tapers and, if I may say so, this demonstration of faith in the survival of our beautiful country was one of the more moving experiences in our life. Likewise, the police were deeply moved by our show of loyalty and the Station Commandant made a short address of thanks from the steps of the police station. If you have heard malicious rumours that the police were frightened of us, or that the march was illegal, or that the police should have arrested us, kindly laugh that off. The police were happy to see us. It is not exaggerating to say that strong men wept tears of joy. Afterwards they joined with us in the singing of the National Anthem. Perhaps when you next see your friend, Dr Owen, you would reveal some of this for I am sure the British press will have suppressed the news. Tell him we are ready. Our watchword is: White Man Awake! And whether our enemy comes by land or by sea – and I don't have to remind you of my special expertise in aquatic defence – we are ready. Let Owen and his friends come. The bullets and the spear-gun await . . .

Looper made a note of the address and then he tore the letter into small pieces. There was no doubt what his father and his political friends wanted. They were dreaming of a putsch!

He took a cab to Friedrichstrasse. He was without much hope of locating Frau Katie's former apartment. Even from the little he had seen so far, he knew the Berlin which Frau Katie delighted in had been utterly destroyed. The crying, keening voices of the dead, somewhere between the song of whales and the signals received from deepest inter-stellar space, all told him that. There were occasional glimpses to be had of the old style and substance. There was the cold and somehow waxy perfection of the restoration that had gone on in Fasanenstrasse, in the houses near the Pension Dolores,

where the eighteenth- and nineteenth-century details had been em-
balmed with heavy reverence. There was the more breezy, casual
and refreshing survival of the old Berlin in the colours and styles
of Bleibtreustrasse. But there was, more strongly than any of this,
a sense of things gone under, gone before . . . the fragment of the
Synagogue embedded in the wall, the dead voices calling from the
dark, the singing stones, the eerie silence which was of that kind
that persists at the site of some great catastrophe.

The driver of his cab was very fleshy, genial and spoke good
English with an American accent and he paid Looper the compliment of appearing to be extremely surprised that he spoke so
little German. Doubtless the leather outfit was a most convincing
camouflage.

They were driving through an area apparently desolate and
deserted. The driver pointed to a stretch of muddy, wind-swept
waste ground.

'That's the Potsdamer Platz. You've heard of it?'

Of course he knew the name from Frau Katie's prints and
postcards. Only her pictures had not looked like this. Her pictures
had showed a great concourse full of cars, trams, taxis, crowds,
buses advertising Persil and on one corner the imposing bulk of the
Palast-hotel. This must mean that they must be getting close to the
Wall. This battered, desolate place looked like a battlefield where
the fighting had only just recently stopped – no, not stopped, but
paused . . . The Potsdamer Platz had been a roar of buses, trams,
men and machines, the Trafalgar Square of Berlin. Now there was
nothing. A few muddy pools, some scrubby greenery, and a cold
wind driving across the dirty water gave it the look of skin on sour
milk.

'This is not a development area,' said his driver.

In the middle of that dreary, flat expanse stood the remnant of a
building surrounded by a low fence. Grass and trees grew around it
and came up through the floor. Trees also grew on the roof, saplings
sprouted from the brickwork. The building had been gracious once,
he could see the neat brown bricks, the elegant and solid entrance
arches, the circular windows now gaping to the sky and several
headless statues on the roof. Only one had not been decapitated.
This was a male figure, presumably once white marble, but now
green. It raised a hand in casual salute, it seemed almost an ironic
wave.

'This was the old Anhalter Station. Major railway station, you understand. Sixty trains a day, forty thousand passengers, off to Dresden, Leipzig, Karlsbad, Prague, Vienna, Rome, Frankfurt, Nuremberg and Munich. If you can believe it . . .'

'I can believe it,' said Looper. He was very struck by the trees, really rather large trees, which grew from the roof and out from the walls of the old station. How tenacious they must be to take root there! How strange this stunted relic with its gaping portals. You looked straight through the entrance and out the other side. How confused the ghosts of its former passengers must be as they hurried in for their trains – only to hurry right out again. How very silly. And how sad.

'Then over the road we used to have the old Hotel Excelsior. Right across the way from the station,' said the driver. 'Grand place, so they say. You can picture it – not so? This was the place where they would wait for their trains. Imagine how long they would have to wait today! Real mad they'd be, too. In those days they were the sort of people who weren't used to waiting, right?'

Right. How angry the ghosts must be. How they must howl in this mockery of a station. What a cruel blow it must seem, this removal of the particular and peculiar certainties which distinguish the modern age of travel: the punctual express and the great station. And over the road the grand hotel. He could picture it. Solid columns, elaborate menus, warm beds, clean linen, cheerful copper, polished brass, neat bricks, hot water, bags, trunks, portmanteaus, porters. A comfortable night for the traveller. Then across the road to the Anhalter. Timetables, a big accurate clock, iron, steel, steam, flags, whistles and waves. Gone, all gone. There were no trains to Leipzig anymore. Oh yes, the ghosts were angry. He could hear them again. Their thin, anguished cries sputtered, their mourning was communicated in sharp, electric probes, spikes of sound penetrating under the eyeballs and into the skull. Looper held up the plastic bag to the window of the cab. Let her shout too, he said to himself. Let her add her outraged wail to the ghostly static which pierced him. No doubt as she surveyed the ruins of the Anhalter she considered the cure worse than the disease.

Once upon a time in Germany there had been other trains, and others who waited for them. Indeed those who waited for the trains could, in those years be divided into two very distinct groups. Those

191

who prospered and fumed as they waited impatiently for the train that was to carry them to Munich and pleasure, and those who waited for the trains that would carry them to oblivion. He remembered that Krepl and his family had waited for the trains day after day in the deserted brickyard that had become their prison. Day after day, Krepl said, longing for the trains, praying for them to come, begging for them to take them away from the filth and the fear of the brickyard ghetto, looking for them as one might look for holiday trains come to carry them away to the seaside. But these people who waited had never been on holiday, many had never been on the train, none had ever seen the sea. No doubt these ghosts, too, added their bitter note to the shrieking chorus that hurt Looper's head. To think of Germany at that time was to realise that it was inseparable from its trains and those who waited for them. All the passengers of all the trains, good and bad, were destined for the grave, those solid substantial souls who had expected the trains to run on time to Leipzig, and those who left for unheard-of destinations, to Buchenwald, to Belsen. Krepl's people paid with their lives for their optimism, for their ignorance, their excessive hope, and perhaps more than anything for their longing for modernity. They died not knowing where they were going. Frau Katie's people on the other hand knew where they were going and perished for their adoration of order, timetables and efficiency, for their unquestioning faith in themselves. The Germans, Frau Katie liked to declare, feared nobody but God. In fact, with Luciferian arrogance, they had even disposed of God.

There was no way now, of course, for Looper to tell which set of ghosts cried more loudly or more bitterly. Who had lost more, or regretted more bitterly their loss. They moaned, lamented, squeaked and gibbered their pain together. And Looper heard it. Not in his ears, but in his mind, because that was the receiver which was tuned to pick up this static. It was all very well as positivists and logicians had done in safer places to write off the mind as a fiction, to say they recognised only the brain, to say that the mind was really no more than the ghost in the machine and in so doing to write off ghosts as well. And for this reason those positivists had nothing interesting to say. But here in this wasteland the question of mind was the only important thing: the question being whether you were in your right mind or out of it. In this place who could not fail to hear the shriek and whine of the lost souls, the dying notes of those who had gone before and, all too often, had gone screaming?

They trundled down the windswept length of Friedrichstrasse. Snow began falling steadily. They were looking for number 55, Looper told the driver, the house of an old friend. It was a long, straight, grey thoroughfare. Looper felt he should have known it, recognised it. After all he had walked its length with Frau Katie very many times before. But here there was nothing that caught the eye. All was grey, dripping, anonymous. He counted the buildings. Number 25, 30 . . . a kebab house, a police station, a bleak little café. Was this all? Where was the Restaurant Siechen and Pschorrhaus famous for its Pschorr beer? Or the Bavarian Lichtspiele cinema? Of course he expected much to have gone. He did not dare to hope that they would pass the House of a Thousand Armchairs, where Frau Katie had taken him dancing, or the seedy Bouillonkeller, the Soup Kitchen where you did not go for soup, or the Wintergarten or the Kempinski Delikatessen . . . But something must have survived . . . They were at number 40 and nothing familiar was to be seen. And now, up ahead he could see police and soldiers. The driver was slowing down. What was this?

The cab stopped. 'We can't go any further. This is where our Friedrichstrasse ends. This is the end of the line.' The driver pointed to the barrier, the soldiers, the watch towers, the Wall. 'This is Checkpoint Charlie. That is our Wall. It looks like your friend lived in the East.'

'Does Friedrichstrasse continue on the other side?'

'Sure.'

It was his first sight of the Wall. It was much thicker and more solid than he had imagined, curved at the top and painted over with vivid, garish pictures of a fantastic and violent kind, showing men and half-women, dogs, crosses, guns and bombs. There was also a lot of graffiti. Someone had written: 'What are you staring at? Haven't you ever seen a wall before?' He climbed a wooden tower and stared across to the East. There was not one, but two barriers with a level area between. This was where the mines lay buried. On the other side there were also towers, manned by soldiers. When a pretty blonde girl in a thick fur coat mounted the steps to the top of the tower the East German guards came to life. They trained their binoculars on the West and you could almost see them grinning. This was the front line, here were the trenches,

193

the barbed wire, no man's land. The blonde knew she was being examined. She smiled. The guards on the other side scrutinised the enemy. On the Wall someone had written: 'Tötet Botha'.

The cabby took him back to his hotel. They turned into nearby Wilhelmstrasse, another blasted, muddy ruin. It began to snow. A dismal sign caught his eye. On this site, the notice proclaimed, stood the former interrogation and torture centre of the Gestapo.

'We lived in Friedrichstrasse so as to be close to my husband's work,' Frau Katie had told her Hottentots.

On the corner of Fasanenstrasse was a shop where Looper saw a collection of black urns standing on plinths. This sombre sight depressed him and reminded him that he had failed to return Frau Katie's ashes to a decent resting place. In the foyer of the Pension Dolores he saw three Christmas trees behind the stairs, lying on their sides, still in their pots still covered with tinsel and powdered in dust. Thudding rock music from the Club Mon Coeur pounded through the hotel.

He spent the evening in the club. It proved most useful. In the club he met Ingrid, for whom he bought several very expensive drinks. They watched a floor show in which two men in black leather vests performed an extremely complicated dance with riding crops.

'Where are you coming from?' Ingrid enquired gazing with interest at Looper's wiry red hair and his black leather coat.

'I am a Hottentot,' said Looper. 'From Southern Africa.'

Ingrid was entranced. 'How wonderful! I thought all the Hottentots were dead.'

'All but me,' he said.

Ingrid was dressed in a pink jumper, tight white slacks and long white boots and her American English was fluent. It was Ingrid who told him that the best way of crossing to the East was to take a bus tour from around the corner in the Kurfürstendamm. Foreigners did not have difficulty going to East Berlin. It was Berliners who struggled to get in, or out. And it was Ingrid who later that night covered his body with hers, pressing it into the deep wide bed while outside, though Looper did not hear it, the snow was falling steadily, patiently, as if building by the steady accumulation of thousands of minute particulars, the facts of some irresistible argument.

CHAPTER 14

Looper sat on the upper deck of the coach. It seemed a good idea. You saw more from the top of a bus. The tour began in the Kurfürstendamm under the genial stewardship of a young driver who collected passports and warned the passengers not to take photographs when they came to the crossing point at Checkpoint Charlie. If they were seen to do so the East German guards would take them off the bus, confiscate their cameras and quite possibly detain them. His audience sat on the edge of their seats. This was more like the Germany you saw in the movies! Maybe now they would be seeing real Germans. Germans who shouted *raus!* and hit you with their rifle butts. Not Germans like you saw on this side of the Wall, who smiled at you and spoke English with American accents. He had seen it happen before, said the driver. The passengers were American, Greek, Italian and many were impressively laden with photographic equipment which they continually touched, pressing and stroking it with the absent-minded affection and sure-fingered confidence of lovers, as if they cradled in their hands or carried slung around their necks small sleeping pets, or papooses. It was difficult to tell who was the more pleased: the guide at being able to give such a solemn warning, or the passengers to feel that this was no ordinary tour. Looper was grateful he had no camera. Every time he blinked he took a picture. It was something to do with the place.

The plastic bag was on his lap. He had no idea what he would do once on the other side. It would have been so much easier if he had found Frau Katie's former residence on the western side of Friedrichstrasse. He might have sprinkled her ashes in the darkness. Last night's snow now piled everywhere would have done the rest. Or he might have been bold enough to have left the entire bag with its contents on the steps of her former apartment, rather in the way that people abandoned babies in the porches of churches and at the doors of hospitals. He might have pinned a note to the bag: 'This lady lived here once. I love her dearly but I can't support her any longer. Please take care of her.'

It all had to do with the question of going home. What you meant by it. And what you were prepared to settle for. That had always been Mona May's answer to the questions reporters put to her: 'What do you want, Mona?'

'I want to go home.'

So did Frau Katie. And he had achieved something like that for her. He had brought her back to Berlin. Wasn't that enough? Did he have to take her back to the actual house in the very street where the old story began? And if her house had been blasted to bits in the war did he have to locate the precise site? Was not this desperate pedantry? Was it not also sentimentality of the worst sort? Yet he would damn well do it. Well, he would do *something*. He owed her something. Besides, it appealed to the devil in him.

For people like him, and Mona, there was to be no return. Their cities, their homes, streets, neighbours would vanish as surely as the lost kingdoms of Africa: the City of the Zanj, the golden dream of Monomatapa, old Azania and Great Zimbabwe – as surely as Lourenço Marques and Salisbury . . . What would become of them once they were lost he could not say. Whether they would fall to ruin or merely into disfavour or change their aspect and become something entirely other, this was not yet clear. But undoubtedly there were people already planning the changing of the names. I and my kind will have vanished. It will be as if we simply never were, thought Looper. Best not to make too much of it. It had happened to other people, in other ages. It had happened most painfully to Frau Katie. But with other people, and particularly with Frau Katie, this profound change had more weight and had taken longer. Perhaps because Frau Katie and those like her were undoubtedly original, were therefore harder to root out, they resisted more fiercely and so the job took longer. Genocide as a programme had the weight and seriousness which history recognised. But in our case, Looper told himself there is no such seriousness and no such weight. History simply isn't interested. It was out when we called. We provided no occasions to which it could rise. We are going to be shifted aside more quickly and forgotten much faster. In our small corner of Southern Africa we have never taken proper hold. We were like men who moved into a house and somehow never got rid of the builders and, watching them pull down the walls and put up new ones every day, we persuaded ourselves that in a young country this was normal living, so we got used to it. We told ourselves that

196

this was no more than the inconvenience to be expected by the newly settled. Then one day we realised that the house was not being built for us. But it was too late. Our secret suspicions had come true. We were in the wrong place altogether. Apparently there had been some horrible mistake. Doubtless this was why the idea of returning Frau Katie to her original married home, or its exact location, so appealed to him. Unnecessary, quixotic, probably bound to fail, none the less it intrigued him. How very good it would be to get her home, in spite of the odds. To spit in the face of history. That was the devil which urged him on.

Looper's rather vague plan had been to reconnoitre the area on the other side of the wall. He had been assured that they were going to see the area around Unter den Linden. He knew from his map of the whorehouses and clubs that this was all once Frau Katie's stamping ground. He hoped to be allowed to leave the bus and walk along the remaining length of Friedrichstrasse.

Now they were back in the area where the taxi had taken them the day before. Here was the muddy waste of what was the Potsdamer Platz. Here was the Anhalter Station with the trees that grew out of its face and the figures on the roof waving for help, or goodbye. Here was Wilhelmstrasse and quite possibly the site of von Sturz's office, the Gestapo torture chambers. Oh what if Rose knew that! Frau Katie's story was even worse than she had guessed. Then again it might have been coincidence. Sheer coincidence. There was the Wall, fat, squat, pale, hideously painted, as if it had been attacked by demented children. Friedrichstrasse again. Mean and grey. Here was the sign that warned you were leaving the American sector. A tall pink house on the right was the Checkpoint Charlie museum of the Wall. Ahead were what looked like customs sheds. Or marshalling yards. The buildings around about were ruins. This was a war slum. Here you felt the fragility, the foolishness of human ideals. You felt the barbarians waiting to fall upon each other. Up in their tower the Americans watched them leave. The war went on. He was visiting the front.

The East Germans watched as they arrived. The coach turned into a large parking lot and the driver killed the engine. A guard clambered up on to the coach, then another and then a third. They wore blue uniforms with green flashes. One guard came upstairs and began poking among the coats on the luggage racks above their heads. He looked under the seats. Down below Looper could

197

hear them opening the luggage compartment at the rear of the bus. He saw another guard wheel up a cunning little caddy on which was a mirror. This mirror was slid beneath the coach and its undersides were examined. The guard on the top floor collected their passports and began checking them, peering closely at the photograph and then back at the passenger. It was slow, careful work. The man checking the passports stopped at Looper's seat. He seemed to spend an extra long period checking and rechecking the photograph. Looper was wearing his black peaked leather cap and had no intention of removing it. Eventually the man was satisfied, but just as he was moving away he noticed Looper's bag. His eyes widened and he frowned. Looper tightened his grip on the bag and stared straight ahead of him. The guard turned on his heel and walked away. A few moments later he came back with the courier.

'I'm afraid, sir, that the officer has asked if he may examine your bag.'

Outside the window he could see that it had begun to snow again. The first few flakes drifted nonchalantly between the little huts and sheds which comprised the inspection area. Looper sat shrinking in his leather coat. He could hear the leather creaking. 'I've got nothing that could possibly concern them.'

'I'm afraid he insists. You must give them the bag. They will not permit the coach to leave until it has been examined.'

Looper now understood how Frau Katie must have felt all those years ago in Berlin when she was stopped by the man in the street who demanded to see her papers and she had taken him home to Bleibtreustrasse. However, unlike Frau Katie, he had no way of dealing with this challenge. Even so he felt obliged to try.

'In that case I do not wish to continue on this tour. I will leave the coach myself. I will not cross to the East.'

'But I'm afraid, sir, we are already in the East. Please give me your bag.'

Looper gave it to him. 'It's a plain, ordinary shopping bag. Nothing that could worry him.'

The courier handed the bag to the guard. He opened it and pulled out the box of ashes.

This is it, thought Looper. Now the whole thing collapses.

The officer opened the box and looked inside. It was a cursory glance. He poked about with his finger. He sniffed his finger. He flicked a little ash from his finger. Then he fell to examining the

198

bag. He held it up to to the light from the window, he rustled it at his ear. With his ashy finger he traced the letters upon the glossy purple surface. And then astonishingly, he handed the box back to Looper and stamped off the bus.

They sat in the gathering snow for about ten or fifteen minutes. Looper put the box on his knees and watched the full, fat flakes slipping by with their casual nonchalant grace. It was as if the wily host, the invading army, believed this tentative approach might deceive people into thinking that they were not gathering in force and number all the time. Looper began to relax. He wanted to laugh. This snow could pretend as much as it liked. He knew what it was doing. It was marshalling its forces.

'They can't understand what the name means.' The courier was back, apologetic, slightly impatient now. 'They think maybe it's some kind of propaganda exercise. *Liberty* . . . They want to know what it means.'

'I told you, it's a shopping bag. It comes from a store in London. Liberty is the name of the store.'

A few minutes later the courier was back again. 'They say we can leave. However, they will keep the bag. You may realise from this they found it difficult to believe my explanation.'

Looper shrugged. 'I think they just liked the pretty colour.' He couldn't believe his luck. Of course it was not his. It was the luck of Katie Brahm.

The coach started up and they left the area of ugly, ramshackle little buildings that comprised the border post. The coach twisted, manoeuvred and stopped again. Their courier now left them and there clambered aboard a small dumpy lady in a brown uniform. She introduced herself as their Berlin guide. She sat downstairs and addressed them through a microphone. It was Looper's first experience of the fact that what the West Berliners referred to as East Berlin is called by East Berliners themselves, simply and grandly, Berlin. It was a memorable introduction to the way in which, once across the Wall, conceptions and names changed utterly. They were now not in East Berlin, or in East Germany, but they were driving through Berlin, the guide repeatedly told them, capital of Germany. Looper hugged the box on his knees. That was more like it! Frau Katie would approve! In the old and seemingly derelict buildings surrounding them nothing had changed since the war. There were bullet holes everywhere. The dull, smoky bricks were gouged by shrapnel. The war might begin again any moment. What they were experiencing was merely a lull in hostilities.

Beyond the border zone the buildings took on a far grander aspect and scale. Their guide's English was fluent, her tone sharp and hectoring. They were there to learn. Here were the showpieces of the capital. A small and rather sad painted fountain in the middle of Alexanderplatz surrounded by the deeply depressing architecture of the 1950s. The fountain had been switched off and the open space of the square was cold and empty. Now here was the Brandenburg Gate, standing like a stage prop, or a huge papier mâché construction on a Hollywood film set. It didn't look real. Nobody passed through that gate any longer. Through its columns he got a very clear view of the Wall running behind it. Everywhere you looked there was careful and impressive restoration and reconstruction. But unlike, say, the British way of making the best of old things, preserving them, propping them up, living in them, which is the special flair of a people bound by a sacred, inescapable duty to the past which so conflicts with their natural aversion to the present, here the emphasis was on the restoration of public monuments. The city hall, the German State Opera, the Old Library – grand substantial ghosts. It did not matter whether they were used or not. Restoration here was a mixture of ideology and conceit, a process whereby progressive forces, 'the future', kept up, in a disdainful way, a few of the more redoubtable and interesting landmarks of what was regarded as a sad, brutal, wasteful,, foolish and hateful epoch. The young revolutionary state preserved a few of its aged, mummified relatives on permanent display. The guide's voice, high, earnest, precise, left the audience in no doubt that they were a band of idiot Martians. There was something in the tone of her voice that made Looper feel quite homesick. It was not unlike the truculent yet patronising manner of the underpaid, overworked and ill-educated government officials of his own country, where the customer, client, supplicant, victim was always judged to be guilty of something and therefore in no position to make demands; where the mechanisms of the state, ill-understood, mystifying, terrifying and unutterably boring, claimed precedence over all human activities. This woman could have fitted easily into a post office in the Orange Free State or behind the passport desk of some embassy abroad. She combined so perfectly within herself a feeling of certainty in all that she knew and believed, and contempt for those she was expected to educate in the way of wisdom, that she became for him the embodiment of those functionaries, so common in police states, who are conscious of representing in their persons the unassailable might of the regime and who exist in order to tell you what to do, in the accents of the kindergarten. 'Come home with me,' Looper longed to say. 'You will like it where I come from.'

Here they were still changing the guard Unter den Linden, still doing the goosestep when the guard paraded outside the Grecian columns. In Frau Katie's picture the soldiers wore blue coats, black trousers and shiny helmets. Today they wore jodhpurs, boots, white scarves on army grey, and rather curious steel helmets whose shape reminded him vaguely of metal anthills. The building was now called the Memorial to the Victims of Fascism and Militarism and, it seemed, was guarded night and day by soldiers carrying machine-guns in their white-gloved hands. Though the snow was falling heavily now there were still groups of people about on the streets. He couldn't help noticing the numbers of young couples pushing prams. Something in the way they stared at the coach suggested they were looking at a high-ranking delegation from outer space. Their stares disturbed and faintly embarrassed him. How odd the cars looked! Box-like little dinky cars. They drove now down some broad, straight boulevard lined with large, tall apartment blocks which lay along its length with the massive indifference of funeral monuments of some alien culture. The postwar architecture seemed to blend these two distinct strains, massive solidity with a kind of dull aggressiveness. What Looper found everywhere absent was any sign of a human touch as they toured these immense avenues of giant achievement. Looper knew what this tour was about. They used to run tours like this in the black townships years ago. Government tours, aimed at convincing visitors and businessmen of the solid accomplishment of the regime and of the happiness and gratitude of the people.

It was with some relief that Looper saw they were leaving the-heavily built-up area and moving into a greener, wooded region. They had been shown the Brandenburg Gate, the State Opera, they had been invited to admire the new TV tower and they were now on their way to the Soviet Memorial in the park at Treptow.

The Memorial to the Soviet Fallen, at Treptow, is an impressive sight. Surrounded by woods and fields, an avenue of grass and flowers leads the eye to the gigantic statue of a Russian soldier who presides over hundreds of thousands of dead here proudly commemorated. The young colossus is placed upon a conical chamber, or bunker, inside which the names of those who fell in the Battle for Berlin are recorded. His right hand holds a sword and in his left arm he cradles a small child. The soil out of which the gardens are made has been brought from all parts of Russia and mixed with the soil of Germany. This is without a doubt a monument raised upon a grand scale, an assertion of triumph and victory, as well as a warning. It has the kind of strange intermingling of religious and nationalist sentiments found in memorials raised by those who have survived and won against what seemed impossible odds. The mausoleum which, in Looper's mind, closely resembled in spirit and size the memorial to the Russian dead in Treptow Park was the weighty commemoration in stone raised to the memory of the voortrekkers on a hill outside Pretoria. You felt no sadness in such places. They were, in a way, too big for that. The anguish and grief were buried with the fallen. What chocked you here, pressed around you like an iron band, was a sense of determination – and, worse still, of bitter exultation.

Although it was snowing hard the passengers clambered down the stairs of the coach and set off to inspect the Memorial. Looper decided to go downstairs. He had no intention of leaving the coach. He wanted to find out about Friedrichstrasse. Perhaps their guide would help him. She might know something about the state in which it had survived the war. Perhaps she could tell him how best he might arrange to visit the street on foot. He found her, in her brown uniform, with her scraped-back hair and school mistressy manner, seated at a small table near the door, selling postcards and stamps.

Looper bought a pack of stamps and a postcard with a montage of the sights they had seen that day, ranging from the Brandenburg Gate to the Treptow Memorial. Leaning on the guide's desk, he wrote:

Dear Father,
Wish you were here. Read with interest your news of Pure Race party and March Of Gratitude to the Police Station. Have taken the liberty of telling friends here about you. Your homeland awaits!

Caleb

It was his little joke. Everyone should be allowed one little joke. Why should only Frau Katie be allowed a joke.

What made him turn around then he did not know. Maybe he felt the long, cool scrutiny of the dark brown eyes. Looper stared into them helplessly. He was sitting at the very back of the coach and with the crowd aboard would have been perfectly hidden. Even if Looper had decided to sit downstairs it was likely in that crowded space he would not have picked him out. He was wearing an expensive camel-hair coat, white woollen scarf, and a checked flat cap. It was the Zulu.

Now the Zulu got up slowly out of his seat and sauntered up to Looper. Looper turned back to the guide and asked her if letters could be posted to South Africa. She looked surprised. 'Sure they can. No problem.'

Looper stuck several large, flimsy stamps on to the card and gave it to her for posting and began walking to the door.

The Zulu mumbled low and relaxed behind his right ear: 'What are you doing, man?'

'How did you find me?'

The Zulu chuckled happily. 'It wasn't easy to begin with. I had to get down to that Hottentot Club of yours and listen hard. What surprised me a little was their attitude. The thing is, they hadn't noticed that the ashes were gone. You beat that? You run off with the mortal remains and her own daughter doesn't notice! Mind you, they had the builders in and the place was a mess. I mean – hell! – how long does it take someone to get around to recognising that her old lady's gone? Anyway when I heard about the ashes then of course I knew where you were. I think we all knew where you were then. There are a lot of people looking for you, Caleb. I'm just the first to get to you. We've been really worried. We want you home. Say you'll come home, Caleb. It will save a lot of grief. Now – this is the way. You come quiet or you come stiff. Up to you. You choose. You got no further to run, Caleb. This is the edge and there's nothing out there now but down. Is that your friend you got with you? In the little box? You're a loyal soul, Caleb. Let's keep it that way.'

The Zulu reminded Looper of Frau Katie's husband, Erich von Sturz. Another policeman. Happy in his job. He always wanted to sort things out, to get things straight. He wanted to straighten out his career, so he divorced his wife. Then he wanted to get his wife straightened out so he gave her a gun. Each day he left his house and walked over to the Gestapo interrogation centre. That was his routine. It was his job. Clearly he was the man to go places. So was the Zulu. This man was bound to forge ahead. And it was just possible that therein lay his one weakness. In his huge ambition to rise above ordinary human feelings he might be encouraged into the wrong conclusion. The Zulu was uneasy with Looper. He was almost embarrassed by his own abilities – so much greater, richer, than those of his prey.

'I think I'll go and have a look around. You want to take a walk?'

The Zulu shrugged. Of course he did not wish to take a walk. He did not bother to follow Looper. He knew Looper had nowhere to go and, besides, he hated the snow. Altogether he was having enormous difficulties in coming to terms with the European weather. It brought on him a form of mild depression. So he returned to his seat and peered out into the gathering, swirling gloom watching Looper, still carrying his box, join the little knot of tourists at the entrance to the mausoleum beneath the colossal warrior.

The gamble had been delicately judged. Reassured by the invitation to accompany him, the Zulu had paid him the compliment of not bothering to trail him any further. By all the factors upon which the Zulu judged, and almost invariably judged correctly, Looper was well and truly trapped. And now it was that Frau Katie played her last hand. Now she gave him her one and only gift. 'Keep your eye on me,' she had told him. Of course! Where do you go when there is nowhere to go? How do you answer the call? No – how do you even hear the call?

She showed the way. For now, although he walked up the steps of the monument, Looper did not enter but slipped around the side of the great carved wedding cake of its base. There were trees beyond and in the falling snow and fading light no one saw him go. The trees provided excellent cover and by the time he had walked through them it was quite dark and the snow was falling with a fury. By now, he reckoned, the others would be back on the bus. He would be missed but he doubted very much that the Zulu would alert the guide to his disappearance. It would be the Zulu who was trapped now. What could he say without the risk of attracting some kind of scandal, possibly even danger, to himself? Looper was gone – and this time no one would be taking him back.

Looper stopped walking. The snow was driving into his eyes and ears. When he breathed it rushed into his nose. He took the top off the box and with one wide sweep scattered the ashes. Then he hurled the empty box into the darkness. He did not move. He was now totally enclosed by the snow. He could not see. He was deaf. His lips were icy. Now he began to walk again. Several times he stumbled but managed to get to his feet and continued, while the snow, invisible, terrible, everywhere, flung itself upon him as if determined that this blind but still warm and moving life struggling in the darkness should be stopped, and obliterated.

EPILOGUE

The call is from afar unto afar. It reaches him who wants
to be brought back.

Heidegger

The opening of the new premises at 31 Antaeus Street found English Rose in her element. On the Saturday evening the official in-
auguration was held and the founder members of the Colony took
pleasure in admitting to themselves their enormous satisfaction at
the considerable success of the venture. The weeks of feverish work
done by Ignatius Plotz, 'Refurbishers since 1879', had been a triumph. The club had stayed open throughout building operations,
which had been extensive. Night after night Gerrie the barman
stood in the rubble behind a makeshift bar and served drinks. It
was to this consistent open-house policy that those in the know
credited the retention by the Colony of its original Hottentots.
English Rose certainly believed this to be so. The tribe liked con-
tinuity, she said – it was in love with tradition. By keeping the
place open throughout renovation she had honoured that con-
servative spirit. At the same time she had 'put the place to work' –
at long last. It was said by a few others that the half-price drinks
offered during the transformation had also played their part – but
Rose dismissed this as cheap cynicism. She made a little speech of
welcome from the steps of the club to the first-night guests who
stood somewhat uncomfortably on the pavement conscious of the
curious stares of passers-by – West Indians, tourists and clientele of
the Joustings, waiting for the pub to open. Rose bade them rejoice
at the 'advent of a new era', and quoted Dame Juliana of Norwich:
'. . . all shall be well and all manner of thing shall be well . . .'
Words which puzzled her audience though they gave her an appreciative round of applause because they sounded right, somehow.

To marry tradition to modernity had been Rose's brief to her
architect. The result was a dancing area which commemorated the
packed sand floor of a traditional African hut, beneath a thatched
canopy – or at any rate, a fibre-glass canopy so like the real thing

no one could tell the difference. A central pole supported the conical roof. Blackened cooking pots hung from the roof. There was an open hearth and food set out on the glowing embers. Aromatic techniques, developed by the Viking Museum at York, ensured that the food gave off the scents of home-brewed beer and maize porridge which, mingling with the real sweat of the dancers, meant that the place not only looked, but smelt, authentic. The smart young members of the Colony, who came from Dulwich and Tottenham, swayed to the reassuring beat of records played by a West Indian DJ in a silk shirt and creamy sombrero. It was music made by English singers from Manchester who related in confident American accents the pangs of love and exile while coloured lights played among the glass-fibre sheaves of the roof, illuminating their dense, biscuity texture. When the records stopped, the Amandla Three took over.

Gerrie the barman in his new uniform: tropical whites, a pith helmet and a red sash, looked rather like the drum-major of a Royal Marine band, lacking only mace and medals. Rose had amused several of his customers by teaching them how to pronounce his name: 'Germishuis'. The first bit, she said, was spoken almost like another name for bacteria – *djermis*, and the other bit in the way certain members of the royal family are said to pronounce the word 'house' – as if it rhymed with 'lice'. People gathered to admire the curious creature behind the bar in his striking costume and dark glasses. The glasses Gerrie wore because his eyes were still red from weeping. The news of Looper's death had grieved him. That he should have died alone in a foreign country was bad enough – but that he should have perished alone in the snow made it seem more horrible still. It was an alien death. 'So far from home,' Gerrie lamented. Where exactly home was for Looper he was no longer entirely sure but the snow emphasised his distance therefrom. Gerrie matched his customers, of course, drink for drink while they mispronounced his name and enjoyed the muscular yet somehow chilling spectacle of this former South African boxer in his ice-cream suit, while they queued for the cocktails he had invented especially for the opening of the new club: 'Congo Cup', 'The UDI', 'Jamieson Raid', and 'White Man's Grave'.

The bar itself was made to resemble some out of the way boozer in a small African town. There was a big wooden counter, brass footrail and mirrors on the back wall, their cobwebby glass painted

207

over with advertisements for De Reske cigarettes. A stubby roof of corrugated iron slanting down over the bar counter completed the décor. As a final touch, a ridge of red sand filled the corrugations of the roof where they met the wall, as if driven there by the hot, dry African wind. Fierce lights bouncing off the corrugations further added to the effect of some heat-stung African watering hole. When Gerrie leaned across the counter to serve a customer the harsh spotlights pinged off the brass buttons of his tunic.

In the upstairs room where Frau Katie had died, a dining room had been fitted out with ferns and spittoons. Broad-bladed fans idled overhead. At the neat tables sat handsome young men in designer shirts wearing shoes without socks. They dined with spiky-haired companions, who proved to be the personal assistants of leading politicians or perhaps young account executives from the advertising agencies among which Morrison had articulated the good news of the coming of the Colony. These creatures talked of who had taken the beer account from whom, of who was up and down in the sanitary towel market, of windsurfing holidays in Provence, while they studied their wine and their companions and their competitors with steady, shining eyes. Then there were young men who turned out to be actors, pogo-sticked to fame in the most recent of the unending series of historical costume dramas by which the British television services signalled their notion of excellence to the outside world. There came also to the Colony, on that first night and thereafter, editors of weekly political journals, sloe-eyed and cherub lipped, young men and women with low foreheads wearing premature frowns, creased as if by the unexpected descent of authority on such young shoulders – yet whose visitation empowered them to write witty vignettes, bristling with knowing asides and nicknames, on some recent financial statement by some minister or his shadow in the Opposition. Their jeering catcalls from the political columns were enjoyed – especially by the cats.

This clientele liked the Colony. They liked the fact that it was somewhat out of the ordinary without being the usual sort of glitter dome, a poor man's lazerium, a batscave of black leather, or high-tech tat, or Nazi Kitsch beloved of the boots and braces brigade – which was the conventional method of suggesting something nicely muscular to the onwardly and upwardly mobile brigade. The Colony was exotic without being foreign, modern without being brutal, political without being boring. It was positively, wickedly, *historical* – without hamming it up, stylish without the dregs which usually went with street style. It had marrow. Any club which is presided over by a sweet lady in a flowing gown of snowdrops upon an apple-green ground, her blonde hair set high and shining in flowing lines that looked at once soft yet metallic, which services its bar with a cashiered drum major and offers to one's view the sight of a portly philosopher in an arab jellaba, has something to say. The Colony had something to say without saying what, and it had imperial camp. It was literate. It knew the parameters within which it moved. More importantly, it knew the parameters within which its guests moved. Guests who did not need to be told, in short, what was and what was not, on. Thus – if you knew what such words meant, it was in a word, English. Though the fact that this was a word which came to nobody's lips was of course an unspoken compliment to the triumph of English Rose.

She had put together a package of marketable nostalgia and high-tech gloss. A concept which stripped off saleable assets of the imperial past and married them to the software of the eighties – but one which remained oddball enough to allow the politically literate to read the deeper message which wrily disclaimed both past and present as things only fools and foreigners took seriously. And so for its new clients the Colony became, in a word – and what other word would do? – acceptable.

What other club, after all, offered an authentic black group like the Amandla Three, a rough township trio who put together the best drumming and stomping heard in London since *King Kong*, or was it *Ipi Tombi*? Well, whatever that successful Zulu musical had been called. It was not widely realised how popular such musical offerings have proved to be on the British stage. The reasons were always quite embarrassingly straightforward and that was perhaps why these reasons have never emerged. Their appeal lay in the drumming and the dancing and, some more sophisticated observers noted, in the rhythm of the thing. And, of course, there was all that energy, the dash, the spectacle, the sheer exuberance of many knees raised in shining unison, the thunder of a hundred heels, the excitement of drums, spears and shields. People liked it. It was hot, noisy and fun. And in the case of the Amandla Three, politically pointed. If the audience thought it was vaguely Zulu, then so much the better, for Zulus retained a special place in the English imagination. It was, to be sure, an affection not shared in Southern Africa where the Boers detested them and the other black tribes feared them. But for the English the Zulus were a special case. What could be more satisfactory? An old enemy they had fought against, lost to, and finally vanquished. In fact there was not a drop of Zulu blood in the Amandla Three – who would have been outraged at the suggestion that there might be. In tribal terms Oscar, Sipho and Zeke were, respectively, a Fingo, a Shangaan and a Tswana. In politics they were radicals who maintained that Zulus, in their experience, were bloodthirsty reactionaries in the sway of their chiefs who were government stooges. But they did not know what the friends of English Rose were thinking and the friends of English Rose knew nothing of the complex animosities that so invigorate South African politics. They knew only that they loved the pounding thunder made by the black trio in the corner. Their music made the Colony that much more interesting. It made it, in the words of the merchant banker from Gimpel Fils, 'somehow more *echt* . . . to know these musicians have suffered for their beliefs'.

To his surprise Rose bridled at this. 'What do you mean – *echt*? Why *echt*? I hate this way of tossing about foreign words when there are perfectly good words of our own.'

'I only meant it looked more real. Authentic, if you like.'

'But I do like, Julius. *Authentic* is fine. I only wish you'd said that in the first place.' The expression on Rose's face as she surveyed the room was one of bright composure. 'I prefer plain English. Call it ethnic, if you like.'

'I see,' said Julius, quite shaken by her tone. In fact he did not see. All he knew was that he had said something which had made her angry. 'In my case I hate the term "ethnic", but each to his own, I suppose. At any rate you're to be congratulated.'

'Say what you most like,' Rose urged.

'All right. It's the way a bright, clean, efficient idea has been counterpointed by these rather satirical references to the Colonial legacy. The grass roof, the cooking pots . . . It's the Third World subtext that amuses me. And hell, Rose, it works!'

'It's going to pay, Julius. It's viable! That's what really thrills.' Her eyes were bright sky-blue now and her full pink lips parted to reveal her rather large white, and somehow fearless, front teeth and he could hear her breath coming in little musical whistles. 'I do believe even my mother would have had to admit that this place is on its feet. At last!'

'Even your mother's friends would have to admit that. And they proved it by staying on. In the main.'

'In the main,' she echoed him gratefully. For the most part, Julius possessed the most beautiful tact. She laid her hand on his arm and squeezed appreciatively. Then she punched him playfully on the shoulder. 'Not even my mother could point a finger now. Look – even old Hossein has stayed on! As you know, he's the most political of them all. The one most likely to object on ideological grounds to new management and ideas.'

'I can't imagine that your mother would've felt anything but intense pleasure. Her club's preserved. Its colonial connections, even its old clientele are all in evidence. As for Hossein, I rather get the feeling that he's had some sort of marital flare-up. It's booze, loneliness, the need for companionship, sentiment, that brings him here and keeps him propping up the bar rather than any particular love of efficient management. That, and a certain degree of lust for that thin, pretty girl with big eyes dancing with the media man.'

'I don't care if Hossein is here for the beer, boy scouts or Hassidic students,' said Rose with succinct brutality. 'I only ask for his paying support. I don't care where he puts the rest of himself. He could have a weakness for nuns, or fornicate with all the holes on a golf course, and I'd not turn him away whilst he paid for his drinks.'

'I wasn't thinking of his sexual tendencies, but more of his politics. He's a puzzle.' Julius spoke hastily. 'It's odd to think that someone who's dedicated his life to the overthrow of the system and the institution of a people's state back in the beloved country is sitting here knocking back pretty cocktails at a couple of quid a throw.'

'That's unkind.'

'But true.'

'Has it occurred to you that perhaps he enjoys being here?'

It did not look as if Hossein was enjoying himself. He was slumped over a drink, his eyes darting from left to right. A large black man in the corner studied Hossein with amusement. If carefully observed he could be seen to be stealing glances at the dance floor where the 'thin pretty girl with big eyes' was dancing with a youngish, cheerful and slightly portly man with fair thinning hair and a broad forehead. This was Biddy Hogan. Her friend was a man named Wen, the producer of a television religious affairs

211

programme called *Believe It Or Not*. This department produced Sunday programmes which saluted the day on which they were broadcast by examining issues such as the scandal of the child carrot pickers, soldier priests, lesbianism among nuns. These programmes could be described as 'concerned', but defended themselves against the charge of being even slightly religious by employing a bright, abrasive approach and a cool scepticism which undercut any tendency to piety, waffle or metaphysical fancy. This refreshingly irreverent approach was credited to the new producer Wen, who had been recruited from a very successful programme on the money markets which had made his name. Biddy had invited him to the opening of the Colony feeling he was the sort of person English Rose would really like. She bought him a 'Jamieson Raid' and he talked to her so knowledgeably about the politician priests of South America and the misuse of western loans to enslave famine-struck African countries that she positively blushed with excitement. When they first met she had not of course known that he was in television – by the time the evening ended she could not have cared less.

She would maintain, in later years, that she had had her eyes opened more widely in those few hours than in all her years at university. Within a week she had joined the team of *Believe It Or Not* as a researcher. She thought of Looper, when she thought of him at all, that he had been considerably deeper than she could ever have guessed. She bitterly regretted her denunciation of him to Hossein. Not because of any injury it caused to Looper, but because it had re-established relations between herself and Hossein just as she was getting over their affair.

On the night in which she had in desperation flung herself upon the windscreen of his car as he careered down Antaeus Street she had succeeded in persuading him of Looper's treachery, while he had persuaded her into his bed. Later it had come to seem to Biddy, in her confused feverish state, that the one had been dependent on the other. Wyngate had traded off his co-operation for her compliance.

In actual fact, Hossein had been shattered. Like many South Africans he firmly believed that political events were tied to moral defects – his humiliation through the treachery of Looper became linked in his mind to his own betrayal of his wife. He had thought himself deservedly punished. On the night of Frau Katie's suicide,

212

jealousy had prevented him from admitting Looper's betrayal. But Biddy's evidence, on second presentation, seemed overwhelming, Looper had a ticket home. Hossein had seen that ticket with his own eyes. If Looper was the deportee he had always claimed to be, then he was not allowed to return home. Just when all seemed clear, hot and close upon this fact had come the realisation that Looper had been very friendly with his wife, Gladys. There was his help in the matter of her photograph album. If Looper was working for Pretoria then it meant that they now had a complete dossier on many of his friends and acquaintances, and many of their most important friends around the world. It was typical of Hossein that this realisation of a possible betrayal of Gladys by Looper reminded him of his own betrayal – yet that the effect of it was not to make him more guilty, but to grow even more wild with anger against Looper. He gave orders. Looper was to be found and his mouth closed. Altogether Hossein acted with what seemed to him all speed and commendable ruthlessness. He telephoned his orders to his lieutenants immediately, and only then did he go to bed with Biddy Hogan.

But from one day to the next Looper disappeared. Hossein feared the worst. The man must have got home after all. There would follow the triumphant, jeering news conference at which the Pretoria regime would unveil their super spy and recount in detail how he had penetrated into the heart of Via Afrika. How he had made monkeys out of the enemies of South Africa in their plush havens abroad. Hossein trembled. It would all come out. His abrupt departure from the Room on the night of Frau Katie's funeral pursued by Biddy had alerted Gladys to his renewed relationship and Gladys had not taken it well. But Looper's disappearance made matters incalculably worse. Not only the business about the photograph album, but other, more personal, details would become public knowledge. His affair with Biddy Hogan for instance.

The few days between Looper's disappearance and the news of his unexpected end, Hossein spent drinking. He considered suicide. He turned away from Biddy Hogan with a feeling of revulsion. She had been the messenger who brought the news of his downfall. He had slept with her. For her he had left his wife. Now he tried to return to his wife, as if by re-establishing relations he could in some way expiate his political sin. Gladys, unfortunately, was not impressed.

'You've been sleeping with that skinny chicken woman again, haven't you, Wyngate? Can't think why. There's no accounting for taste. So now you get just right back to her and jump in her bed and bury your head between her itsy bitsy little white tits and see where that gets you. Stupid old man! You've got no sense, you know that, Wyngate? I think they must have knocked all your sense out of you when you spent those years in jail. The Boers have injured your brain!'

It was this explanation he found himself offering to himself a few days later when the news broke that Looper's body had been found in the snow in an East German field. Suddenly Looper presented no threat. He was no traitor. He had died, it seemed, faithful to his convictions. It was likely that he had been in East Germany to make contact with certain acquaintances and there had been murdered, probably by South African agents. That was the official rumour believed by many of the Hottentots and by some South African newspapers and by many exiles and expatriates who had known and admired Looper. Hossein thought maybe Gladys was right, maybe the Boers had damaged his brain. How else to explain his foolish behaviour? His baseless suspicions, his remorse and despair, his drinking, his betrayal of his wife and his ridiculous attachment to a political *naïve* like Biddy Hogan? How, for that matter, to explain that after all that had happened, after all he now knew, he still ached for that pale, bony body – skinny chicken, or not?

So that was why he now sat at Gerrie's bar, under the slanting roof drinking whisky and watching Biddy nuzzling up to the insufferable, prancing man who did something on the television. Hossein longed for the old regime of Frau Katie and the law forbidding couples. How wise it seemed now. Even Mona May and Elize from Zimbabwe cuddled quite openly and no one turned a hair. Mr Govender and his daughter Anagupta stared into each other's eyes across a table shining with silver, green with Perrier bottles and occasionally one of them would reach out a finger and touch reflectively the earlobe or lower lip of the other in a way he found deeply suggestive and then, as if in order to emphasise the depth of their passion, one of them would lick just the tip of his or her forefinger and then with the wet tip glistening in the candlelight lightly touch the other on the eyebrow or chin. He became so intensely embarrassed watching this intimacy that he had to turn his head away.

214

Rose took an unexpected line on Looper's death, declaring that he died for love. He had taken her mother home to Berlin and perished there. Yet however deeply touched by his romantic mission, she could not overlook the fact that Looper had, without consulting her, removed her mother's remains from their final resting place and absconded with them. Her first thought was to repatriate the ashes and she had got the Foreign Office, through the intercession of a client of Gimpel Fils, well-placed in government circles, to bring pressure to bear on the East German authorities for the return of her mother's remains. However the East Germans denied there were any ashes. There was only the body of a man, Looper. And a plastic shopping bag. They offered to return them both but Rose said she certainly was not going to accept the responsibility for taking Looper back. There was, she believed, a father still alive in South Africa. Perhaps he wanted Looper. Let the South Africans handle it. However Looper remained a deported person and the South Africans also declined to accept the corpse. Then Rose received a letter from Looper's father, the ageing inspector of mines:

Dear Miss Brahm, I'm afraid that you have directed your enquiries to the wrong place. The man you knew as Looper was no relation of mine. Might I suggest that you direct your enquiries to Dr David Owen. He will undoubtedly deny involvement, but that would be no more than par for the course. Should you speak to him, give him this message. We are ready. Whether he comes by land or sea, and I might add that I am a trained sub-aquatic fighter of some renown – despite my advanced years.

P.S. The imposter Looper has written to me from East Germany. As a result, certain colleagues are very perturbed. I don't blame them. Under the circumstances, I would be too. No clearer proof is needed that the forces of international Communism allied to the worldwide Jewish conspiracy are determined to discredit patriots.

It was Morrison who volunteered to go and fetch Looper. But, as things turned out, it was Morrison himself who went on a far longer journey. Morrison had been driving home one night when he saw a group of black youths stoning a blazing sub-post office. A group of Asians were in their turn battling with the black boys, while white residents in the area, awoken by the noise and the smoke, tumbled on to the street and watched helplessly. What had happened next was unclear. Some witnesses maintained that Morrison had attempted to pacify the stone throwers. Others said he had attempted to place himself between rioters and the post office. A few witnesses said Morrison had attempted to enter the blazing building in order to rescue the family trapped upstairs. At any rate, when the fire brigade arrived Morrison was found unconscious. Again, evidence as to what happened was vague. Some reports spoke of an attack on Morrison by rioters. Others said the building had collapsed and he had been hit by falling masonry. Still others declared that Morrison had been mistaken for a looter by the police, who had arrived by this time, and had been assaulted by several officers with truncheons. It is likely that the only one who knew what had happened was Morrison himself but he was in a coma from which he never emerged.

He died some days later in hospital. Dreaming, one would like to think, that he was in Africa again, back in the midst of the fray in the old struggle. *Advertising Man Dies in Riot* said the headlines. But it had really been Father Morrison, the crusading priest, who had died fighting the good fight once again and one could not but hope that he died happy.

So Buffy Lestrade went to deal with Looper. He looked plumper now and even more like a Buddha though his looks were quite disturbingly at odds with his fleshy pushiness. Except on traditional occasions such as the opening of the Colony he had left behind the white flowing garments he had once favoured and now wore dark blue suits and floral ties. He smiled broadly, still drank Russian vodka and when he laughed his musky aftershave cologne drifted off his meaty cheeks in thick waves. He had bought a stake in a small health-food establishment known as Gulag Foods. It had once been a shop for Catholic Vegans. Gulag Foods had the vegetarian business at the Colony and Buffy got on very well with the rising young clientele of the club. Everyone agreed he was a far more likeable character since he stopped philosophising and became a caterer.

Buffy dined out on his trip to the East.

'I identified our friend Looper while he still lay in the fridge where they kept him since his discovery. His eyes were open.

216

Nothing, they said, had been touched. His eyes were so open and fixed, staring at me. You know, I got the feeling that he'd like to catch my eye, if I'd let him. He had the air of a man who has a point he wishes to make. I kept feeling this. I know it sounds odd – I felt he wanted to buttonhole me. You remember Looper's gimlet stare? Well, it was still there. His hair was neat and crisp. Yellow as always, with that slight reddish tinge and I remember he had icicles in his beard stubble and the jaw set in that somewhat pugnacious jut. You remember? It was Looper all right. Dressed not as we so often used to see him here, with that combination of respectability and slight truculence, in a speckled brown and green tweedy suit and quiet tie. No. Now he was dressed like the old man in the nursery rhyme – all in leather. And rock solid. Petrified! No doubt of that.'

'Where did you sprinkle his ashes?' It was Rose's question.

'In some potter's field.'

Nobody commented. No one said that the reference to a potter's field might well have alluded to the burying place of Judas Iscariot. Perhaps no one knew this.

Biddy Hogan's friend Wen did, it was true, pick up the reference, but he preferred not to mention it because he knew it would upset Biddy who still had a bad conscience about Looper's flight and death. To take her mind off things he had got her down to work on a new project for his series in which he intended to explore the compulsory circumcision of women in certain African cultures. It was to be called *The Unkindest Cut* and would be very searching. This therapy worked very well and Biddy threw herself body and soul into the project and cheered up immensely.

The big man in the other corner of the bar raised his glass to Wyngate. 'Happy, happy, Mr Hossein,' he said. It was an old Christmas greeting from the days when people flooded out from their backyard rooms in the white suburbs and knocked hell out of the lamp-posts to celebrate the New Year.

'Wish I were,' said Wyngate, surprised that someone should recognise him. Pleased too. It never hurt. He marked the fellow up a notch.

'Where you from?'

'Zululand.'

Zulus meant one thing to Hossein – numbers. They had more than anyone back home and they showed little sign of playing ball when payday came around and the white man handed in his cards. But he liked the look of the stranger and he was still pleased at having been recognised. So he said: 'You must meet my wife some day. She's Zulu.'

'Glad to,' the Zulu raised his glass again and they both drank.

On the bar sat a green telephone entangled in its cord which it trailed like a long tail. The phone began to ring. Its high-pitched purr did not so much intrude into the room but rather blended with the music and the conversation. Gerrie nodded his boxer's jaw in its direction.

'Maybe it's for you.'

For the first time that evening Hossein grinned. 'Not likely!'

English Rose and Julius Bafney came dancing by.

'Is someone going to get that?'

No one answered her and she danced on.

Lestrade came by and leaned heavily on the bar. He glanced at Gerrie. 'Maybe it's for you?'

Now it was Gerrie's turn to laugh.

The phone continued to ring. It was like a curious little green animal crying for attention, whimpering to be picked up. The others ignored it as they might have done a wilful baby.

'It's an old joke,' Hossein explained to the Zulu who was looking puzzled. 'Once, when this club was still for Hottentots, we used to make a joke with a friend of ours. When the phone rang we said it must be for him.'

'Thing is this friend of ours never did get any phone calls. No one called him, ever.' Gerrie beamed at the thought of it.

'In fact,' said Lestrade, 'the calls we got here in those days were usually from irate wives, or wrong numbers, or tourists, or creditors. The calls were likely to be threatening and unpleasant. So we never took them. We offered them to Looper because he never got any of his own.'

'Not one?'

'Not one.'

The Zulu looked as if things were suddenly clear. And to show them that he understood, he bared his big square white teeth in a wide grin, as if he really had seen the joke.